THE SECRET HOOK-UP

PIPPA GRANT

Editing by Emily Laughridge, HEA Author Services
Proofreading by Jessica Snyder & Jodi Duggan
Cover Design by Qamber Designs

For the romance-lovers who swoon for cinnamon rolls and slow burns.

Addie Bloom, aka a professional baseball batting coach who has made some choices...

So this is it.

This is how I die.

Death by suffocation from being wedged in a formal gown at an upscale boutique, my arms stuck over my head while I try to remove a dress with too-small armholes and absolutely zero give.

I should've known.

When the sales associate started using words like *sheath* and *sleek*, it should've been a clue that this was not the dress for me.

Dress shopping and I aren't regular acquaintances, but I'm not a newbie at this either. I know better.

There's a specific type of dress necessary for the

woman who was once asked to sub in for the Beast when her high school did the *Beauty and the Beast* musical. *You're built right for it, Addie. You have the wide shoulders that fit the costume best.*

I know this.

I do.

But the sales person held up that gorgeous shimmery eggplant-hued dress and said, "this will make men salivate at your curves," and she was so excited that I decided maybe, just maybe, this would work better than the last time I tried a *sleek sheath*.

Making men salivate isn't my primary goal.

But feeling fancy and beautiful?

Doesn't every girl need that now and again?

I love how it feels when I find a dress that fits me right. When I can stand in front of a mirror and see everyday baseball-uniform-wearing Addie transformed into feminine Addie with strong curves and killer collarbones and good boobs and a secret soft underside that I generally stifle when I'm at work.

I grunt and try to get a grip on the slippery fabric again, succeeding only in turning in a circle in the small dressing room and banging my hands on one of the walls, the noise reverberating in the small space.

That high school memory doesn't dissipate despite my work at visualizing myself in the dress that I wore to the Fireballs championship dinner a few months ago, when I looked absolutely *fabulous*.

"Hello? Ma'am?"

I didn't ask the salesclerk her name.

Are they called *salesclerks* at upscale dress boutiques?

And why is it that while I'm rapidly losing my ability to breathe, I'm more worried about if the employees at dress boutiques are called *salesclerks*?

"Get it together, Addie," I mutter to myself.

Bad idea.

Shouldn't waste breath talking to myself.

The lower half of this dress is wrapped around my chest. The upper half is holding my arms over my head like it's a straitjacket. Breathing is becoming harder and harder.

I twist.

I turn.

I contort.

I bang into the wall again, harder this time, and my breath whooshes out of me with another grunt.

The dress does not budge.

Now I'm starting to hyperventilate.

Only you, Addie, my oldest brother's voice chuckles in my head, which is irritating as hell too. If women are allowed to have swagger, then that's what I have.

Swagger.

Earned swagger.

I don't get stuck in dresses. I don't trip and fall into random men while walking to work like some romcom heroine. And I certainly don't intend to die in this dressing room.

But right now, I'm having flashbacks to hyperventilating during an MRI, and I am not okay.

"Somebody? Help?"

No answer.

None.

Heat floods my cheeks as another memory from high school takes hold.

What are you wearing? Is that a dress? Since when do you even know what a dress is? And why do you keep looking at Jacob? Oh-Em-Gee! You have a crush on Jacob! Baddie Addie has a crush on Jacob!

Would you look at that?

Apparently when you're dying of suffocation while trying to wrench yourself out of a formal gown, your last memories are the worst times of your life.

"Not today," I huff to myself while I twist and contort myself again, trying desperately to get any kind of grip on the fabric. I slap at the wall, looking for one of the hooks. If I can get this dress anchored to something, I can use that to pull it off.

I'm Addie Fucking Bloom.

I eat professional athletes for breakfast. I hold my own with the rest of the coaching staff for the Copper Valley Fireballs professional baseball team. I can bench one-fifty and squat two hundred. I can run a six-minute mile.

And it was a long time ago that I realized it didn't matter how other people judged me and my natural body shape and my honed athleticism. I get to wear pretty dresses too.

"I. Will. Not. Die. Here. Today," I basically order myself as I bang around the dressing room.

Bad idea.

Need that oxygen.

And I can't find a hook.

Why can't I find the hook?

Also, banging around in here isn't helping the oxygen situation.

"Ma'am?" I call once more. "*Help*. Please—help—me!"

For all that I can lift in the weight room, I can't get myself out of a stupid dress.

I can't rip it. I can't shimmy out of it. I can't pull it. I can't tug it.

I'm stuck.

And I'm going to die.

Right here.

I fling myself at the door, my groan of frustration getting higher pitched than anything I let myself express when I'm at work.

Where the hell is the sales associate?

This is one of *those* places that's supposed to have the best support staff.

"You should go to 118 Willowstone," Cooper Rock said to me this morning when I ran into him at Fireballs headquarters. And no, that's not the address. That's what the boutique is actually called. "Waverly says it's really great for personal attention. She shops there too."

My first mistake today was taking advice from Cooper Rock.

My second mistake was taking advice from Cooper when it involves his wife, who's an amazing person that I feel comfortable calling a friend, but also one of the biggest international pop stars to ever exist.

My third mistake was forgetting that sheaths and I will never be friends no matter how much I like wearing dresses.

"Let. Me. *Out!*" I shriek.

Am I hyperventilating? Are there dots dancing in my vision?

I do believe there are.

Where the hell is the sales person?

It's time. It's time to get out of here and go searching for help. I bang into the door with a crash that echoes through the fitting room.

No, that's another crash. Then a bigger crash, and then a man's voice.

"Let her go!" he barks as the door hits me right back, sending me flying backward against the opposite wall. "You don't get to assault a woman in—oh. You're alone."

I can't see him, but he's definitely a man. Vaguely familiar voice.

Familiar enough that goosebumps break out on my arms.

Or possibly everything feels familiar when you're about to die.

"Saleslady," I gasp.

There's a very, very long pause.

Or possibly it feels that way because every breath is getting harder.

"Where is she?" I ask.

"I—I don't know. I've been looking for her too."

Mother. Fucking. Fucker. "Get. Me. Out. Of. This."

Morphing into Addie-in-Charge mode and issuing orders is second nature.

It's what I had to do for years to survive coaching professional male athletes alongside professional male coaches all day long.

Give no quarter. Do not smile. Don't let them think you're weak.

I've loosened up after five and a half seasons with the Copper Valley Fireballs, but lately, I've been getting home just as exhausted as I was my first year here.

"You want me to go look for her again?" the man says.

That voice.

That voice.

It feels like a lifeline and an anchor, but also like danger. There's something in the gruff way he's speaking that's lifting the fine hairs on the back of my neck.

"No." I'm panting. *Dammit.* I can't draw a full breath. And I'm not wasting it asking him to find out where she is when she's clearly not close enough to hear me calling for help. "Just...get...me out."

Modesty doesn't exist inside locker rooms, so there's zero chance in hell modesty will be the reason I die.

I want to get out of this dress.

I bend over so my arms are in the direction of his voice. "Tug," I say. "For the love of championship rings, please tug me out of this."

"Fuck me," he mutters.

I tell myself his *fuck me* isn't about the fact that a woman in granny panties with a dress trapping her arms and upper body wants him to help her. I try to peer at him, but actual pinprick dots of light dance in my vision and everything's dark inside the dress.

"Hope you're...strong," I add.

He makes a noise I can't interpret but that vaguely reminds me of a movie I watched recently with a cranky billionaire hero who catches a strange woman waxing her beaver in one of his many mansions.

"Please...get me...the fuck...out...of this thing," I repeat, having to draw a breath between practically every other word.

I'm losing my no-nonsense edge and veering into panic territory. Next step is crashing out of the shop and onto the sidewalk to see if any random passers-by will help me out of this. Modesty might not exist in my world, but going out onto the street in only granny panties and a straightjacket dress is a bit far.

Plus, that's the sort of thing that gets you fired.

But if my choices are getting fired or death, I *will* have to choose getting fired.

He blows out a massive, audible breath. "Yeah. Fine. *Of course*, I mean. Yeah, I can…tug here, right?"

I feel him grip the dress, and I almost tear up in relief. Which also doesn't happen often. Generally only when my fellow coaches tear up as we either win the whole damn championship or are eliminated from the playoffs. Or when one of my brothers' wives has another baby, which I only cry about in private. And those are tears of joy.

"Yes," I say. "Right there. Hold it and don't move. I can do the rest."

I cross my fingers that he's strong enough for this, and then I heave myself backward.

While half bent over.

Something twinges in my lower back and there's a subtle *rrrrrrriippppp* noise from the dress, but I don't care.

It's working.

He grunts.

I grunt.

My arm gets stuck weirdly and I have to contort my upper body even more, but I twist and snort and groan and don't care how unladylike I sound.

"Thing's on really tight," Mr. Cranky mutters.

"It's not—built—for girl guns." I'm panting and wiggling and it's coming off.

It's coming off!

Today is not the day I die.

I try to make my shoulders as small as humanly possible. *Think tiny thoughts, Addie. Think tiny thoughts.*

Right.

Tiny and I will never be acquainted.

I like my body. I'm strong. I'm fast. I'm capable.

And I will never be the kind of woman who should set foot in any dress shop except my normal boutique back home in Minnesota, where Mrs. Gerardi understands my body shape and has helped me with every dress I've ever bought.

Or I should acknowledge that I'll once again wear the same dress I've worn for every other formal event since I arrived in this city just east of the Blue Ridge Mountains in southern Virginia.

Yes, it's fabulous, but I wanted something new for the auction.

Something different.

A girl deserves more than one dress that makes her feel like a queen, doesn't she?

"Does that hurt?" the dude asks, still gruff. "This looks like it hurts."

"I'm...fine."

I heave one last time with a massive shimmy, pulling one arm free, but also pulling something in my upper arm that makes me yelp.

Fuck.

Fuck.

Not again.

I drop to my knees, barely registering that I'm gasping for breath, free of the dress, as pain radiates through my shoulder.

This is not a good day.

This is not a good day at all.

And that's before the guy squats in front of me, his grim face coming into focus through the dots in my vision. "Thought that sounded like you."

Fuck.

Me.

Fuck me upside down and sideways and over a barrel and inside a fish tank.

No.

No no no no *no.*

I hope he's strong.

Of course he's strong.

He's Duncan Lavoie. The curly-brown-haired, bright-green-eyed, smiling-at-everyone-but-me goddamn *captain of Copper Valley's hockey team.*

It feels like three lifetimes ago that our friends-with-benefits situation went sour. But with him squatting in front of me, grim-faced, while I suck air into my lungs and cradle my left arm, the slash to my heart feels brand new.

"Thank you for your assistance," I say as I realize I'm flashing him.

My boobs are hanging out.

My boobs and my white granny panties.

"Shoulder dislocated again?" His voice has a dead feel to it, like he doesn't want to be using it but he has to because he's Duncan fucking Lavoie. If there's a problem in a five-mile radius, he thinks it's his to solve, no matter how competent the people with the problem might be at solving it themselves.

"No," I lie.

My shoulder is absolutely dislocated.

I need to get to the ballpark. Today's a rare summer day off—no baseball game—but the medical staff will still be in working with the players on the injured list. They can handle me too.

But I need to get dressed first.

And call a ride.

And figure out how to pay for the dress that definitely ripped while I was taking it off.

"Looks dislocated," Duncan says.

He'd know.

Professional athletes see a lot of injuries.

Plus, he was there the last time my shoulder dislocated.

It's the whole damn reason we called it quits on our secret fling.

I drop back against the mirrored wall, still cradling my dangling left arm and trying to convince myself it's just a little strained muscle when I know that's not the case at all.

Go get a new dress for the charity auction, Addie, I said

to myself this morning. *You have the whole day off to be a girl.*

"What are you doing here?" I'm stalling while I catch my breath and contemplate the likelihood that I can get dressed on my own.

"Picking up a dress for my niece. Can you put your shoulder back in place, or do I need to get you to a doctor?"

"I've got this."

He snorts.

I actively ignore him and order myself to quit feeling the pain in my left shoulder. To not remember how long it'll take before I can use my arm fully again. To not wonder how difficult my job will be one-armed for the next few weeks. To not think about how I'll be interviewing for the manager position with my arm in a sling.

Dammit.

I can't put this back in place myself.

Correction: I know that I *shouldn't* put this back in place myself.

I tried the first time it happened.

It didn't go well.

And he knows that because I told him so on our way to the hospital the last time it happened.

Heat and hurt and guilt that I cannot convince myself I shouldn't feel gather in my chest.

I liked him.

I liked him more than I knew was safe. More than I knew was healthy for me.

I knew better than to like him as much as I did.

He did me a favor when he got mad after I refused his suggestion that we move in together so he could take care of me. He didn't like that I didn't want to define what we were and that I still didn't want anyone I worked with to know we were hanging out, so he left my apartment telling me if I was so damn determined to do everything on my own, then fine, I could do everything without him.

Unfortunately, that favor came with a very sharp reminder that I'm not built for relationships, and all they do is cause pain.

Duncan grabs my pile of clothes off the small bench in the corner of the room. "You want your bra or not?"

"You can send in the sales associate."

"If I could've found any sales person to send in, I wouldn't have come in here myself to stop someone from beating up a woman in the dressing room."

"Wouldn't you?"

Those green eyes snap to mine.

If I were at work and he was one of my players, I'd stare right back at him until he blinked.

But I'm not at work.

My lungs are still working to catch up on all of the air I missed while I was stuck in the dress on top of how someone has now also ripped a scab off of my heart.

My arm hangs uselessly at my side.

And seeing Duncan again hurts, dammit.

I duck my head and squeeze my eyes shut, and then I swallow the dregs that are left of my pride. "Yes, I'd like my bra, please."

I don't know what I did to today to make it hate me, but it was clearly something.

As soon as I figure out what, I'm never doing it again.

2

Duncan Lavoie, aka a hockey player who didn't have saving his secret ex-girlfriend on his bingo card today

I'D SAY it's nice to see that Addie hasn't changed a bit, but I'm too busy being pissed that I'm thinking about Addie at all.

Thinking about Addie existing.

Thinking about Addie being in the dress shop I had to stop at this morning on an errand for my niece.

Thinking about how I yanked too hard and hurt her shoulder *again* and how much I don't want that guilt in my life once more.

Thinking about arguing with her about helping her get to a doctor.

Thinking about how I'm going to make this right for someone who never wants my help. Who never wanted *me*. At least not enough to admit in public that we were dating.

I stifle a growl of frustration.

Were we *dating*? Were we?

We were definitely about more than just sex. For several months, we talked. We cooked for each other. We passed out on our couches watching TV together when we were both too tired after long days of coaching or conditioning to put the energy into getting naked.

But we weren't enough to do anything in public together.

"I can make it from here," she says as I pull into the players' parking lot at Duggan Field, which is the first thing she's said to me since we got into my vehicle. "Thank you for your help."

I'm not fucking stopping at the far end of the parking lot to let her walk to the door when she's in this condition, so I ignore her hint to stop and drop her. "My pleasure."

My pleasure.

Pulling her out of that dress and then actively avoiding staring at her mostly naked body while I helped her back into her clothes was not *my pleasure*.

It was *my torture*.

Botticelli couldn't do her curves justice. Her luscious ass and full breasts. Collarbones that could cut glass and biceps that say *try me*. The long legs with the thick muscles that I can't look at without remembering how they feel wrapped around my hips, regardless of how long it's been since we were together.

Even her plain white panties are evoking memories I don't want of the first night we met. The night when she slipped through the crowd around me to buy me a drink at a bar where I'd just taken over the stage to goof off with my guitar.

When she asked me if I was some kind of local celebrity or if the people at this bar truly liked pop song covers this much.

If I wanted to join her at her hotel and give her one good memory of the city after she'd bombed an interview.

That night, I lied to her. I told her my standard line —that I was a lazy bum who just liked music.

Not long after, I spotted her on television when I was hanging with a buddy who had the Fireballs game on. Shocked the hell out of me, but I was happy for her. I had her number but didn't do anything with it. She was a fucking badass. If she wanted me, she'd reach out, and I had my own shit going on.

But the next season, when I was asked to toss out the first pitch at a Fireballs game, I saw her in person again for the first time.

The look on her face—the *oh my god, I know you, but I didn't know who you were* look—told me everything that was echoed in her text to me later that night.

HOCKEY PLAYERS ARE NOT LAZY BUMS. Oh my

god. Apologies. I never would've hit on you if I'd known. Can we pretend that didn't happen?

I texted her back, turned on the charm, and that's when things got fun.

For a few months. In secret. At her insistence because she didn't like the optics of being with a professional athlete who was friends with a lot of her players.

Until I offered to teach her to ice skate and everything went to hell.

For the four years since, I've mostly managed to avoid her. I quit going to the bar where we met. If I hang out with any of the Fireballs players, I do it on my turf at Mink Arena or at one of our houses. When the Fireballs ask for one of the Thrusters to toss out a first pitch, I suggest someone else on the team.

I didn't know my heart could be shredded as thoroughly as this woman shredded it. And considering how I felt after my divorce a few years before that, that's saying something. But when I realized Addie was completely oblivious to the way I was hearing wedding bells in our future, that she didn't want me as anything other than someone to let off steam with in the bedroom, I broke.

And I apparently shouldn't have been neglecting the sessions with my therapist that I started not long after our breakup because seeing her again today fucking *hurts*.

Like it was last week that I walked out of her apartment for the final time instead of four years ago. And also as if I've spent every day since both last week and four years ago waiting for her to text me and tell me that she misses me and her life is better with me in it and she wants to try to have a real relationship.

Add in the guilt at knowing I've hurt her arm again, and I can barely stand to be in my own skin.

I pull my new Mercedes SUV into the loading zone as close as you can get to the staff and player entrance of the ballpark. When I kill the engine, I'm also actively ignoring the soft scent of lavender that's permeating the air between us, courtesy of this woman who's once again making my heart pound and my palms sweat and my balls demand to know why it was wrong that we had the audacity to like her so much.

Because that was the problem.

Casual is all I have to give. Baseball is my first true love. I'm living out my dreams, and they're not you.

I mentally shake myself.

This is one trip down memory lane that I don't need right now.

Especially when that wasn't exactly what she said.

It's what I heard, but it wasn't what she said, which it took me months to admit to myself.

"I can make it from here," she repeats.

Her *I've got this* voice brings back more memories that I don't want, and I reach deep to hear my old therapist's voice instead. *Being in a relationship isn't about*

20

codependency, Duncan. It's about the enhancement to both of your lives that you can't get on your own.

Better.

Except not.

Addie made my life better. I wanted to make hers better, and she wouldn't let me.

"There are seven cars in this parking lot," I say. "If one of them isn't the team doctor, I'm taking you to urgent care."

"The doctor's here."

"Which car is theirs?"

"He takes public transportation." She reaches her good arm across herself to try to unbuckle her seat belt, grimacing as she struggles to reach it, and that pisses me off too.

I pulled too hard.

I pulled too hard on the dress and I didn't listen to the sounds she was making because I recognized her body and her voice and I knew who she was while I was tugging.

And if it hadn't been her body and her voice, the pink-and-white lady's slipper tattoo on her hip was the final clue. Her homage to her home state and its flower.

And I was pissed.

I was pissed that in the one dress shop in the entire city where I had to pick up Paisley's dress for this weekend, where there seemed to be no one at all in the boutique so I could just grab it and go, that it sounded like someone was beating up a woman in the dressing

21

room, and most of all that it turned out to be Addie fighting herself trying to get out of a dress.

That she'd tried to get into a dress that clearly didn't fit her.

That there was seemingly no one in the shop to help her.

That I could see all of the smooth skin on her belly. Her trim hips. The way her thigh and ass muscles were straining with all of the effort.

That I nearly popped a boner when I spotted her tattoo.

And I didn't care that she was grunting and making little gasping noises.

I just wanted to get her out of the damn dress so I could leave and not have to see her any more than necessary, a knee-jerk reaction telling me I'm *not* over her the way I've insisted I am for the past several years.

And now she's reinjured her shoulder.

I was reckless and irritated and I hurt her.

Again.

I'm not leaving her alone until I know she's in good hands.

The sooner we find those good hands, the better.

I hit the button on her seatbelt, earning me a half-hearted glare that fades quickly into a sigh. "Thank you."

I don't answer.

I'm already halfway out my door on my way around to get her door for her.

Naturally, though, she's climbing out herself by the time I get there.

She's tall—the top of her head is level with my mouth—and absolutely capable of getting out of the car herself. But I don't miss the way her eyes pinch with the effort.

Shoulder has to hurt like hell.

And there's nothing like reinjuring the same thing— for at least the third time—to spike frustration.

Her normally smooth chestnut hair is sporting flyaways around her crown, and her thick ponytail is crooked. She reaches behind herself to pat at her back pocket, then cringes again.

"Forget your ID?"

"No."

I look at her ass and spot the outline of a card in her left back pocket.

The bad side.

I reach into the pocket, actively tell myself to ignore the firm ass muscle under the denim of her jeans, and whip the card out so fast that it goes flying as I lose my grip on it.

We both bend to pick it up off the pavement at the same time, and our heads clunk together.

"Fuck," I mutter.

So does she.

"I've got this," she grits out. "You can go."

"As soon as someone else is helping you."

She snags the card and straightens with another

wince. "Ballpark isn't abandoned, Duncan. Someone can help me."

"I'm not trying to insult your independence."

"Didn't say you were."

"So why won't you let me help you?"

"You *dressed me*. And you drove me here. I think you've helped plenty."

Of course she doesn't want me walking into the ballpark with her.

She'd have to admit she knows me.

When we were together, she didn't want to tell anyone. *You're not one of my players, but you hang out with them*, she said. *This could impact my job, and I've never loved a job the way I love this one. Let's just keep this to ourselves for now.*

I still don't know if that was the whole truth, or if her insistence on discretion was code for *I don't publicly admit to my meaningless flings.*

There I was, falling head over heels for a kind, sexy, playful woman who spent her workdays wearing an *I'm a hardass* mask to take on the world and win it over one day at a time. She was helping take her team on a path to greatness and glory for the first time in their entire history, while showing me her soft side at home, but I was ultimately nothing more than someone to scratch an itch.

"Will you at least text me later and let me know you're okay?" I ask.

She doesn't look at me. "Yes."

"Thank you."

"You're welcome."

I should turn around, walk back to my car, get in, and leave.

But I can't.

Not until she's inside.

And she's not moving very quickly to get inside.

I rub my head. Fucking thing aches where it hit hers, and I'm used to taking knocks to the head. Hers probably doesn't feel too awesome either.

"I'm sorry," I grunt.

"Not your fault."

"I pulled too—"

She looks over her bad shoulder at me, brown eyes igniting as hard as her jaw is clenched. "It. Is. Not. Your. Fault."

I've heard my buddies on the baseball team talk about her from time to time since she started here over five years ago.

Don't get on her bad side.

Coach Addie is a baller.

She ate and left no crumbs just by waking up this morning.

But every one of those *she will flay you alive* statements is said with utter reverence and generally followed with *if she ever quits, none of us will be able to bat right again.*

Or *she really got me through a tough time last season.*

25

Or *I didn't know it when she first started on the team, but she gives good advice if you just ask.*

Every time, I nod or cringe or mutter complaints with them, whatever seems appropriate, as if I've never met her before.

As if I've never seen her shake her ponytail out and sigh in relief as she scrubs her fingernails over her scalp. "Relieving the tension," she said once.

As if she didn't fall asleep on my shoulder still mumble-singing along to one of the songs in *Pitch Perfect* on one of our early dates when she'd just gotten home from a three-week road trip right after training camp started for me.

As if she hadn't laughed until she cried while telling me the story of Brooks Elliott showing up for on-field batting practice once with a Fireballs cape draped around his shoulders, wearing a thong over the outside of his pants prominently featuring their old mascot stretched across his cup. "I couldn't let them see me crack, or they would've known they could push me around," she'd said.

Or something to that effect.

I know this woman's soft side.

But that's not the side she's giving me now.

Now I get why she's sometimes called *the marble statue*.

She's not fucking around. She's all business. And that business is getting rid of me.

I hold up my hands in surrender even though I feel

like an ass. "Great. You've got this. Glad to be useless again."

I expect more glaring. Foot stomping. Eye rolling.

Instead, a muscle ticks in her jaw and her eyes take on a shine.

"Yo, puckboy, that's an illegal parking job," a familiar voice says from the doorway. "This guy causing you headaches, Coach Addie? Want me to have one of my security guards take him down?"

Addie jerks her attention to the door and starts toward it. "Hello, Cooper. Nice baby."

Her pace increases as she strides the last few steps, supporting her arm with the other one as she approaches the dark-haired, newly-retired baseball player wearing a baby in a sling at the employee door.

"The best baby," Cooper replies with a grin, rubbing his large hand over the baby's fine dark hair. She's nestled against his chest. "She gets it from her mom. What are you two doing here together?"

"Long story," Addie says before I can answer. "Thank you for holding the door."

"You find a dress?"

"The saleslady got food poisoning and couldn't help me today."

That much is true.

The woman running the shop finally appeared as we were leaving the dressing room with Addie back in her normal clothes. The woman had looked like death. Pale, sweating, and weak. She apologized and said she was going to have to close for the rest of the day.

We waited until someone picked her up before I drove Addie here.

Cooper looks at me, then at Addie, who's past him now and is disappearing inside, and then back at me. "Why are you here, and what did you do to piss off Coach Addie?"

"Long story." Might as well stick with what Addie said. I nod to Cooper's chest. "Cute baby."

He squints one eye at me. "You're pissed."

"I'm Canadian. We're never pissed."

"That's why this is weird."

"What's weird is thinking of you as part-owner in this club."

Mentioning his relatively new change in position with the team distracts him.

Dude smiles so big, I want to punch him in the face.

I don't usually resent other people being happy, but seeing Cooper Rock marry one of the world's biggest pop stars, happily go into baseball retirement at the end of last season without a care in the world about what came next, take on fatherhood like a natural, and then his wife gifting him a minority share of the team he's loved from birth feels like more than one man deserves.

Especially when the last woman I let myself be obsessed with won't even let me make sure she gets to a doctor safely and when I shouldn't care as much as I do.

"Surreal, man," he says. "It's like every day is better than the last, and the last was pretty freakin' awesome."

I nod. "Happy for you."

"You still look pissed."

"Haven't had poutine in too long."

Cooper looks down the hallway that Addie disappeared into, then back at me once more. "You give her a ride? She was going dress shopping. Were you at the dress shop?"

"Wrong place, wrong time." I pull out my phone like someone's calling. "Gotta take this. See you around."

I like Cooper most days.

Today isn't most days.

Today is *go home and work out until I can't move so my brain shuts off*.

While I wait for the text from Addie that won't come.

And while I know I'll turn on the Fireballs game tomorrow night to see if the cameras pan to her, so that I can see for myself that she's okay.

3

Addie

THE DAY I interviewed for my position with the Fireballs, I was positive I blew it.

That I said all of the wrong things. That my philosophies and experience were insufficient for the highest levels of baseball. That I'd accidentally insulted the new owners. That I wasn't good enough.

Considering that the Fireballs were the worst team in baseball at the time and had been for basically decades, it took a lot to feel like I'd bombed an interview with them.

I'd gone back to my hotel, called my favorite sister-in-law to vent, and then decided to hit a bar for a single self-pity drink by myself.

That's the night I met Duncan.

He was jamming out on an acoustic guitar on stage, absolutely slaying some Levi Wilson pop song.

He stopped after two more songs, and since I had nothing more to lose that day, I waded through the crowd of women, and what I realized much, much later were hockey fans, to offer to buy him a drink.

Because he was cute.

And he could sing.

And I just *wanted* him.

He came back to my hotel room with me. We banged. I told him I'd never be in Copper Valley again. Before he left, he gave me his number and told me to ping him if I was wrong.

I had no idea he was the captain of the Thrusters.

When he popped a dimple as he grinned and told me he did as little as possible, I thought he was probably an account executive at some industrial firm or an engineer or a teacher who liked playing bars for fun when he wasn't at work.

Much to my surprise, the Fireballs *did* hire me. It's been the best professional situation of my life. I love the team. I love being on the ball field every day of summer. I love my fellow coaches and the team we've built and the support we get from management.

An even bigger surprise, though, came halfway into my second season. I was out on the field, soaking in the sun and smelling the grass and talking to one of my players about what he was likely to see from the opposing pitcher that day, when Duncan strolled out of the dugout in a Fireballs jersey. I was so startled to recognize the guy from the bar that I almost tripped while standing still.

And I don't trip.

Dislocate my shoulder, yes. Trip, no.

Our eyes met, and his jaw dropped, and I forgot what I was doing, which is the last thing I ever need to do on a ball field.

Standards are higher for me than anyone else on the coaching staff.

I don't want to be that *token woman coach*. So I don't fuck up.

Ever.

But while I'd kept his number and thought about him occasionally, I hadn't texted him before that night.

Mostly because I don't date.

But I had to text him, to ask him to please not mention that he knew me.

And when I said something along the lines of *you didn't tell me you were a professional hockey player*, he responded something like *you didn't tell me your interview was with the Fireballs, but I'm glad it was. Wanna get a drink and catch up?*

The right answer was no.

I picked the wrong answer because he was friendly and funny and flirty over continued text messages, and I thought it couldn't hurt to ask him in person to please respect my professional boundaries.

And instead of setting those boundaries, I

completely lost myself in enjoying what he called a *cookie date* at his place, and then we banged again.

And then kept seeing each other.

Casually.

I thought.

Until I got hurt while he was teaching me to ice skate and he offered to move in with me to help take care of me, since *we're going to move in together eventually*, and I freaked out and said I wasn't ready to be serious, and he freaked out right back and asked what the fuck we were doing if this wasn't serious?

But that's my world.

Baseball first, fun second, commitment never.

Not when I saw firsthand what blind commitment did to my mom. And not with my dating history.

And my dating history is exactly why tonight is going to be awful.

Tonight, I'm out of my league.

That interview that I was sure I'd bombed five years ago has ultimately led to me being in a private hotel suite with Waverly Sweet, international pop star and wife of one of my former players.

And my friend.

She's helping me reposition my arm into a glittery pink sling that goes with the new dress she insisted one of her costume designers make for me when the truth came out about how I injured my arm four days ago.

I didn't think a dress could be made that quickly.

Apparently anything is possible when you have enough money.

"Does this hurt?" she asks as she finishes tying the sling.

"Not at all."

"Good. No one's even going to notice you're in it."

"If they don't look at me."

She smiles. "They'll all be looking at you."

"Hooray."

My sarcasm earns me a laugh from the shorter woman. "You just wait. You're going to bring in more money than anyone else tonight."

Baseball's All-Star break started today, so those of us from the Fireballs who aren't playing or coaching in the big game are still home here in Copper Valley for the city's annual athlete charity auction to support local youth sports teams.

All of the local professional teams have players and coaches offering experiences. I've managed to avoid this for the past five seasons, but not this year. This year, I was selected as the Fireballs' coaching staff representative.

"Yes, I'm sure an afternoon of playing *Croaking Creatures* at a teahouse will bring in the big bucks," I mutter.

I was supposed to offer an afternoon of axe throwing.

Guess what's not happening now?

"You'll be shocked at how much you go for," Waverly says.

"Do *not* bid on me."

"I won't have to. The minute you walk onto the stage, half the men in the room won't be able to keep their paddles on the table."

"Is that a euphemism?" Cooper yells from the next room.

"It wasn't, but it could be, couldn't it?" she calls back. "We're dressed. You can come in now."

Cooper sticks his head through the doorway, dressed up in a black tux. He looks at Waverly and smiles that dopey smile that he's had ever since she gave him a second chance during my second season with the team. The season that Duncan happened. The first season the Fireballs went all the way and won the whole damn World Series.

"You're wearing my favorite dress."

She smiles back at him. "This is new. It can't be your favorite."

"It's my new favorite. And you should definitely not leave this room without double the security agents. Actually, you shouldn't leave at all. You should stay right here, with—"

"Please don't finish that," I interrupt.

Cooper swings his gaze to me like he forgot I was here.

Which he probably did.

And then the asshole whistles. "Coach Addie, looking good tonight."

Since he's not one of my players anymore, I flip him off. Even my bad arm is still good for that.

Then I cringe. "Sorry, boss." It's not so much that I keep forgetting that Waverly talked the team's owners into selling her a ten-percent stake in the club for Cooper as it is that it's weird for him to have gone from player to part-owner in a matter of months.

"You'll always be my coach first, Coach Addie," he replies with a grin. "Flip me off all you want."

"I won't let him fire you for it," Waverly adds.

He slips an arm around her and kisses her head. "She won't," he agrees. "How's the arm?"

"Immobilized." Waverly's team also did my hair and makeup for me.

"If we win you tonight, can we take a rain check until you can throw axes again? My form needs work."

"I'll go throw axes with you when I'm better if you don't bid on me tonight."

"You'll go throw axes with my wife because you like her better. Legit. I get it. I like her better than me too. But I'm never sure if I get to tag along. I wouldn't want me to tag along if I were you."

"I appreciate your self-awareness."

He blinks once.

Waverly giggles.

I smile, which isn't something I would've done four

years ago. But the longer I've been with the Fireballs, the more I've felt like I've found where I belong.

Mostly.

I still have days where my old insecurities rear their heads and warn me not to get too comfortable. But tonight, I'm determined to simply enjoy what I can of the evening. "I would have fun throwing axes with you too, Cooper."

"Hot damn, she cracked," he says.

"Must be the painkillers," I deadpan.

"Nah, it's all of this Cooper Rock innate charm finally getting past your defenses."

I like Cooper. Always have. He was talented enough to get paid five, seven, even ten times as much by other teams early in his career—*winning* teams—but he insisted on playing for the Fireballs because he loved them.

Even when they sucked.

You can't buy that kind of love and loyalty.

And that made it easier to relax around him even when he was still one of my players. When a guy who loves a baseball team possibly even more than he loves his pop star wife repeatedly insists you're the best batting coach he's ever had, you start to believe him.

You know what he wants. He wants to win. He wants *his team* to win. There aren't ulterior motives.

By extension, it was easier to make friends with Waverly than it was to get close to the other wives and girlfriends.

They're all lovely, but my default friend group should not be my players' significant others. And now that Cooper's part-owner in the team, I know I *should* have better boundaries with Waverly, but she's worn me down over the years.

"I'm not the same kind of woman in a man's world as you are, but I know a little about feeling like the standards are higher for us than they are for other people," she told me during the first spring training after she and Cooper started dating again. "So if you ever need an ear, you can have mine, okay?"

I've taken her up on the offer more times than I ever expected, and I've always been grateful for her support. She says having friends who treat her like a normal person is all she needs back, and after getting a front-row seat to her life while she accompanied Cooper on road trips the past few seasons, I get it.

She's been a good friend.

Waverly's security detail pops in and tells us it's time to go. They escort us down to the ballroom in the Madison Towers Hotel, where there's a roped-off VIP section that we access through a back door.

Jimmy Santiago, the Fireballs' head coach, is already there, as are Tripp Wilson and Lila Valentine, the husband-and-wife team who hired me before they got married, when Lila inherited the team and was forced to take Tripp on as her president of operations.

Lila's a redheaded bombshell in an emerald-green

dress and a confident smile. Tripp's exactly what you'd expect of a forty-ish former boy bander with two kids from his first marriage—fit, well-dressed in a custom suit, and starting to get a little more silver mixed in with his brown hair.

Tonight's about having fun, but I'm still very aware of the fact that I'm on display tonight as a potential candidate to replace Jimmy when he retires at the end of the season. So when Cooper offers to get me a drink, I ask him to get me what Waverly's having.

She introduced me to her favorite cranberry seltzers at Cooper's retirement party over the winter.

Delicious, with no fear that they'll leave me tipsy.

Tipsy is for *not* work hours.

Not when I'm hoping for a promotion.

It's still an easy, comfortable atmosphere as I chat with my fellow coaching staff and a few other VIPs from around town who have been cleared by Waverly's security team to be in the private section. Heavy appetizers are passed around by the catering staff. I'm laughing at a story the women's soccer coach is telling Waverly and me about her daughter's wedding when that spot between my shoulder blades starts itching. It's that one that you can't scratch even when you have use of both of your arms.

I glance around for something to rub it on, and that's when I realize why it's itching.

Duncan.

Duncan Lavoie is here.

While it's no surprise, I hoped that hanging out in the VIP section with Waverly and Cooper would mean I could avoid him.

But based on the way he's talking to the security guard, I'm gonna guess my luck has run out.

4

Addie

I TRY NOT to watch as security lets Duncan and a young woman into our roped-off section.

A *very* young woman.

The itch gets itchier.

"Addie?" Waverly whispers. "You okay?"

I slam the rest of my second drink while the soccer coach excuses herself to go talk to one of the rugby guys.

Would be nice if my drink had alcohol in it, but see again, this is a work function. "Shoulder itches," I murmur to her.

"Want me to—"

"Waverly." Cooper joins us, and *fuck*.

He has Duncan with him.

"Have you met my hockey buddy, Duncan?" Cooper says. "And this is his niece, Paisley. She's a big fan."

"Of yours?" Waverly asks with a cheeky grin.

"Of *yours*." Cooper's grin back is even bigger.

The one person not grinning?

Paisley.

She's pale and barely audible as she whispers, "*Huge* fan."

She's an inch or two taller than Waverly, but an inch or two shorter than me, wrapped in a red dress that matches her lipstick. Dark curly hair, just like her uncle. Green eyes, just like her uncle. But unlike her uncle, she is absolutely overwhelmed as she stares at Waverly.

"So nice to meet you, Paisley." Waverly smiles at her, hands her drink to Cooper, and takes the girl's hand. "Do you live here in Copper Valley?"

Paisley shakes her head. Then nods. Then shakes her head again.

"She's heading into her first year at Copper Valley University," Duncan supplies.

I remember him talking about his older sister and how much he adored his niece. He must be happy that she'll be close.

And that is none of my business.

Friendly isn't a word I would've used to describe our interaction the other day, which is for the best.

Waverly keeps smiling her kind smile. "Oh, how

wonderful that you'll have family nearby. What are you studying?"

"Sports management." Paisley's voice is still barely more than a whisper.

"No. Way. For real? You have to meet Addie. She's a coach for the Fireballs." Waverly turns her smile on me.

I used to think it was her pop-star smile, but it's not.

It's her normal smile. She doesn't hold anything back when she smiles.

"Hi, Paisley," I say with a smile of my own, though mine is definitely more reserved.

"Duncan, you know Addie?" Cooper asks while Paisley whispers a soft, "That's fire," and shakes my hand.

"We've met," I say shortly in answer to Cooper's question.

Fucking Cooper.

He knows we've met. And the mischief dancing over his face says he's about to have fun figuring out why Duncan dropped me off at the ballpark a few days ago. With my arm in the shape it was in, Cooper didn't push for details.

That courtesy is apparently over now.

"Was it a nice meeting?" he asks.

"I'm the reason she's in a sling," Duncan says.

Even Paisley snaps out of it to look at him.

"He is *not* the reason I'm in a sling," I say to Cooper.

"I am." Duncan's voice is so cool it could freeze antifreeze.

"Odds are extremely high that I would have dislocated my shoulder regardless of who was in the vicinity." I'm still talking to Cooper.

Pretty sure Duncan is too. "I pulled too hard trying to get her out of the dress."

"In a dress store while I was trying on a dress that I knew was a bad idea."

"I had a pocketknife on me that would've been more efficient."

For the love of the baseball gods. I snap a look at him. "You can't just cut up a dress in a store."

He shifts his gaze to me, cool as ice. "Why not?"

"It went on. It could come off."

"Clearly not."

"And then you have to pay for it."

"Oh, dear me. How would I have ever afforded to pay for a dress that I cut off a woman in a dress store? I'm so broke. It would've left me destitute and homeless."

"Stop being an ass."

Yep.

I just said that with an audience.

While I was provoked into this conversation, it's starting to feel like my mouth has taken on a life of its own. Confident, capable, in-charge baseball coach Addie has left the building, and *Addie who finally says all of the things she thinks* has taken her place.

Stop talking, I order myself.

A giggle in the back of my brain is the only answer I get.

What the *hell*?

"Maybe if you'd let someone *help you* for once in your life, the people around you wouldn't feel the need to be *asses*." Duncan's icy tone has turned sunburn hot.

"Oh my gosh, Addie, your shoulder was itching!" Waverly exclaims. "Which shoulder was it? I've got it."

"Good luck with that," Duncan mutters.

Like that was our problem. That I wouldn't let him do enough for me.

When the real problem was that I liked him more than I've ever liked any man in my life, and it was terrifying.

I liked him enough that I kept agreeing to see him even while that little alarm in the back of my head was reminding me that the longer you go, the harder it is to extricate yourself. That the man he showed me every day likely wasn't the man he'd be for the rest of his life.

Everyone's on their best behavior when you first start dating. But what about three years down the road? And five? And fifteen? When you have kids together and one of you is carrying the entire load of doing everything for the kids *and* her husband while trying to have her own career too and she's so tired and worn down that when she says she wants to go on a Caribbean cruise and he says *no, I won't be stuck on a boat with that many people*, so she just says *okay* and drops her dreams and desires instead of going by herself or with a group of friends instead, and then she never gets to go because he always told her no and she always listened.

Shit.

Get out of your head, Addie. This isn't about Mom.

Waverly scratches at my spine just above my dress.

Both of my shoulders hitch, sending a jolt of pain through my left shoulder that I actively ignore.

Cooper's looking between me and Duncan, wide-eyed and clearly amused. "Can you make sure your uncle doesn't have any glitter bombs at his house?" he murmurs to Paisley.

Freaking Cooper. I channel some inner *take no bull-shit* and look him square in the eye. "I thought you were never saying the word *glitter* again after what Waverly did to your house to prove to you who's top prank dog."

"Desperate times require interventions."

"I don't do pranks with players. On *any* team." Even if I sometimes want to. That's one line I still don't feel comfortable crossing. Despite how comfortable I feel with the entire Fireballs staff.

Cooper's eyes are absolutely sparkling with mischief. "Yet. Everyone has a tipping point."

"I—*oh yes,* right there. You're a goddess. Thank you," I say to Waverly.

She's found the itch, and she's scratching it.

It's not helping as much as I'd like, probably because

the source of the itch is still standing there beside me. Doesn't matter that I'm not looking at him.

He's still there.

He's still staring at me.

And his niece is staring at me too.

One of Waverly's security detail takes my empty glass and hands me a refill.

"Better?" she asks me.

"Yes. Thank you."

"I had an outfit for a photo shoot once that wouldn't let me move my arms higher than this." She holds her arms out about six inches from her sides, demonstrating. "Getting itches was the worst when I was in it."

"I would've scratched your itches," Cooper tells her.

"You scratch all of my itches now."

They're so cute that they're gross.

I didn't know that was possible. I've definitely never thought that about any of my brothers and their wives.

If Cooper doesn't carry an equal load in their domestic household, I will—

Nope.

Not my marriage. Not my place to have any opinion.

I need to get out of my own head here.

"Are you offering anything tonight, Duncan?" Waverly asks.

I slide a look at her as I try not to gulp the drink like it's liquid tolerance.

I don't need liquid *courage*. I need liquid *tolerance*. Patience. Something to help me resist the lull of being provoked.

Because I'm at work.

And at-work Addie doesn't bicker with hockey players.

Even if it's easy.

"He plays guitar," Paisley blurts, her voice finally above a whisper.

"Acoustic or electric?" Waverly asks.

"Acoustic," Duncan answers.

"And he sings," Paisley says.

"Not as well as some people."

"He's *really* good," she insists.

"It's just a hobby."

Just a hobby. He's fucking amazing. And I say that as someone who didn't go to see him play, but as someone who was completely blown away by how sexy he looked on that stage the first night we met.

"You're auctioning off a private concert?" Waverly asks.

"A night out with me at one of my favorite bars while I'm playing," he answers.

Fuck me.

I think I'm seeing red.

Or is it green?

Shit.

It's green.

Which is stupid. First, *he left me*. I can take being

48

rejected, even if it hurt. I'm *grateful* that he rejected me. Made it easier to move on. Second, it's been four damn years. And third, he has no say in who I see or sleep with, so why should the fact that I've seen him twice in a little over a week now mean I get any say in who he sees or sleeps with?

I'd question why I think it's a foregone conclusion that any woman who wins a night of being a groupie while Duncan's playing at a bar would end up in bed with him, except it's obvious.

A strong, tall, green-eyed, curly-haired, dimple-cheeked hockey player strumming a guitar while that voice comes out of his mouth?

He's sexy as hell when he's playing.

Of course they'll end up in bed together.

Maybe she'll even be the marrying type, and they'll settle down together and he'll retire from hockey to support all of her hopes and dreams and goals and they'll have three perfect children and two perfect dogs and one perfect cat and they'll live perfectly ever after.

And *what is wrong with me?*

I don't care.

Or, I'm not supposed to care. I do a very good job of actively not caring most of the time.

Tonight, I care. It's like all of the feelings and long-ings that scared the shit out of me when I started to feel them toward Duncan four years ago have sprouted new wings, tumbled free of their cages, and are flop-ping around this ballroom on full display.

I picture them like flying fishes and I almost giggle.

Again, *what the hell is wrong with me?*

A microphone screeches, and we all look toward the stage. "Ladies and gentlemen, please refill your glasses, visit the buffet if you need any more food, and then take your seats," Levi Wilson, tonight's emcee, says. "The bidding will begin in fifteen minutes."

"Oh, wait," Waverly says. "Paisley, let's get a picture before you go sit down."

I shift away.

I'd like to shift farther away, but the VIP section has gotten more crowded than I realized as the night's gone on.

And I finally let myself steal a full look at Duncan while he snaps a photo of Waverly and Paisley on a pink-cased phone that I assume belongs to his niece.

His rugged jawline is clean-shaven.

Fresh haircut that only hints at how curly his hair will be when it grows out another half-inch again.

Dark blue suit that fits him like a glove, right down to his powerful hockey thighs and ass, built up from a lifetime of being on skates.

Tie featuring the rocket-powered bratwurst mascot of the Thrusters hockey team. And I'd bet the socks match.

Soft smile on his face as he looks at the phone.

He's not just hot as hell, he's also a good guy.

In the short time we spent together, I would've said he was one of the best men, in fact.

Until he couldn't handle my utter terror at the idea of my life becoming what my mother's was. I couldn't explain it to him either.

Not that I tried.

And I don't know if I kept it to myself because I was afraid of what other truths would tumble out of my mouth if I'd started with that one or if I was afraid he wouldn't understand.

Probably both.

Waverly hugs Paisley, then lets her go and slips to my side as we're led to a set of tables near the back of the ballroom just outside of the VIP section. "Don't disappear. You're sitting with us, okay?"

"Sure."

"Have I told you how much I love this color on you? You are absolutely sparkling tonight."

I blush. "It's my favorite," I confess quietly.

As if liking the color pink is something to be embarrassed by.

Of course it's not.

I love wearing dresses when I get the chance. I love wearing *pink* when I get the chance.

But I don't admit it out loud to other people.

The last time I said it—back in college, before a dinner with the athletic director and several talent scouts—my softball coach cornered me and warned me to never say it again.

If you're going to be a woman in a man's world, you

cannot be feminine. Not yet. Prove yourself before you let them remember that you're a girl.

Her advice offended me to the core.

And then I learned the hard way in my first few jobs after college just how right she was.

Wearing a dress to the Fireballs' first championship dinner celebration was among the scarier things I've done, but everyone—players, fellow coaches, admins, board, and owners—treated me no differently than if I were in my baseball uniform.

It was surreal.

And while I've let my guard down regularly with the team since then, that paranoia still holds a grip on me.

While I've started wondering if this is a *me* problem, if the Fireballs truly are different enough as an organization that I'll be judged on my merits as a coach when I interview for Santiago's position, I can't fully drop my barriers.

I don't want to set myself up for failure by ignoring all of the lessons life and my fellow lady coaches have taught me over the years.

No matter how much I want to believe what you see is what you get with the Fireballs.

"Loving what you wear is why you glow." Waverly squeezes my good arm. "It just feels good. So how long ago were you and Duncan together?"

The way I want to answer that question so badly

and ask her opinion on which of us was right and wrong all those years ago…

But instead, I take a swig of my drink.

"I still don't know you well enough yet to know if that means *recently* or *a long time ago*," she murmurs.

"It means it's irrelevant," I reply.

"Hmm."

"No *hmm*. It's irrelevant."

"Was he a dick?"

"No more than any other man." I slide a look at her, then add on a grumble, "Probably less than any other man."

She squeezes again. "Did he hurt you?"

"I…I think we hurt each other."

"Cooper hurt me once," she says softly.

"I know."

"Giving him another chance was worth it."

"I can regret that we hurt each other and still not want to give him another chance to hurt me again."

"Because you love your life the way it is, or because you're afraid the potential hurt will be worse than the potential joy?"

Did you let him go because it was easier to face the temporary hurt of a breakup than it was to be brave and admit to him that you were afraid he'd hurt you even worse the longer you stayed together?

It's the question that haunts me when I let it. "This is not a conversation I'll ever have when I'm sober."

She grins at me. "Then I'm glad you're drinking tonight."

"I'm not—" I freeze.

I *am*.

I look at the drink in my hand. "I wanted what you're having. You like cranberry seltzers. You liked cranberry seltzers at Cooper's retirement party."

Her mouth forms an *O*. "I was pregnant."

My mouth forms an *O* right back. "And you're not now."

"I'm not even nursing. It hurt too much and I couldn't make enough milk."

"I can't get drunk." I stare at her in horror as I realize exactly what picturing my emotions as flying fishes means. It means I'm tipsy. "*I can't get drunk at work*."

She grabs me by the cheeks and goes up on her tiptoes. "Listen to me, Addie Bloom. You do *not* have to hold yourself to such high standards that you can't enjoy your life. If *anyone* tries to use *anything* from tonight against you, they'll have to go through me. Understand?"

I try to nod, but it comes out as a shake of my head.

Am I drunk?

I don't think I'm drunk.

I tend to hold my liquor pretty well.

But I haven't had much to eat. Just a few bites off of the hors d'oeuvres trays the servers have been passing around.

But I also had a massive argument with Duncan by way of staring at Cooper for most of it.

I would not have done that if I were totally sober.

Would I?

How did that argument start again?

I try to nod once more. "Can you just make sure I don't do anything stupid tonight? I have to get up on stage."

"You're constitutionally incapable of doing anything stupid. Just relax and have fun, and everything will be fine."

Everything will be fine.

I hope she's right.

5

Duncan

I HAVE A PROBLEM.

Her name is Addie Bloom.

She doesn't have the decency to bid on me while I'm on stage, which shouldn't be a surprise.

Her coaching salary can't compete with the big donors in this room.

Plus she doesn't want me.

And I shouldn't want her.

I shouldn't.

But every moment I'm in the same breathing space as her, she's all I can see. All I can concentrate on. All I know.

That pink dress—just fuck me. She's goddamn

gorgeous. And she still smells like lavender. And the way she was laughing before she saw us—I miss that laugh.

I miss *her*.

I never should've left her the way I did. I should've gone back and apologized for getting mad that she didn't think we were serious. We went from *let's hook up every few weeks* to me telling her I should move in with her and she should wear my jersey to the Thrusters' preseason opener.

She was in the midst of a personal crisis, worrying she couldn't do her job while the Fireballs were headed into their second playoffs with a team that would go all the way and make fucking history.

And I asked her to put me and our relationship at the top of her priority list when she was feeling the pressure of being a young coach for a historically terrible team that was being watched and analyzed by the entire damn country.

I thought I was taking care of her, just like I take care of everyone in my life to the best of my ability. And she didn't want me to.

Her rejection—the way she didn't need me at all—was so foreign a concept that I couldn't handle it.

"Most people don't scowl after they go for ten grand at an auction, Uncle Duncan," Paisley whispers to me as I retake my seat.

"My shoes are tight," I mutter back.

"Those ugly things you've had for as long as I've known you? *Now* they hurt?"

"Yes."

I shoot another look back at Addie's table.

She and Waverly are whispering about something, and whatever it is has Waverly cracking up.

"Dude, if Cooper Rock realizes how much you're staring at his wife, you're fucked next season," Rooster Applebottom says on my other side. "He'll pay guys to fuck you up on the ice."

Rooster's fun. He's offering a chance to go skydiving tonight.

"He's not staring at Waverly," Paisley tells him. "He's staring at the woman with her. Maddie, right?"

"Addie," I correct without thinking, then shift a look at my niece, who grins.

"*Addie*," she says, zero shame in the mischief shining through her. "*Right.*"

"You're obsessed with the Fireballs' lady coach?" Zeus Berger asks from Paisley's other side.

He retired from the Thrusters a few years back, and now he and his wife, who's an even bigger badass than Addie, are raising quadruplets.

Quadzeuslets, Z-man calls them. He's close to seven feet tall, built like a dump truck, and he's equal parts troublemaker and teddy bear. His identical twin, Ares, played for the Thrusters for a few years before and after Zeus. He retired at the end of this past season. Time to focus on his wife and kids as well.

All these guys I played with forever are moving on.

While my agent's starting to ask what I want to do when my contract is up with the Thrusters at the end of this coming season.

The contract I signed when I was hooking up with Addie.

The contract I signed when I thought it would be my last because I thought I'd be leaving my own hockey career to spend more time with my badass wife and our kids.

"He stripped her in a dress shop last week," Paisley tells Zeus.

I slam my glass down too hard. "Not what happened."

"Gonna have to tell us what *did* happen then," Zeus says.

Joey, his wife, who owns a flight adventure company giving people a chance to experience zero gravity like they're in space, gives me a stern *spill it now* look.

And since it's fucking awesome to fly in her jet as a floating passenger, I oblige the order in a way I'm sure she'll appreciate. "I did a good deed with unintended consequences. The end."

"Up next for your bidding pleasure, we have one Ms. Addie Bloom, representing the Fireballs coaching staff," Levi Wilson, emcee for the evening, announces.

Levi's a former boy bander who's on hiatus from his solo musical career while he, too, focuses on his wife and family. I like playing his music when I'm jamming on my guitar. His brother, also his former bandmate in that boy band and majority shareowner of the Fireballs, roped him into running the show tonight. If the Thrusters had been in charge, Zeus and Ares would have been the emcees.

Maybe next year.

I look back at Addie and Waverly again.

They're whispering furiously.

Addie snatches Waverly's paddle.

Waverly's security agent takes it back and hands it to Waverly, who laughs and uses it to shoo Addie.

"All good there, Coach Addie?" Levi says.

"Can we disqualify pop stars from the bidding this round?" Addie's voice carries naturally through the room.

She can be so soft and quiet and delicate, and she can also command a room.

I always liked that about her. You can't put her in a box. She knows when she needs to shine, and she knows when to step back. She's bold where she has to be, and she's quiet and vulnerable when she's home.

I fucked up.

I fucked up so bad with how I left her.

I had regrets immediately, but I blamed her. By the time I realized it was my own fuckup, it was too late.

The regrets are resurfacing, but they're coming with something else.

Determination.

I thought I had closure.

I don't.

Levi puts a hand to his heart. "I can't bid on an evening of playing *Croaking Creatures* with you at a tea shop?"

Fuuuuuck me. That wasn't what was listed on the auction website yesterday.

But I suppose throwing axes won't work for her now.

And instead—

"Isn't that your favorite game, Uncle Dunc?" Paisley whispers.

"No," I lie.

"It's an *afternoon*," Addie says to Levi. "Not an evening."

She's making her way through the crowd toward the stage, and I don't like it.

She can do whatever she wants.

She wants to offer an *afternoon* of playing a hand-held video game at a tea shop, fine.

But what I don't like are the murmurs going up around the ballroom.

The way the men at the tables around me are sitting straighter.

Reaching for their paddles.

Addie's hot as fuck tonight.

She's glowing in a shimmery pink gown, her arm in

a matching sling. I don't know much about makeup, but I know she's wearing it. Her lips are a deeper pink and her eyes pop in a different way than they normally do. And her hair—all of that thick chestnut hair is tied up in an elegant knot that you'd never see her sporting on a baseball field.

Addie Bloom is the sexiest secret hiding in Copper Valley. Now, because she put on a fucking *dress*, all of these nitwits are noticing what I knew years ago.

My fingers curl around my paddle.

Not my business.

If she wants to get fancied up and have men drool all over her, tough shit for them.

She won't give any of them the time of day.

And she can take care of herself.

"Sit back, boys, this one's mine," a guy at the next table says.

He's graying at the temples. Custom-fit black suit. Beady little predatory eyes tracking Addie as she makes her way to the stage. Thin mouth. Soul patch that makes him look like he has an ashy turd under his lower lip.

He's oozing *bad guy* as he taps his bidding paddle on the table.

"You play *Croaking Creatures*?" I ask him.

The look he gives me is pretty easy to interpret.

No, you fucking moron.

But he doesn't say anything out loud.

Just goes back to tracking Addie.

"You've been having some fun with my friend Waverly back there," Levi says as Addie finally climbs the few steps onto the stage.

"She's a fun person," Addie replies as he shifts the microphone to her.

"Are you a fun person?"

"No. I'm boring as hell."

Levi grins.

Addie grins back, startling the hell out of me.

"I have to be a hard-ass," she told me more than once. "If they see me crack, they'll walk all over me."

And here she is, smiling for all of Copper Valley's biggest charity supporters to see.

"How long have you been playing *Croaking Creatures*?" Levi asks her.

"Since day one."

"Do you all know the game?" Levi asks the crowd.

The halfhearted murmurs of response suggest the majority of this crowd either doesn't know it or doesn't play the game.

Fucking shame.

It's hilarious.

It's a sim game about building an island to host your favorite creatures, except shit goes wrong and the creatures croak.

"Well, there's still the tea part of your offer," Levi says.

"One thousand dollars!" someone yells from the back corner of the room.

Addie pulls a face.

Levi half chuckles. "We haven't started bidding—"

"Two thousand," the fucker at the next table says.

"I was going to ask if your arm's okay," Levi says to Addie.

"It's fine," she answers as he holds the mic in her face. "My doctor says I can't arm-wrestle bears anymore though. National Forest Service says the same. Apparently wrestling bears is a federal misdemeanor or something. Especially when you beat them."

Paisley giggles. "She's funny."

I scowl.

Addie being funny used to be my personal secret.

And how two-faced am I for being mad at her for wanting us to stay low-key while also wanting how funny she is to be my secret?

Fuuuuuck.

I am so not over this woman.

"Five thousand," someone hollers from the center of the room.

"Ten," the dude next to me says.

Levi looks out over the crowd. "You're in demand, Coach Addie. I haven't even told them exactly what you do for the Fireballs and Copper Valley sports yet."

"I don't play soccer," she says, which gets a laugh.

The only other women offering experiences tonight are from the Scorned, Copper Valley's women's soccer team.

"We've hung out before," Levi says to her.

"I had to kiss your ass since your brother's my boss," Addie agrees.

I catch myself before I join everyone else at my table in laughing.

Half the room is laughing, actually.

Including Levi's brother—her boss—at that back table with Cooper and Waverly.

"Eleven thousand," someone yells.

Addie leans into Levi's microphone. "That's a figure of speech. Ass-kissing doesn't come in this package. Literal or figurative."

"How long have you been the Fireballs' batting coach?" Levi asks her.

"This is my sixth season."

"And that's how many championship rings?"

"Three."

Levi smiles at her.

I know the wide smile she beams back.

But again, not because it's one you usually see on her in public.

She should smile though.

Three rings is something to be proud of.

Almost as good as my four.

"Fifteen thousand dollars," the douche-muffin next to me says.

"He looks like the kind of person who'd follow a woman home," Paisley whispers to me.

My fingers clench around my paddle.

"Is it true you fixed Cooper Rock's swing?" Levi

asks Addie.

She nods. "Crowning achievement. He's notoriously difficult to coach."

"Accurate," Cooper calls from the back of the room.

"Any chance you're offering batting tips while you're playing *Croaking Creatures* and sipping tea?" Levi asks.

"Not until I quit wrestling bears," she quips as she uses her good hand to gesture to her bad arm.

"Twenty-five thousand dollars," someone from Waverly and Cooper's table yells.

"Bro, your wife is sitting right next to you," Levi says. "And you can't bid on your own batting coach."

"My wife and I both object to how the Thrusters' owner's looking at her," Tripp replies, prompting all of us to crane our necks to get a better view of my team's owner, who's also sitting near the back of the room. "If she can teach Cooper to hit a ball better, she can teach a bunch of puckheads to score better too. I don't want him stealing her from us."

"Accurate again," Cooper yells. "Twenty-five thousand one hundred."

Addie flips him off while color rises in her cheeks, which I know is from the compliment she just got from her boss.

The crowd roars with laughter.

"Thirty thousand dollars," the fucknugget at the next table drawls.

"I think I need to start the bidding," Levi says to Addie.

"I think you're falling down on the job. It already started without you," she answers.

"Okay, folks, I've got thirty thousand dollars at this table to my right. Do I have—"

My paddle flies up before I've decided I'm definitely doing this. "Thirty-five."

Addie visibly chokes. "That one didn't count," she says to Levi.

He squints at me. "Why?"

"He's Canadian."

Levi grins. "That's a shitty reason."

She doesn't grin back. "Give me a beer and five minutes, and I'll come up with a better answer."

"Forty thousand," the wank-nut next to me says.

"Forty-five." I'm being an absolute fuck myself.

But none of these assholes—*none* of them— would've given her a second glance if she'd walked on stage in her baseball uniform.

Fuck. Them.

They don't deserve her.

And I have a metric ass-ton to unpack when I make my next appointment with my therapist.

Addie doesn't want me. She wanted us to be a secret. She's given me zero signs she still thinks about me at all. She doesn't do long-term relationships.

And that's what I want.

I want what my friends have. I want a wife. I want

kids. I want pets. I want to *see my partner* more than three hours a week.

Even if Addie did serious relationships, we wouldn't have worked. We're both too busy.

So why am I doing this?

Closure, half my brain says.

A second chance on her terms, the other half of my brain says.

"Fifty thousand," Waverly Sweet calls.

"She can't bid on me either," Addie says. "Pop star rule, remember?"

Levi chuckles. "Any of them can, Coach. Even the Canadians are using American dollars tonight."

"People usually listen to me when I use my stern voice."

"You can use your stern voice on me, baby," the shit-waffle mutters.

"Seventy-five thousand dollars," I hear myself say.

A small gasp ripples through the room.

"Are you for fucking real?" Addie gapes at me.

"I need to up my *Croaking Creatures* game."

"You do *not* play."

"Porty Picky's my favorite character. What's yours?"

Her mouth goes round. "You just googled that."

"I was late to an orientation thing because he was trying to get a double-death one day last week," Paisley yells.

"Eighty thousand dollars," Mr. *Not Gonna Win Tonight* barks.

"One hundred." I stare straight at Addie, my paddle still up in the air. "Ten more if you tell me your favorite character."

"Fluffle Bucket," she says. "And I got a *triple*-death before I came here to get dressed."

"You can play one-handed?"

"I can do a lot of things one-handed."

Fuck. Me. Again.

I just popped a boner.

Worst part?

Betting I'm not the only one in this room that just happened to. And if I find out who any of the other boner-sporters are, I'm kicking their asses.

"That was hot," Rooster murmurs.

"Quit looking at her if you don't want to lose your eyeballs," I murmur back.

Every last one of my friends at the table turns and stares at me. Paisley does too.

"One hundred and ten thousand dollars," Levi says. "Do I hear one-twenty?"

The fucker beside me throws his paddle on the table and glares at me.

Makes me wonder if he had that eighty to begin with.

"Going once," Levi says.

"Waverly, you can bid on me again," Addie says.

"I lost my paddle," Waverly calls back.

"Going twice…" Levi's laughing as he says it.

Addie stares at me.

"You're a fucking ass," the actual fucking ass at the next table says in my direction.

Zeus stands up to his full six-foot-nine height and glares past me. "Say that again to my buddy's face. And then I'm gonna rearrange yours."

"And sold," Levi says. "To our very own captain of the Thrusters, who apparently has secret hobbies that all of the pundits will be asking about as soon as hockey training camp starts this year. Nicely done, Coach Addie. Way to beat the record for highest bid ever recorded at the annual athletes' auction."

"This wouldn't have happened if I wore my baseball pants," she replies.

The crowd laughs again.

But she's not wrong, and it's pissed me off since the minute she stood up to walk to the stage.

"Sit down," I tell Zeus.

"I don't like the way he's looking at you."

"I can take care of myself," I assure him.

"I'm really in favor of Zeus handling this for us," Paisley says. "You're getting old, and you don't have a sugar mama yet, so you still need your dashing good looks."

Addie strolls off the stage to cheers and claps from the rest of the audience.

Joey stands up next to Zeus and glares at the fucker at the next table too.

I don't pay attention to him at all though.

I'm tracking Addie as she circles the other side of the ballroom, never once looking my way.

She hasn't glanced over here at all by the time she retakes her seat next to Waverly, accepts a drink from the Fireballs' head coach, and slams it.

Half the people at her table are staring at me, but she doesn't.

She sits back down, back straight, and looks at the stage while Waverly leans in and says something to her.

"All good over there, Zeus?" Levi says in the microphone.

Zeus lifts an arm and flexes. "Showing off before me and my lady hit the stage," he says, still glaring at the turdnugget at the next table.

"Not getting soft at all in retirement, are you?" Levi says.

"I lift quadzeuslets for exercise daily," Zeus says.

"How about you and the missus get on up here so she can tell us what she's offering that you're taking half credit for?"

"I'd call you out on calling me out, my dude, but you're still my number one boy band crush. No offense to other former boy band dudes in the audience." He sends one more glare to the fucker at the next table, who flips him off with an eye roll.

Paisley scoots closer to me while Zeus and Joey head for the stage. "We are *totally* talking later about your history with Coach Addie."

"Nothing to talk about."

She snorts in *you're such a liar.*

"I would've bid entirely too much for you too if someone like the fuckarello at the next table was looking at you wrong," I tell her.

"You're such a softie, Uncle Dunc."

I'm not a *softie.*

I'm the guy who's paying over a hundred grand for one more date with the last woman I let into my heart.

6

Addie

SOMEONE REPLACED my brain with a dying sloth.

But that's not the weird part.

No, the weird part is that the dying sloth in my brain is jackhammering in my ears.

You'd think a dying sloth wouldn't move fast enough to operate heavy equipment, yet here we are.

I whimper as it pounds again.

My mouth tastes like rotten cranberries. My arm aches. There's a crick in my neck.

And I'm still wearing last night's dress.

I pry my glued eyelids open enough to verify I did, in fact, make it to my own apartment last night, though I didn't make it to the bedroom.

Not that I've been sleeping in my bedroom even when I'm sober.

It's easier to sleep in my recliner while I'm supposed to keep my arm immobilized.

The sloth pounds once more, and I realize it's not a sloth jackhammering.

It's someone knocking on my door.

I hit the button to make my recliner go back into its normal upright position with my brains sloshing around the whole time.

I'm never touching alcohol again.

Not for how it likely made me look in front of all of the Fireballs' staff and board and owners last night, but for how it's making me feel this morning.

I push on one ear to hold my head together. Pushing on both would be more effective, but that doesn't work with the damn sling. I move around my simple gray couch adorned with all of the bright throw pillows that one of my sisters-in-law quilts for everyone she knows. My dress rustles too loudly. Sunlight streaks through the slats of the white wooden blinds, and I squint against the audacity of the sun shining so brightly today.

Whoever's at the door isn't giving up.

They knock again.

I can't squint through the peephole—my eyes aren't working well enough—so I fumble through unhooking the slider and fiddling with the tricky deadbolt, and I peer through the crack in the door.

And then I utter a *dammit* that's too loud for my own ears.

Duncan quirks a half smile at me that has more audacity than the freaking sun.

He's solo—no niece with him today. And he's slouching, hands in his jeans pockets, plain maroon Thrusters polo hugging his pecs and biceps, chin tipped down, eyeing me like he's half ready for me to tell him to pound sand, half ready to let his smile reach full smile status depending on what I say next. His broad shoulders and over-six-foot height make the hallway outside of my apartment feel smaller than it is.

And he's so damn gorgeous my nipples ache.

Or possibly that's my hangover.

"I like your pajamas," he says.

My good hand grips the doorknob tighter as I remember he bid over a hundred thousand freaking dollars on me last night. "You didn't bid enough to own me outright," I blurt.

The man who seemed furious at my very existence a few days ago is now sucking in his five-o'clock-shadowed cheeks like that'll stop him from laughing. "How much do you remember from last night?"

"Touch grass."

He lets that full smile fly, and god help me, he's using the dimples too. I hate his dimples. They're fucking glorious.

"I've never been told to touch grass by a hungover raccoon in a prom dress."

I'd flip him off, but he'd probably have something cheeky to say about that too.

And I'd probably laugh.

Just like I did when he would've said something like that to me back when we were secret-flinging.

Instead, I order myself to not wonder how my makeup is faring this morning or how much it'll cost in dry cleaning to get this gown back to its original shape and try to channel Baseball Coach Addie and all of her badass attitude.

"What do you want?"

There was a time when he'd knock on my door and I'd grab him by the collar and haul him inside so we could strip each other out of our clothes and let off steam and just *be*.

With no expectations.

Or so I thought.

I wonder if that's what he's thinking about now too.

"Just checking in to see how you're doing," he says.

"Not much different than when I saw you last night."

He stares briefly at my face before his gaze drops to my dress—to my cleavage?—then lifts to meet my eyes again.

"I can see that. Can I come in?"

Most things about last night after me being on stage are hazy. And that means my priority needs to be getting cleaned up, texting Waverly to ask if I embarrassed myself and need to apologize to anyone, and then doing whatever she tells me I should do.

The idea of getting cleaned up makes my eyes water though.

In the bad way.

It's fucking hard with my left shoulder immobilized.

Duncan takes advantage of my silence to slip past me and into my apartment.

He glances around, and I stiffen, which annoys both the crick in my neck that I'm starting to feel from sleeping in the recliner and also my shoulder.

Time for pain meds.

And coffee.

Three or four vats of it.

"Take it you haven't seen the news," he says as he casually strides through my living room toward my small kitchen. Dishes litter the counters and sink. I live alone, so I don't go through a lot of trash. Usually, anyway. Since I got hurt, I've been living off of takeout and prepackaged meals, so my garbage can is over-flowing.

Cooking one-handed is a pain in the ass.

So is taking out the trash.

And then my sloth brain catches up to what he just said. "What news?"

He lifts an empty to-go cup from a café down the street and waves it at me before putting it back on the counter. "You still drink coffee?"

I don't answer so much as I whimper in *yes, please*.

He opens the white cabinet door next to the sink and pulls out my coffee beans, then digs my coffee maker out from the lower cabinet under the row of cabinets separating the kitchen from the living room.

And then he does something even worse than starting my coffee for me.

He searches the back of the freezer for my stash of premade egg muffin sandwiches.

I whimper again. "Why are you doing this?"

"You need coffee and food before I piss you off." He pops a single sandwich into my microwave. The beeping pierces my skull and makes the very center of my brain ache.

And the aching is why I cave and sit on one of the barstools opposite him at the long countertop. I'd lay my head down, but I'm not sure my shoulder would like it.

"You're here to piss me off."

"I'm here because you'll be pissed when I tell you what I have to tell you. Even though I'd rather it not piss you off, but you're within your rights to be pissed about it."

Is my sloth brain still sludging, or is he absolutely perky about pissing me off? "And you're going to enjoy it."

His smile slips. "Not at all."

"Then why are you in such a good mood?"

"Acceptance."

"Acceptance?"

"Hold that thought." He grabs my coffee grinder and the bag of beans, and he carries them out of the kitchen and into my bedroom.

I don't argue.

Not even when he shuts the door.

The man is grinding coffee beans in another room while I have the hangover from hell.

Which means he's either here to sprinkle ground coffee beans all over my bed, or he's thoughtfully keeping loud noises as far from me as he can.

My eyes water again.

I hate depending on people. I hate needing help. I hate vulnerability as a general concept.

Too many people have used it against me, so I make it a point to not need anyone else.

Want is fine.

I can *want* to be friends with someone. I can *want* to sleep with someone. I can *want* to share parts of my life here and there with the people who come and go.

But I never want to *need* it.

Needing it is what gets you in trouble. Needing it can destroy your life.

The coffee grinder whirs to a halt, and moments later, Duncan strides out of my bedroom.

He gets the coffee maker prepped and hits the button to turn it on as the microwave beeps that the breakfast sandwich is done.

Before my sloshy brain can contemplate moving, he

opens the microwave to stop the beeping, grabs a plate from the cabinet next to it, and grins at me again while he gets the food on the plate.

"You want one of those too?" he asks.

I gawk at him.

"Kidding. I didn't come here to raid your kitchen."

"*Why* are you in such a good mood?"

I already asked him that.

Shit.

What did he say?

He said—

"Acceptance," he repeats. "I think I was an ass when we broke up. And I regret that. But I don't regret that we're back in each other's lives. I'm looking forward to what comes next."

"Whoa, buddy, slow your roll." I blink hard, mostly because I don't want to have this conversation.

I want to go into my bedroom and flop down and sleep for another three days.

Which I can't do comfortably because I still can't move my shoulder for nearly another week.

"You buying an experience with me," I say slowly, concentrating on every word, "does not equate to you buying your way back into my life."

He slides breakfast to me. "Yep."

"Yep, you understand, or yep, yep it does?"

"Both."

I look down at the plate with the egg sandwich to

distract myself from Mr. Puzzles, and I whimper at how good it looks.

And don't ask how it smells.

There is nothing on earth that could smell as good as this microwaved egg sandwich.

It's making me drool.

I suck at my lip while I make a quick swipe with a napkin that I'm reasonably certain I used to wipe up spilled cheese dip the other day.

But it's sitting there.

So I use it.

"Eat," he says. "Coffee will be ready in a few."

The scent of egg and cheese and bacon tickles my nose, and my mouth waters more. There's a part of me that would generally argue on principle, but that part of me is still hungover.

So I do as he's suggested—not told, *suggested*—and I pick up the sandwich with my good hand and take a bite.

And *oh my god*.

Absolute.

Freaking.

Heaven.

I don't look at Duncan, but I don't need to.

I know he's smirking like he's Captain Hangover Cure to the rescue.

I do shoot a look at him when I realize what he's doing now though.

He's putting my dishes in the dishwasher.

"I was getting to that," I say around another bite of my breakfast sandwich.

"Can't be easy managing your life without full use of one of your arms."

Every time I injure my shoulder, I realize how much I take two working arms and two working legs for granted. "Temporary inconvenience. I can do my own dishes."

The expression he aims at me needs no words to accompany it.

You can, but it's easier for me, and I'm here, so I'm doing your damn dishes.

Today.

Today, he'll do my dishes.

That was my issue when we were—whatever we were. Dating? Flinging? Situationshipping?

He'd do nice little things, and while I always said thank you, and I always appreciated it, I didn't *trust* it.

You do nice things when you're trying to impress someone.

Doesn't mean it'll last.

God knows my mother learned that lesson long before I came into my parents' lives. I was baby number five after four boys. And she was already done, except she wasn't.

She wasn't allowed to be.

She had mouths to feed and bodies to bathe and

clothe and endless laundry to run, and my father thought that since he made more money, he didn't have to do any of those things.

And she willingly spent her life sacrificing her own happiness for the sake of everyone else's.

I force the memories of her out of my head and concentrate on my breakfast instead.

Eating takes longer than normal both because the sandwich is pretty hot and also because my body is moving at the same speed as my brain this morning. So Duncan's finished the dishes and is squishing the errant napkins and food containers from my countertop into my trash can before I'm done.

He also gets the trash bag tied up and sets it next to the door, then replaces the bag in my can.

Pours me a cup of coffee when it finishes brewing, using the last clean mug on my mug tree next to the fridge.

Wipes my countertops with a soapy wet dishcloth while I'm lost in the bliss of a cup of coffee that someone else made me.

Which isn't necessary.

It's not.

I can make my own coffee. I appreciate my own coffee.

I'm just exceptionally grateful today that Duncan made it faster than I could've made it or gotten down the street to buy a latte.

And I finally remember to say thank you.

Which prompts my snail's-pace brain to remember the other thing about Duncan being here. "We should pick a date for me to fulfill your experience."

He smirks.

He freaking *smirks*.

"I don't care how much you bid on me, it doesn't come with sex," I say dryly.

"You already texted me about setting up a date," he says. "Remember?"

Oh, shit.

I don't.

I don't remember.

Which means I could've said anything.

I reach for my phone in my pocket, but I'm still wearing my dress from last night.

Which has a pocket.

Waverly's costume seamstress is a freaking goddess for that.

However—my phone isn't there.

"Your phone's on the charger in the bedroom," Duncan says. "I saw it."

That's good news.

I autopiloted plugging my phone in.

Good job, me.

Also, *who else did you text while you were drunk last night, me?*

"You can look at your calendar later and get back to

me," Duncan adds. "I'm pretty open the next few weeks."

"Not golfing every day?"

He grins. "For you and *Croaking Creatures*, I can cancel a tee time."

Croaking Creatures is a little niche. It started as a mockery of a popular sim game where you pick what animal you want to be, then go live on an island and grow fruits and vegetables and hunt and fish and raise livestock and build your dream house. The creators of *Croaking Creatures* had been playing the original game and started wondering what would happen if your character had an accident with an axe or didn't fully cook their recipes and gave themselves salmonella. But it's morphed into utter chaos in the years since launch.

It seems there's a new way to hurt yourself and die —and respawn, naturally—every week or so.

Morbid, but hilarious and fun.

And seriously good stress relief.

"You do *not* play." He said he did last night. He named a favorite character.

I remember that part.

He hunches over, leaning his long, corded forearms on the countertop. "Our last away trip, we were on the plane, it's like one in the morning because we were coming back from the West Coast, and I crowed so loudly in victory when my creature impaled himself on a tree branch while simultaneously having his slingshot malfunction and hit him in the eye that I woke up half the plane and had to buy them all dinner after the season was over."

I stare at him for a very long beat, and then I crack up, which hurts, but I don't care. "Double-death! Paisley was serious."

The man has the nerve to hit me with the full force of his smile. His fucking gorgeous smile that comes with those killer dimples. The smile that swooned me right out of my panties the night we met.

"I'm going for triple next," he says smugly.

I scoff. "I was out swimming, looking for a treasure chest with the black hole in it to plant at Dorcas's house because she's so annoying, but a seagull pecked my eye which made me crack the chest with the black hole, and my medicine turned out to be a poisonous mushroom since I bought it at the market instead of making it myself, but not even that ultimately did me in. That was the day the flying kitten of death attacked as soon as I surfaced with the black hole trying to suck me back in."

He laughs, and it's like we're once again the two people who hung out and enjoyed each other's company in a totally chill way a few years ago.

No pressure.

No expectations.

It's why I kept hooking up with him longer than I would've normally let a guy stay. He was just so easy to be around.

Before I hurt him.

"You did the triple," he says. "And with the flying kitten of death?"

"I had half an idea she was the flying kitten of death when I adopted her, but she was so cute, I didn't care."

If anyone who doesn't know the game were listening in, they'd likely think we'd been dipping into edibles.

"I never adopt anything," he says. "I'm afraid it'll eat me in my sleep."

"That's *the whole point*. And why we have unlimited lives." Half the fandom is lobbying for an option to die so many times that you get to be a ghost for a day, but so far, the creators aren't having it. I'm holding out hope though.

"I can handle it if I drown or if my slingshot malfunctions and takes out my eye, but there's something about being eaten by a pet that doesn't work for me."

"You must've been a crazy old cat lady whose pets ate her after she died alone in a previous life."

He chuckles and shakes his head. "Must've been. You feeling better?"

I blink once. Then again. "I am. Thank you."

"Good. Time to ruin it. Sorry."

He pulls out his phone, thumbs over the screen, and then slides it in front of me.

Athletes' Auction Breaks Record and Brings the Drama.

I take another gulp of coffee before setting the cup aside so I can use my good hand to scroll.

Auction opened as normal, blah blah. Decent food. Levi Wilson made a great emcee. Blah blah blah.

But the real excitement began when Addie Bloom, batting coach for the Fireballs, stepped on stage draped in a pink dress with a matching sling that she's been sporting for unknown reasons. The sassy L'Addie and her quick mouth on stage sparked a bidding war that ended with the unexpectedly feminine coach fetching the highest price of the evening, beating even an offering from pop star Waverly Sweet and her husband, future baseball Hall of Famer Cooper Rock.

Adding to the unexpected, she was won not by a local real estate magnate twice her age, but by the captain of the Thrusters.

Is an afternoon of playing a second-rate video game truly worth over a hundred grand? Or is there something more going on here?

I shove the phone away. "Who cares what the gossips say?"

"It's the lead headline on the paper's website. Written by a sports guy."

My fingers prickle.

So do my toes.

Will Santiago see that?

And Tripp and Lila?

Also— "'*Sassy L'Addie?*' What the actual *fuck?* That reporter should be fired."

Duncan clears his throat. "The comments indicate people around Copper Valley have decided to call us…*Daddie.*"

I'm in my sixth season with the Fireballs. I've seen grown men launch glitter bombs in locker rooms. Use jock straps as slingshots to send plush mascots flying at each other. There's a hat that makes its rounds in the locker room every year with a stuffy attached that looks like a dick and balls, thanks to the mascot contest management ran my first season with the team, when they tried to convince the city that *Meaty the Flaming Meatball* should be the Fireballs' new mascot. More than once, we've been subjected to the entire team wearing mascot thongs over their pants.

It takes a lot to make me gape in disbelief.

But I'm actually speechless as I stare at Duncan.

"I already called the Thrusters' PR team to ask what they can do about it."

"*Daddie?*" I shriek loudly enough to re-spark my own headache. "*Daddie.* Oh my god. Do you know how this looks?"

"You didn't do anything wrong."

I squeeze my eyes shut and try to grab my head with both hands, but my left shoulder reminds me it's not supposed to move. "*Fuck.*"

What did I say on stage last night?

I can't remember.

But it's probably on the internet by now.

He shifts around the kitchen again, heading toward my bedroom once more.

I don't stop him.

I automatically thank him when he emerges and hands me my cell phone.

I want to check my text messages to see what I drunk-texted who last night, but the missed calls catch my eye first.

People don't call me.

I don't call people.

Not unless it's an emergency.

So six missed phone calls?

Those are top on the priority list.

There's one from Santiago, one from Tripp Wilson, and one from the Fireballs PR number.

"They wouldn't be talking about us if you hadn't bid over a hundred grand on me," I mutter while I click over to voicemail.

"It's fine. You can hate me forever for that."

I glance up at him. "Why *did* you bid so much on me?"

He wiggles his eyebrows at me.

Whatever reaching *acceptance* means, it's clearly working for him.

Nice to see him happy again.

Even if I'm flipping him off at the eyebrow wiggle, which makes him snort in amusement.

I look back at my phone and skim the automatic transcription of my voice messages.

Santiago wants to know if I've seen the news and if I'm okay. He also wants me to know it's fucking stupid that the press is having a field day with me when they wouldn't if I were a man, but also, if I were a man, I wouldn't have fetched such a high price, and that's fucking stupid too. He thinks he should've gone for over a hundred grand last year.

Tripp wants to know if I saw the news and if I can swing into the office today to discuss a potential opportunity to turn the shitty side of the article into a positive. And he also wants me to know he was uncomfortable with some of the things he heard men saying about me, and he'd prefer that I don't offer experiences again in the auction so long as I'm a member of the Fireballs staff.

Sadie in PR reiterates what Tripp said, that she's been speaking with management and they think they have a spin that'll fit in well with a new community outreach program, and could I please call her back?

Waverly's left me a message telling me to not look at social media and to trust that someone else will be tomorrow's front-page news.

My sister-in-law wants to know if she should fly in *now* to help me handle everything.

And someone's left me a message about my car's extended warranty.

I thought we were done with that scam. Fuckers.

When I look up from my phone, I have to turn around to locate Duncan.

He's picking up used tissues scattered around my couch and straightening the pile of books on my end table.

Little things he used to do when we were together too. Things I never told him I appreciated because I didn't know how to balance the weirdness of having a man straighten for me—my father and brothers would *never*—with my unwavering need to take care of myself.

"You don't have to do that," I say quietly.

"I'm a figment of your imagination. When I leave, your apartment will be messy again and you can do all of the dishes and picking up yourself."

I stare at him while my heart does a funny thing in my chest that I don't like at all. "You're not funny."

"I am, but you're Coach Addie-ing me with all of your walls up. It's fine. I know you think I'm funny under the badass glare. All good with the Fireballs?"

This man. He's not wrong, and that bothers me more than it should. I test my head as I rise from the stool. "Boss wants to see me."

Duncan eyes my dress. Then my face, which I haven't looked at myself yet today. "How soon?"

I wince, which makes my head throb, which makes me wince harder. "ASAP."

Duncan looks at my dress again.

Then at my face again.

And then the bastard smiles that dimple-popping smile. "Need a ride?"

"I need a shower."

His smile fades, but his eyes—fuck me.

His eyes stay kind.

And I know what he's going to ask before the words come out of his mouth, and unfortunately, I know how I'm going to answer.

Out of necessity.

Which means my eyes are watering already as he says, "No innuendos, no ulterior motives, if you need help, if it'll make showering faster...I'm here."

7

Duncan

I CLEARLY HATE MYSELF.

Or I didn't expect her to say yes.

But she did, and so here I am, stripped down to my boxers in Addie's bathroom, standing in her shower with her, shampooing her hair.

Nothing I haven't seen before, I said when she gave me a side-eye at my offer to help her shower.

About the same as showering with all of the guys in the locker room, I said when I started to sense that she wanted to say yes but didn't trust one of us. Or maybe both of us.

"Waverly's stylist fixed my hair yesterday," she says, obviously trying to keep this normal by pretending we're having an everyday conversation where she's not totally naked and I'm nearly so. "First time it got washed since…that thing that wasn't your fault."

My dick is holding the majority of the blood in my body right now, which means my brain is operating at about ten percent of its normal capacity. And eight percent of that capacity is going toward suppressing the shivers that come with being wet but not in the direct flow of hot water in the shower.

This is one of those corner shower numbers next to the bathtub.

Small.

Almost too small for me to keep enough distance so Addie doesn't notice the boner from hell.

Worth it though.

I fucked up four years ago. I don't want to fuck up again.

"How much longer are you in the sling?" I ask.

"Five to seven days. Depends on the scans."

I make a noise that I hope is acknowledgment mixed with sympathy.

Pretty sure I sound like a drowning goat instead.

"Surgery?" I ask to cover the noise.

"Depends on the scans."

I gather more of her hair near her head, rubbing the suds into it against her scalp.

She makes a noise herself.

It's like a stifled moan.

I'm studiously counting the drips of water on the white fiberglass shower wall so I don't look at her naked body any more than necessary.

That ass—*fuck me*, that ass.

I loved holding her ass back when she let me in her life.

And now it's mere inches from me, and I need to stop looking at it and thinking about it and being aware of its existence.

I meant it when I told her I woke up this morning with acceptance.

But what I didn't tell her was how long I stared at myself in the bathroom mirror, contemplating life in general.

How I'm creeping closer to my late thirties.

How much I feel that pang of jealousy in my chest anytime I visit my teammates who've retired and are loving their domestic lives.

The way I feel more sluggish in general, like my body is telling me it's time to slow down.

The way I've always figured I'd be married with kids by the time I retired, but I'm realizing that's not my path. Retirement from hockey is coming within the next few years regardless of what my personal life looks like.

So I made a choice.

I choose to take responsibility for my part in breaking up with Addie. I choose to acknowledge I put her in an awful position. I choose to forgive myself for it too, because I can't be good for anyone if I'm busy beating myself up for my mistakes instead of learning from them.

I choose to find out if Addie's still the woman I fell for.

I choose to do everything I know to do to see if I can fit into her life.

To see if we can complement each other as easily now on purpose as we seemed to by accident four years ago.

Seeing her last week wasn't an unfortunate coincidence.

It was the universe's way of telling me to quit lying to myself when I say I've let her go. When I say it was her fault we broke up. To face the fact that I've consciously or subconsciously compared every woman I've dated in the last four years to Addie Bloom, and every last one has come up lacking next to her.

"What did I text you?" she asks the spray of water hitting her front.

Where she has the most glorious breasts known to man.

Which I am also not thinking about holding.

Licking.

Sucking.

Not *yet,* anyway. Not until I've earned my way back in.

I clear my throat. "I could tell you, but I might get something wrong."

"High-level overview."

"That we need to set a date to fulfill your obligation to me per auction terms."

Captain Lavalier, I have dutifully accepted that you won what I offered, which is only what I offended and nothing I didn't offramp, even though I object to your use of Canadian Ehs as currency in an American auction, and so you can pick one single date lasting no more than 3 hours from sunrise to sunset to get schooled so bad you'll be crying for your mama when my creatures come up with new and inventive ways to murder your creches over tea.

Yes, I memorized it.

Autocorrects and misspellings and all.

It was badass Addie with a hint of *what the fuck just happened* and a dash of alcohol.

But that text isn't what pushed me into acceptance of what I need to do.

No, the privilege of understanding and acceptance came courtesy of the next text she sent me. Which I won't be mentioning.

She can read it herself in her sent messages later.

Her hand brushes mine and tangles in her soapy locks. "It's time to rinse."

"Okay."

"Turn around. I think I can do this one-handed."

I obey, turning my back to her, and I start counting the water droplets on the shower door.

And that's when my mouth decides it doesn't need my brain in order to say things. "I don't trust people who don't see you as a woman until you put on a dress."

There's a heavy pause behind me. I can't hear her breathing over the flow of the water, but I swear I can feel her pulse tick up.

Or maybe that's mine and I'm projecting.

"Okay," she says quietly, but it's more of a question than a statement.

"It pissed me off that it took you putting on a dress for half the city to realize you're a woman. They didn't fucking deserve to win you, and I don't trust what they would've tried if they had."

I was simply almost-naked a minute ago.

Now I'm naked and exposed and vulnerable.

Admitting to the last woman I let myself care about that I overstepped last night.

And I know I overstepped.

I overstepped in stopping by when she didn't answer my texts this morning asking if she was feeling okay.

I overstepped in doing her dishes. I overstepped in fixing her breakfast and coffee. I overstepped in picking up her living room and letting myself contemplate starting her laundry for her.

I'm overstepping in letting part of my brain hope that she's looking at *my* ass now as our positions are reversed.

But she's not calling me out on any of that.

She's not saying anything at all.

And I don't regret overstepping.

Because if I'm going to see Addie regularly over the next few months—which she doesn't know yet, but I likely am—then I'm going to be me.

The real me.

The me she'll get if she gives me another chance.

I'm not much different today than I was four years ago when it comes to helping people I care about.

But I'm very much different when it comes to realizing that I don't yet understand what she needs.

And while I know I like her more than I've ever liked any other woman in at least a decade, I also know that I might have to accept that she might never like me the same.

I look down at the shampoo suds swirling around my feet, which is my only evidence that she's rinsing her hair.

"I get it," I add. "I know. You didn't ask me to play hero. You don't need me defending your honor and you can take care of yourself on a meet-up with someone who won an experience with you. You've got everything under control and you don't need my help. Truth is, I didn't do it entirely for you. I did it for me. So I could sleep better. So I won't worry about things that you'll tell me I don't need to worry about, but things that I can't help but worry about because it's who I fucking am."

She inhales loudly enough to drown out the sound of the shower. "I'm glad you have the resources to help you sleep better."

I glance over my shoulder, get a *don't you dare peek at me while I'm naked* face that's not nearly as irritated as I'd expect it to be, and turn my head back around to not look at her.

Is she pissed about my motives last night but suppressing it?

Or was she halfheartedly glaring merely because I looked at her?

I didn't look at her breasts. Just her face. Which I won't be saying out loud.

Mostly because I wanted to look at all of her, and I can't tell her I only looked at her face without adding that I wanted to look at all of her.

I *will* get to look at her again.

All of her.

But only if I find the right balance between pushing it and not pushing it.

"If you ever do need help, you can call me," I add. "I won't tell anyone. I won't mock you. I won't ask any more questions than necessary to get there and do whatever it is you need me to do."

I can see the vaguest outline of myself in the glass shower door, but I can't see her.

And I definitely don't expect the, "Thank you," that follows a long pause.

It's startling after the number of times she's told me

I've got this or *I can handle this* or *No, I like to do it myself* any time I tried to help her with nearly anything when we were together.

Right up to when she told me she didn't need a caretaker when she hurt her arm.

Which was my fault too.

I insisted on teaching her how to ice skate.

She fell and dislocated her shoulder when I wouldn't let her go as soon as she wanted me to so that she could try skating on her own.

"I'd offer to help all the same for any friend," I say.

"I know."

We lapse into silence again.

I don't know what she's thinking about, but I'm thinking about how miserable my drive home will be, and how much I'm looking forward to rubbing out this boner.

Unless she lets me push her against the wall and take her right here.

I'd be good with that.

We were good together. If she needs the reminder…

"My bosses don't want me participating in any more auctions," she mutters, which is so far from where my brain has gone that I almost don't comprehend the words. "They also noticed people noticing that I'm a woman, and they were…uncomfortable… with certain parts of last night."

Focus, dumbass. Focus. "That's a complicated mess of *not fair.*"

"It is."

"Do you want to offer another experience?"

"Fuck, no."

I chuckle.

"Conditioner time. You can turn around again."

I shift in the shower and take the conditioner bottle she points to, squirt some in my hand, and go to work on her hair again.

I love her hair. It's thick and smooth and gorgeous, and it smells like her.

"My sister-in-law offered to come help me while I recover," Addie says. "I should call her back and accept."

I make a noncommittal noise. She didn't say *will*. She said *should*. And I know she knows I noticed.

"If I don't, you'll keep showing up to try to see me naked," she adds.

"I'm not doing this to see you naked. I'm doing it because you in makeup scares me and that's the other thing that'll keep me from sleeping at night."

I would absolutely come to her house every day to help her shower to see her naked.

I'd do it every day for months without expectation that I'll ever recover from this case of blue balls if that's what it takes to prove to her that she can trust me.

No matter how uncomfortable my junk is as I'm massaging sweet-smelling conditioner into her hair and sneaking peeks at her slender waist and the dimples at the base of her spine and the way her thick ass muscles flare out.

"I'd be offended, but I saw what I looked like before I got in the shower," Addie says.

"You looked gorgeous last night. But you almost always do. In a dress or in your baseball pants or completely naked or in a Minnesota Wild shirt, which I'll deny saying if you ever tell one of my teammates."

"Stop."

"This is called *setting standards* if you ever change your mind about being single forever. Don't settle for anyone who doesn't think you're gorgeous all the time. Don't even do casual with someone who doesn't think you're gorgeous all the time. You're welcome."

She glances over her shoulder at me. Her face is makeup-free again, glistening with the moisture in the shower. Eyes wary. Lips pursed.

I aim for a poker face.

She's gonna be pissed when she looks at her phone again and sees the last message she sent me after the auction last night.

Probably even more pissed now that she's let me help her do her dishes and take a shower.

But that one message is the very root of why I'm here.

That, and knowing what the Thrusters staff wants me to do after I won an afternoon with Addie last night.

I wish you hadn't gotten attached. Then we could've hung out forever. But I don't do relationships because relationships don't benefit people like me. All they do is rob you of your happiness. Ask me how I know. Or don't. It doesn't matter. I hope voice-to-text gets this wrong because I'm going to wish I didn't send this when I see it in the morning.

Translation: *It wasn't you. It was me and something in my past that hurt me.*

So if Addie Bloom would take me in her life so long as I never tell her I want to see her every day, every night, every hour and minute of my life, why would I not try?

Why would I not want to be here with her?

Giving her all of the time she needs to see me as someone who enhances her life?

To trust me enough to tell me who hurt her so badly that it destroyed her belief in relationships.

Forever isn't casual. Forever is never casual.

But if casual is what she needs to believe in for me to stay in her life, then I'll play the game.

The weeks left until I report for training camp will fly by. They always do. I won't have a lot of time for a serious relationship either once my own season gets going.

But the time I do have, I'll be a benefit for her.

Not a drag. Not an obligation.

A bonus.

And eventually, I'll hang up my skates, and we'll see where we go from there.

If she lets me.

"I can finish up," she says.

"You sure?"

She nods.

"I'll wait outside if you need help getting dressed."

"I don't want to keep my boss waiting. Santiago's retiring, and I'm on the list to interview for his job. I can't fuck up."

"Does that mean you want help so you can get there faster?"

She growls quietly.

I take that as a yes.

"No one who's seen the Fireballs play the past few years would think *any* of you on the coaching staff are screwing up where it counts," I say. "And you're Addie Fucking Bloom. You don't piss around anyway."

She looks back at me again. Her hair is shiny with the conditioner rubbed in. Water droplets cling to her thick brown lashes. Wary eyes hold my gaze before briefly dipping to my lips, then back.

So it *is* possible for my hard-on to get harder.

"I fucked up getting drunk last night," she whispers.

"You're allowed to be human."

"I'm really not."

"Addie—"

"People already call me the *token woman coach*."

"Very few people, and those people suck and they're just trying to get under your skin because it makes them uncomfortable that you're better at your job than they are at theirs."

"But am I? *Am I?* Or do people just want *A League of Their Own* and *Field of Dreams* mashed up and come to life? Am I really as good as all of the other women coaches in professional sports, or *am* I the token lady coach?"

I start to assure her she's good at her job, but she shakes her head and looks forward again. "Never mind. I need to rinse my hair and get dressed and get to work."

I put a hand on her good shoulder. "You. Kick. Ass. You're not a gimmick. And if you get promoted to head coach, it'll be because you earned it, not because the Fireballs are trying to be the first team in the league to have a female head coach."

"Will it?"

"Who cares? Once you're there, you'll keep taking the team all the way, every season. That's what'll count."

"What if I don't?" she whispers.

Fuck it.

Just *fuck it*.

I wrap my arms around her from behind, careful with her bad shoulder, and press a kiss to her good shoulder. "Can't control injuries, Addie. Can't control how a rookie or a trade will fit into the team. Can't control the weather. Can't control bad calls. Can't control bad days. But you can control doing the best damn job you know how to do. You're incapable of doing anything else."

Her breath shudders out of her.

She doesn't pull away.

Doesn't tense.

Doesn't rub her ass against my hard-on that's poking her, but she doesn't shriek and yell at me for it either.

Nor does she yell at me for the fact that my forearms are pressing against her breasts.

Or for kissing her shoulder.

This Addie.

This is the Addie I miss. The Addie she doesn't let anyone else see. The one with fears and dreams and a soft side. The one who needs to be hugged and who needs a safe space to get tipsy and laugh with friends.

Is this why she doesn't do relationships?

Because she doesn't know how to let her guard down enough to let someone in?

Or is it more than that?

What has made her so terrified of being vulnerable?

"I need to get to work," she whispers.

"Right." I drop my arms and step back toward the shower door. "I'll get a towel ready."

I don't want to get a towel ready.

I want to stand in this shower and rub soap all over her body and kiss her and touch her and play with her sweet pussy until she's screaming my name.

I want to towel her off and carry her to bed and stroke her soft skin and lick her from head to toe and make love to her while being so very, very careful with her bad arm.

I want to lie in bed with her all afternoon and listen

to her tell stories about the Fireballs and tell her my own favorite stories about the Thrusters from the past few years.

And none of that is happening today.

But maybe—*maybe*—it could happen another day.

8

Addie

I AM NEVER DRINKING AGAIN.

Ever.

Ever.

"It cannot be *that* bad," Francie, my oldest and long-est-running sister-in-law, says to me over my car's speaker system as I drive myself to work after letting Duncan help me get dressed.

Which happened *before* I looked at all of the text messages I sent to various people last night.

Including Francie.

Which is why we're on the phone now. It's not often she gets a random *I love you, don't let my stupid brother take you for granted, you deserve better than what my mom had* text from me.

But she did last night.

And she's not the only person I texted.

Which makes letting Duncan help me shower even worse.

"It's that bad," I tell her.

"Did you also text your first boss and tell him to lick your shoes?"

"Of course not."

"Did you text your current boss and tell him you're the only option he has for manager when Santiago retires?"

"No."

"Did you text Steve Simpson and ask him if he's still good enough with his tongue to temporarily make up for his personality?"

"*No.*"

"So…what did you do?"

"I don't want to talk about it."

She laughs. "You called me to talk about it and now you don't want to talk about it."

"I want to talk about how much I don't want to talk about it." I brake as I approach a line of cars behind a red light a couple blocks from Duggan Field. My hair is still damp.

So is my left armpit.

I wouldn't let Duncan help me dry off as thoroughly as I needed to get dried off because I needed him to leave.

I needed space.

Now I need to not think about how he hugged me in the shower.

About how much I liked the feel of his erection against my ass.

How much more I liked the soft kiss he pressed to my good shoulder, then the way he pretended none of it happened at all after I'd soaped and rinsed the rest of my body and stepped out of the shower to let him help me dry me off.

Maybe subconsciously, I remembered what I texted him.

But *dammit*, I miss him.

The him I believed in before he got butthurt about me being independent.

I can understand being butthurt about me insisting on keeping our short-term fling turned longer-term-quasi-friends-with-benefits thing a secret. About me not wanting to get serious.

But half of it was my independence, and I need that almost as much as I need oxygen.

"Oh my god," Francie yelps. "There's a boy, and you like him."

"I am completely uninterested in boys."

"A *man*. There's a *man*."

The light turns green.

No one moves.

"C'mon, people," I mutter. "I told my boss I'd be there in three minutes, and I cannot be late. Again."

"Who is he?" Francie asks.

"My boss? The big boss. Tripp Wilson wants to talk."

"Tell me you're not crushing on your married boss."

"Ew. No. He's old."

He's about the same age as Sam. The oldest of my four brothers. Francie's husband.

Same number of kids at roughly the same ages too.

"Okay, good," Francie says. "Although, I thought his wife was the big boss and he was the next-big boss."

"Also true, but she was scheduled to leave this morning for the All-Star festivities. So I have to talk to him."

"About?"

"I don't know. Some community outreach thing."

"Ah. I see. So who's your crush?"

I should've known she couldn't be distracted.

The cars in front of me finally move, so I press on the gas too. "No one."

"*Addie.*"

What the *fuck*?

The damn light's turning yellow again.

Already.

I brake with a groan as the car in front of me hits the brakes too.

I'm late. I'm freaking late after getting trashed at a work function and missing three calls and four texts from my boss.

"Never drinking ever again," I mutter.

"Oh, don't say that. I love when we have spiked hot chocolate at the holidays. You're hilarious when you put your guard down."

Yeah.

I'm hilarious.

I'm so hilarious, I texted Duncan that we could've been forever if he'd never told me he cared about me.

Stupid stupid stupid.

And then he showed up and cleaned half my apartment and helped me shower and hugged me and kissed my shoulder and didn't make a single joke about what we could do while I was naked and he was pretending his boxer briefs weren't doing their best to restrain his thick, long, hard erection.

I miss his penis.

He's very good with his penis.

But it comes with the rest of him, including his brain and his protector streak and his heart and our history, and that means his penis is off-limits.

I blow out a breath. Fuck it. I *do* want to talk about this. "What does it mean when a guy you had a casual thing with a long time ago shows back up in your life doing nice things for you but not hitting on you after you drunk-text him that if he hadn't caught feelings, you would've kept having a casual thing with him forever?"

"It means I'm getting on a plane this afternoon

because there is no way that's the whole story and I *am* getting the *entire* story out of you."

"That's it. That's the whole story." I stare at the freaking red light. I'm absolutely running late. Not that Tripp told me I had to be at the office by ten. I told him myself I'd be there by ten. Freaking traffic.

Freaking shoulder.

I grab my phone while I wait for the light and type out a brief *caught in traffic* text to him.

"All three of your other brothers told me some variation of that *it's nothing, it doesn't mean anything* story within months of proposing to their *it's nothing* flings," Francie muses.

Some days I hate having older brothers who are all too similar to me in certain ways. "I'm too busy to have a relationship."

"Mm-hmm," my unfortunately still-favorite sister-in-law says.

I don't dislike my other three sisters-in-law.

I just don't like them *as much*.

Mostly because they haven't been around as long. Francie has been in the family since I was in high school.

She's seen things. She's listened to me cry over shitty situations at work. She's listened to me fume about the males of the species that I mistakenly let myself believe in. She's listened to me rave about how much I like working for the Fireballs.

And I do.

But just because things have been good this far doesn't mean I'll ever let my guard down. I've been screwed too many times in the past to trust that good ever lasts.

And that's my problem with Duncan too.

I grew up watching my mom fade into a shell of herself for all that she gave to the rest of us.

My first high school boyfriend dated me on a dare and told me he didn't really like me when we broke up.

My most serious relationship ended because he didn't like how much time I spent with male athletes.

I lost my virginity to a guy who was seeing two of my college softball teammates at the same time. That was bad on him—he didn't expect us to stick together and confront him.

Hope he learned his lesson.

And then there was the guy who almost ruined my life for the pure joy of being able to do it.

But Duncan—Duncan broke up with me. He knows what I can and can't offer. I'm in no position to help him professionally, and he's in no position to want or need me to. He honestly doesn't have any more reason to like me today than he did the day he left. He doesn't have any reason to show up and help me this morning.

But he's still here.

Implying that he wants to be part of my life.

After I told him I would've stayed with him forever if he'd just kept it casual.

I drum my fingers on the steering wheel and glare

at the red light. "He has a job that demands all of his time."

"Just like you."

"Just like me."

"You have an offseason."

"He's busier during my offseason."

"But you still had time to have a thing that led to him catching feelings."

The light turns green, and I lay on my horn.

The driver in front of me flips me off.

Don't care.

He needs to move so I can get to work.

"Does this guy you had a thing with know about your road rage?" Francie quips.

"It's not road rage. It's impatience *today*. Tomorrow I'll let a dick merge without flipping him off. Today, this fucker needs to *move*."

I get through the light and the next one too while Francie tries to talk more details out of me, and while I get increasingly more stressed about this meeting with Tripp.

By the time I let my sister-in-law go and park in the staff parking lot at the headquarters building across the street from Duggan Field, I'm sweating and convinced I'm getting fired.

Good thing I can be a token girl coach for any team.

And then I shake myself.

Tripp said *community outreach opportunity*. He didn't say *we need to talk about your behavior last night*.

I'm ten minutes late when I finally get to the executive floor. Denise, the executive assistant, sees me straight into Tripp's office, then settles onto the couch off to the side with a notebook in hand.

"Morning, boss," I chirp with a desperate cheerfulness that's absolutely not me.

And he notices too.

His brows go up. "Morning, Addie. You okay?" Tripp owns roughly half the club by virtue of marrying Lila, but every interview he's ever done indicates that he loves the Fireballs almost as much as Cooper Rock does. The only reason Tripp's loved them longer than Cooper is that he's several years older. He runs things and does a good job. And I don't say that just because he hired me.

"Peachy."

"You left early last night."

"Shoulder."

"That's all?"

"Yep."

He stares at me like he knows I don't clearly remember much of last night after the third shot I took with Waverly following Duncan winning me.

Which is something *else* Duncan and I didn't discuss this morning.

I only know Waverly and Cooper took me home last night because it was in a text from Waverly this morning. *You said to text you that you got home safe since you've only been this drunk one other time in your life and you need assurances that you didn't do anything stupid. You did not do anything stupid. I'll fight anyone who says you did.*

Fuck.

Did I do something stupid in front of my boss?

He was there too, but mostly I remember everyone being in a good mood.

"You sure you're okay?" he says. "You seem more stressed than normal."

"I'm good."

"The guys are saying you're not as easy to be around the past few weeks."

I tense.

I know what he's talking about. I know *exactly* what he's talking about.

The minute I heard Santiago was retiring, I knew I wanted his job. And the minute I knew getting his job was a possibility, I also knew it was a possibility that someone would screw me over and I wouldn't get it.

Why?

Because that was my first six years in baseball. Didn't matter if it was farm teams or the highest level in the minors. I got stepped on and overlooked. And if I wasn't cheated out of a position, I was accused of having inappropriate relationships with my players or fellow staff members.

But I've loved my time with the Fireballs.

My first couple seasons, I was all business on the field. No cracking smiles, not even when I wanted to.

No joking with the guys. No possibility that anyone would accuse me of impropriety or of not pulling my weight.

Slowly, I've loosened up.

I don't pull pranks in the locker rooms with them, but I do let myself smile in front of them over the good ones. I don't plan birthday parties, but I donate to gifts and show up for the cake with the rest of the coaching staff. I joke around with my fellow coaches, though I'm still wary of joking in ways that could be interpreted wrong or used against me.

"I can't help fix what's wrong if I don't know what it is," Tripp says.

"I want Santiago's job." The truth is the easiest place to start.

He nods. "You're on the interview list."

"The last time I was on an internal interview list, one of my colleagues overheard me talking out my coaching philosophies with one of my team mentors, interviewed first, used them, and then when I said the same thing without knowing he'd already used my own words, I was accused of using him to get ahead."

Dammit.

Now I sound like a paranoid asshole.

But I'm not done, even though I know I should be. "I was also fired from my first coaching job because I was accused of inappropriate behavior with one of the players. He'd just lost his mother. I'd just lost my mother. I told him we'd both get through it. He asked if he could have a hug, I hugged him, and two days later, I was canned for *not knowing boundaries*. I know I sound paranoid, but I have to be smarter, stronger, faster, and tougher than the rest of the coaching staff, or I'm called *the token woman* on the team."

His lips part. "Addie, if we've made you feel that way—"

"You haven't." I briefly squeeze my eyes shut and will myself not to say the next part, but my mouth has a mind of its own. "*Yet.*"

Maybe I'm testing him.

And why shouldn't I?

I love working here, but if they turn on me too, then *dammit*, they don't deserve me.

I want to work in the majors. I want to spend my springs and summers and falls helping lead a team every afternoon and evening on the ball field. But I have other options in places that will let me be more of myself, even if I wouldn't get the same rush and feel the same sense of accomplishment that I do working at the highest level of baseball.

He leans back in his chair and tucks his hands behind his head. "I can't say that I've ever been exactly in your shoes, but a lot of things about this season make more sense now."

Dammit.

Am I fucking up my own chances by putting up more boundaries? "With the exception of my position here, every time I've had that next big dream within my grasp, something out of my control has taken it from me. I don't want to stand in my own way, but lines aren't as clear-cut for me as they are for other members of the coaching staff."

"If you don't get Santiago's job, will you leave us?"

My heart sinks at the question like not getting the job is a foregone conclusion, but I make myself look him straight in the eye while I shake my head. "The Fireballs have been—this has been my favorite experience of my life. And I'm not just saying that because I like all of the bling."

That gets me a smile.

"I know coaching a single team for an entire career isn't likely. I love working here. I'd like to stay as long as possible. But when we're not a good match anymore, then—then I'll find my next position, and I'll wish this team the best. I don't want that day to be today though."

"We don't want that day to be today either," he says.

That's a relief. And it reminds me— "I don't normally drink as much as I did last night. It won't happen again."

"I don't imagine you generally have men bidding six figures for the opportunity to spend a few hours with you either."

I open my mouth, then close it as I slide a look at Denise, who's managing both her cell phone and the notebook now. I wonder if Lila's getting a line-by-line update of this meeting.

Honestly? I hope so. I think she gets it. Probably even more than I do. She made some decisions that weren't popular when she inherited the team and got a lot of shit for it. Firing the entire coaching staff. Retiring the mascot. Being involved when she didn't know much at all about baseball.

Wonder how many people have apologized to her now that the team has won multiple championships and fills the ballpark to capacity nearly every game.

I'm guessing not many.

They likely give Tripp all of the credit.

"Sadie will be up in fifteen, Mr. Wilson," Denise says.

"Thank you." He rocks in his office chair and looks at me. "Speaking of last night, Addie, is there something about Duncan Lavoie that you'd tell a friend but don't want to tell your boss?"

"That's a very specific question."

"I'd only ask it under specific circumstances."

I straighten in my seat and push aside the confessions I've just made to my boss to focus on a much easier line of questioning. These, I can handle in my sleep. "There's nothing you need to be concerned with that will impact my performance on the baseball diamond."

"That wasn't my concern."

"There's nothing between me and Duncan Lavoie."

He folds his arms and frowns at me.

It feels like being stared down by my oldest brother.

"Duncan's not one of our athletes," Tripp says. "No lines crossed here as far as I'm concerned if you two have any kind of history. What you do on your own time is your business. But last night was outside the realm of expected and normal. It wasn't a problem, but it wasn't normal. So let me reword my question—do you feel safe around him, or is there something you need help with on a personal level?"

"There's nothing in my personal history with Duncan to cause concern."

He lifts his brows again.

I realize I probably look ridiculous.

Hard not to be when we're all willing to acknowledge that if I'd gone on that stage last night as a man to offer an afternoon of playing my favorite video game over tea, I would've gone for a couple hundred dollars as a pity bid.

Instead, my ex-fling who helped me not die of suffocation in a dress last week got into a bidding war over me with an apparent local real estate mogul.

Those are the details my boss is sniffing for, but no matter how much I'm starting to feel relief at telling him I have to hold myself to a higher standard, I don't want to go there with my personal life.

"It's not boss-worthy. Very boring and inconsequential."

"Addie…"

"We hung out for a while, and we don't anymore.

Nothing bad happened. Just no time. Both too busy. Obvious reasons."

I don't supply details of what constitutes *hanging out* in my head.

He doesn't ask.

But he does go somewhere else unexpected. "I heard a story last night about a dress and what happened to your shoulder."

"From who?"

"Cooper."

The bastard. "He was never my favorite."

Tripp cracks another smile. "I look forward to being in the vicinity when you tell him that."

"I'd prefer no witnesses. Except maybe Waverly. She's a good friend. I'd hate to lose her because she has bad taste in men."

Denise coughs. I glance at her, unsurprised to find her stifling a smile.

She's one of my favorites in the office. Honestly, I like her as much as I truly like Cooper, despite what I'm telling Tripp.

And she's being unusually quiet today.

"Why am I here?" I ask her.

"Community involvement opportunity," she replies.

I look back at Tripp. "And this relates to the Thrusters?" I guess.

"It does. Which is why I'd like to know if you have a serious problem with Duncan Lavoie," Tripp says.

"I do not."

"You're certain?"

"He's a good guy who's been put in some awkward positions anytime I've been around him through no fault of his own. There are no hard feelings." Not like his erection this morning, which was *very* hard.

Which I need to stop thinking about immediately.

"We're partnering with the Thrusters for a new community outreach program aiming to get more adults involved with sports for fun," Tripp says.

I blink. "Adults?"

"Adults. Sports are for all ages, and we'd like to promote that more."

"That sounds…sweet, actually."

"Glad you think so. I've been on the phone with Thrusters management off and on all morning. They want you and Duncan to be the primary spokespeople for the program."

My brain is mostly operational, but there's some sludgy goop left slowing things down.

Which is why I stare stupidly at my boss while I process what he said.

"Daddie," I whisper.

Fuck.

Duncan had talked to the Thrusters PR team already.

He knew.

He knew before he ever showed up at my apartment this morning.

Tripp clears his throat. "We would make all official

announcements using both of your names individually and separated by enough lines to not imply anything."

"You don't want a player?" I ask. "From our team, I mean."

"We were leaning toward Diego, but it's impossible to deny the extra press boost that you'd bring instead."

"Because Duncan bid over a hundred grand for me and it's making people lose their minds."

"That was…a very large bid."

"There was no fine print. Just because he bid that high doesn't mean it comes with a blow job."

Mother. Fucker.

I just said that to my boss.

Thank the baseball gods, he snorts in amusement, though he's clearly trying to stifle it.

"We won't put that in any official *or* unofficial announcements unless we have to," Denise says dryly.

"Thank you, Denise," I reply. "Let's make sure we don't have to."

"Agreed."

"You don't have to do this," Tripp says to me. "You already do more community outreach than anyone else on the coaching staff. Officially and unofficially. No one will hold it against you if you'd rather sit this out. And it won't impact your evaluations as we go forward with interviews for Santiago's job."

This is a terrible idea.

I don't know if Duncan was nice to me this morning because he knew about the community outreach program and how the auction last night would affect who he was partnered with from the Fireballs, or if he truly just wanted to check on me.

I know he wasn't happy to see me last week.

Or last night.

But something changed since we ran into each other at the start of the auction.

Question is, is this change permanent, or is it temporary so that he can get through working with me in public?

Until last week, I would've told you the same thing I told Tripp—he's a nice guy.

And I would've meant it.

I *still* mean it.

I can acknowledge he's a nice guy—and that there's a part of me that likes him—and also acknowledge that our lives don't mesh.

Even if they did, I'm not interested in long-term relationships.

Despite my frustrations with being unable to completely care for myself while my arm's tied up in a sling, I like my life. I like my freedom. I like not feeling responsible for anyone's happiness beyond my own.

That's a massive burden.

You can't control other people's happiness.

Look what trying did to my mother.

But the bigger picture for me right now—my boss wants me to do something.

I'm on the interview list for a promotion.

He could tell me they wanted me to partner with a garbage can and I'd do it, no matter what he says about how this will or won't impact my chances at a promotion.

I could ping Duncan. Verify that he knew when he came over to see me this morning.

Or I can do what I need to do for my team and for myself.

I nod to Tripp because there's really not another option. "When do we start?"

"You're sure?"

I nod again.

He studies me for a minute, then looks at Denise. "Let the PR department know they should get going on rewriting the PSA script."

"On it."

He looks back at me. "Tomorrow. We start first thing tomorrow."

"Great. I'll be here."

"You're absolutely, positively, one hundred percent sure?"

"I'm sure."

Baseball is my favorite part of my job. Game days in the sun. Developing players. The thrill of victory and the heartache of defeat.

I love every bit of this game.

But I enjoy the community outreach almost as much. On the days when I wonder if I'm here because I'm a woman, I fall back on knowing I'm setting an awesome example for all of the people who never thought they could fit into this kind of professional sports world.

So yes, I'm in.

And if it means seeing Duncan more often, then I'll figure out how to deal with that too.

The good parts and the bad parts.

9

Duncan

WHEN THE HEAD of PR for the Thrusters said *community outreach*, I thought they meant we'd be out in the community.

Talking to people.

Delivering swag bags to intramural teams.

Running sign-ups for new Thrusters- or Fireballs-sponsored adult sports leagues across a variety of sports.

Instead, I canceled my tee time for today, and now I'm standing at Duggan Field's home plate, fully suited up in all of my hockey gear, right down to my helmet and gloves and freaking skates—blades covered, of course—surrounded by a full camera crew.

Plus a handful of my teammates and former teammates who still live in Copper Valley who were happy to come heckle me today. Couple of my friends on the Fireballs too.

A few rugby guys from the Pounders and some of the women's soccer players from the Scorned.

And sweat.

I'm drowning in sweat.

It's July. Of fucking course I'm drowning in sweat.

"Duncan, let's start from the top. Go ahead and step up to the plate, and then Addie, you come in with your line," the director yells.

"Is this the last take?" I'm so fucking hot that I'm almost cold. We've been out here for what feels like hours and I've said my lines probably three dozen times.

"If you do it right."

Motherfucking fucker head.

He said that three takes ago.

"He won't be doing it at all if he passes out from heat exhaustion," Addie says.

She's showing no signs of the hangover that had her a complete disaster yesterday morning. Her sling today matches her Fireballs uniform—black and orange with their mascot, Ash, a baby dragon who's aged some over the past few years—waving at her elbow.

She's in her Fireballs uniform and she gets to wear sunglasses to hide her eyes.

She's also completely no-nonsense.

It's a mask.

I know it's a mask.

Just like I know she's still off-kilter from having me thrust back into her life.

Wait until she realizes I'll do whatever it takes to stay in her life.

If you hadn't gotten attached, we could've been forever.

She cares. She likes me. She just doesn't know how to admit it.

So I'll be here until she realizes it.

"Then he better get it right this time," the director yells. "Places, everyone."

"Hey." Addie holds up a hand to me. "You okay?"

"I'm good."

She studies me too long. Not *I want to jump your bones* studying either. She's staring at me the same way I've watched her stare at any number of her players. All business, that wrinkle forming on the bridge of her nose while her brows bunch.

"You're sure?"

No, I'm not fucking sure. I'm hot and tired and I want to get out of my pads and uniform.

But I don't mind the part at all where I'm with her.

I wink. "Have we met? I'm a fucking *god*."

After one more long glance, she rolls her eyes and heads to her place for the shoot, and I blow out a slow breath.

Played through worse than being a little hot before.

Probably.

My teammates and I all work up a sweat under our

gear every practice and game, but we're on ice when we do it.

Not standing under the blazing July sun that's so hot, it's evaporating all of the sweat off my face.

The director calls, "Action!" and I take one more big breath before lumbering my way to home plate and lifting my hockey stick like a baseball bat, my pulse ticking higher. This is the last take whether the director likes it or not.

"All right, big guy, let's see what you've got," I call to Silas Collins, a young player from the Pounders who's prepared to pitch me a rugby ball.

Backward, since that's how they do it in rugby.

Addie steps up to the plate too. "You're holding the wrong bat, Captain."

Whoever wrote the script for this knows her well.

I give her a cocky grin. "You mean I'm holding the bat wrong."

Someone off-camera tosses her a baseball bat. She catches it one-handed almost without looking, then flips it to offer the handle to me while she holds it by the barrel.

"The wrong bat. You can't hit a baseball with a hockey stick."

"The word you're looking for is *shouldn't*. I *can* hit a baseball with a hockey stick. But I *shouldn't*." Okay, yeah, despite the heat, this is a fun script. Whoever wrote it knew me well too.

But it's still hotter than balls and I'm about done with this shit for today.

"Actually, with your stance like that, you won't hit anything at all," she says.

"Bet," I reply.

I readjust my stick the way she showed me before we started shooting, digging my skates into the dirt.

Ground crew's gonna hate us.

Not my problem though.

My problem is having enough patience to wait Addie out while she realizes I'm what's missing in her life.

"Pitch it, Collins," I call while Addie shakes her head and backs away with an audible, "Your reputation, Captain."

"Get ready to strike out," the rugby player retorts. He turns his back to me on the mound, then arcs the rugby ball backward toward me.

Fucking weird sport. They never toss the ball forward, only sideways and backward. Unless they kick it, then it can go forward. Dudes don't wear padding. They're hardcore.

I swing for the fucking fences as the ball soars my way, pulling my stick around to connect with that bloated football at the exact right moment.

But the rugby ball doesn't go sailing.

Instead, there's a crack that reverberates in my wrists as my hockey stick splinters and goes flying.

Straight at Addie.

I lunge for her, but my skate catches on the edge of home plate, and I, too, go flying.

The good news is that when I land, I land flat on the dirt.

No Addie beneath me.

No rugby ball beneath me.

No crooked stick beneath me.

The bad news is that dots start dancing in my vision.

Fuck.

I know this feeling.

It's not the impact.

It's dehydration and overheating.

I need water.

Stat.

"I stand corrected," she says over me. "You can, in fact, hit a rugby ball with a hockey stick while in that stance. Nicely done, Captain."

I breathe in dirt and sweat. I should push myself up, but I don't want to.

Not while my head's swimming.

"*Cut!*" the director yells. "Beautiful. That was absolutely beautiful. Nice improv, Coach."

"Electrolytes," she says to someone. "*Now.* Collins. Get over here. I need muscle. Yours better not be all for show."

Shit.

I'm still on the ground.

And I don't want to move.

Fuuuuck. I know what this means.

"Still with us, Duncan?" she says quieter, closer.

"Yep." I try to move my arms, but she puts a hand to one, making me go still.

"Don't move just yet. Did you land on anything wrong?"

"My pride."

"Anything hurt? Ribs? Ankles? Wrists?"

"I didn't fall that hard."

"Hot?"

"Fucking sun. Fucking eighty million takes."

"You still sweating?"

I don't answer because she won't like the answer.

I should roll over. I think I can roll over.

But then the sun would be in my eyes.

My lids drift shut.

Fuck.

"Can we get that umbrella over here?" she calls to someone. "We need shade. Collins. Let's get him out of his uniform. You. Is that a pocket knife? Hand it over. Duncan, sip slowly. Who has a fan? Anyone have a fan?"

Something touches my lips from the side and I angle my head toward it.

My helmet disappears.

"C'mon, Duncan. Take a little sip," Addie says.

My mouth obeys, and sweet liquid flows over my tongue.

Oh, yes.

137

That's better.

"Good job," she says quietly. "Don't sit up. We've got you."

"You want me to cut him out of his jersey?" a guy says.

"I think the Thrusters can afford to get him a new one," she deadpans.

I smile and suck in more liquid.

"Good, Duncan. But not too fast." Soft fingers touch my hair.

Is it Addie?

Is she touching my hair?

Something tugs on my sweater, and then cooler air trickles over my back.

I know better than this.

I do.

Rule number one—don't overheat and pass out.

"Uncle Duncan? Uncle Duncan, are you okay?"

Shiiiiiit.

Paisley's here.

I forgot I invited Paisley to watch.

I grunt and try to lift my head, but it swims in the summer afternoon, and I have to set it back down on the ground.

"I'm okay," I mumble.

"Thanks, Coach," a familiar voice says. I know that guy. He's some front office dude for the Thrusters. "We've got him."

"Why isn't he taking his own pads off?" Paisley says.

Oh.

Huh.

Someone's unhooking my pads.

More fresh air.

Fuck yeah.

"He'll be okay," Addie says. "We'll take good care of him."

"Why isn't he moving? Oh my god, he's so pale."

"He overheated, but he's in good hands. The best hands. Look. Doc's on the way."

"I'm okay," I say to Paisley.

Someone shoves the straw back in my mouth.

I lift my head again and push up onto my elbows.

Still swimmy, but *fuck*, it feels better without my pads on. With a breeze blowing on me. Under an umbrella.

Shade.

She got me shade.

"I'm okay," I repeat to Paisley.

There are three of her.

Four of Addie.

Bad sign.

"Hey, Superman, how about you relax right now and let the trainers and doc do what they need to?" Addie says to me.

Not badass Addie.

Patient Addie.

The same Addie who sat on my couch with me a few years ago and helped me talk through a massive crisis in confidence when I thought the team was going in a direction I wasn't fit to lead them in.

I miss that Addie.

I *want* that Addie.

I'll get her back.

I will.

No matter what it takes.

Right now, pretty sure it'll take cooling off.

"Eighty degrees might be too warm for full pads, huh, sport?" someone new says. "I'm Doc Engleberg. Work with the Fireballs. We're gonna get you inside and get you all patched up. Anything you're allergic to?"

"No allergies," I report.

"He'll be okay," I hear Addie say again. "Right, Duncan?"

I give her a thumbs-up.

"Yeah, that last shot was good. You can take him," the director says.

I switch which digit on my hand is sticking up.

And I debate giving myself that finger too.

This wouldn't have happened ten years ago.

And it's not the first sign I've had about my future.

But as I realize the sniffling I'm hearing is my niece, utter clarity smacks me in the balls.

It's time.

And for once, it's not a terrifying thought.
Maybe, just maybe, because it's finally right.
And this time, I'm not thinking about Addie.
Not directly anyway.

10

Addie

THE BEST PART of the take-no-prisoners attitude that I taught myself to wear to work every day is that none of the hockey players question why I keep popping down the hallway outside of the in-stadium clinic as the Fireballs' medical staff gets Duncan cooled off and pumped full of fluids.

The worst part is that I'd like to head into the bathroom and cry the same way Paisley did as we watched Duncan get helped off the field.

He was so fucking pale.

I knew that last take was a bad idea.

I knew it.

But he stared me dead in the eye and said he was fine.

Worse, he *winked* and said he was fine.

And he's an adult, so I let him make that call, despite my instincts telling me we needed to take a break.

He's cleared for visitors after half an hour or so, and every last hockey player swarms the room.

The next time I pop down the hallway, Paisley is squatting solo against the cinderblock wall, staring at the door across the hallway.

I squat next to her. "You okay?"

"Why are men dumb?"

The question catches me so off guard that I actually laugh out loud.

"It's our egos," Tripp Wilson answers for me as he steps out of the stairwell to our left. "Gets us every time." He nods to the door. "Mr. Hockey gonna make it?"

"It's like he didn't nearly die an hour ago," Paisley said.

"He wasn't in danger of dying," I tell her, which I think is ninety percent true. "He was dehydrated and had the wind knocked out of him."

"I wanted to have my own apartment for school, but now I feel like I have to move in with him to make sure he takes care of his old ass," she mutters.

"Ew," I say.

"Yeah," she agrees.

"And he's pretty dumb too, so you'd have to deal with that."

She shoots me a frown. "He is *not* dumb."

"Maybe not completely, but he's also not smart enough to take batting advice from a pro."

Her frown turns into an *O*, and then she dips her head and laughs too. "How did he hit that ball?"

"It was a big target pitched just right." I nod to the clinic door. "If you want to see him again without swimming in that much testosterone, I can kick his teammates out. They have proof of life now."

She glances at Tripp, then back at me.

This girl watched her uncle get in a bidding war over me just days ago, after watching us argue about him stripping me out of a dress, and now she's sitting outside what essentially feels like an emergency room after watching him let his ego take priority over his physical needs.

She has to have questions.

She doesn't ask them though.

Instead, she pulls herself up. "They don't bother me," she says. "But thank you. I'm gonna check on him one more time, and then I have some things I need to do."

I rise too. "If you like baseball, I'm sure this guy here can get you set up with some tickets for you and your friends without having to take a decrepit old man along with you."

"Absolutely true," Tripp says. "I have a hookup."

She shakes her head. "Thanks, but I have to make friends first, and I don't like to make them with bribes."

Tripp hands her a card. "If you change your mind once you've made some friends, send a note here. The offer doesn't expire."

"Thank you." She looks at me. "And thank you for holding my hand."

"It's scary to watch someone you love hurting."

She nods, then slips into the clinic.

Tripp eyes me.

"I'm fine," I say before he can utter a word.

"Personally or professionally?"

Neither.

I blow out a cheek-puffing sigh. "Do you know how pissed I was when I found out the musician I hooked up with was actually a professional hockey player?"

It's the first time I've ever confessed my secret hookup with Duncan out loud. I haven't even told Francie what happened. Not in so many details.

And I feel like I'm taking a massive risk in telling my boss.

He has the audacity to chuckle. "Speaking as a man who hooked up with a woman who became my boss and then married her...yes."

"That's different."

"Not really."

"*Very* different."

"Failing to see how here."

"Your relationship with Lila didn't affect how the team plays."

"You having a relationship with a hockey player wouldn't affect how my baseball team plays."

I bite the inside of my cheek.

"Makes for great promo spots for community outreach programs though," he muses.

The clinic door swings open, and a string of hockey players exit.

Paisley's right behind them.

She gives us a small finger wave, then follows the men, who are all cheerfully talking.

Either Duncan's having a prostate exam, or he's been cleared to get dressed and go home.

Tripp's phone buzzes. He glances at the screen, and even if I hadn't seen Lila's name, I'd know who was calling based on the smile on his face. "Can you make sure Duncan gets safely to his car?" he says to me. "I don't want another medical incident if he trips on his shoelaces."

"Can I turn him over to security instead?"

"If that makes you happier."

"Thanks. Tell Lila to tell the guys to kick ass at the game."

"Will do. Let me know if *you* need anything after today." He slips back into the stairwell while he answers the phone.

Do I want to see Duncan?

Yes.

Yes, I do.

Entirely too much right now, in fact.

So I catch a security guy and ask him to be available if the clinic needs to hand Duncan off to get him to his car, and then I head to one of my favorite places.

The stands.

The clinic is on the third-base side, so that's where I emerge to stare out at the ball field and just breathe. It's approaching noon, but I find a shady seat high in the lower bowl and let myself hunch over, breathing through the need to cry while my eyes wander over the green grass, the dirt mound, the empty stands, the blank scoreboard, and the dozens and dozens of ads.

The pennants the Fireballs have won the past five seasons wave lazily in a light breeze, but the normal sense of pride in my team is overshadowed by the question *what the hell do I do about Duncan?*

I'm not surprised when the man himself steps into my row of seats. He looks less like a ghost and more like a normal white man, and if he knows my pulse has just shot into the stratosphere at the sight of him, he doesn't give any indication.

I swallow the lumps that keep threatening to make me cry and force myself to channel my inner badass baseball coach. "Feeling better?"

"Yes and no."

My brows lift. *No?*

"Can I join you?" he adds.

"Of course."

He steps into the row and sits with just one seat

between us, then glances at the field. "Your happy place."

"My happy place," I agree.

Mink Arena, where the Thrusters play, is his happy place.

Full or empty.

Or it was, back when we were together. I· can't imagine that's changed.

He's carrying a sports drink bottle, and his complexion is holding steady as we both stare at the field.

So is his breathing.

The two of us are a mess. Me in a sling because of a dress. Him giving himself heat exhaustion for the sake of a video shoot.

I'd laugh, but instead, I suck in a slow breath, not letting myself go back to that terrifying place where he fell and then didn't move.

Second-guessing myself as I leapt into action to check on him.

Wondering if he'd hit something wrong on one of his pads and broken a rib. If he hit his head. If my gut was right that he was overheating, or if it was something else and we needed to not move him at all.

How do you balance caring about someone with knowing that their life doesn't fit with your life?

How do you care without caring too much?

How do you guard your own happiness when you feel like your happiness is denying someone else theirs?

Do. Not. Go. There.

I don't owe someone else their happiness at the expense of mine.

My mother passed away not long after I graduated college, a single year after divorcing my father and stepping into living the life she'd always wanted but never put first. If it wasn't my father making demands, it was us kids.

She chose us. She told me she never regretted what we needed.

But she wished he would've helped out more.

He put such a burden on her for decades.

She finally put herself first, only to trip and fall and hit her head wrong coming down the stairs in her rental house before she could live out even a fraction of her dreams.

I finish my long exhale and turn my focus back to what I *do* know.

Duncan wants to talk.

I can talk.

"What's up?" I ask him.

"I think it's time for me to retire."

A sound I don't recognize slips out of my lips.

Focus, Addie.

Focus.

Not the first time I've heard a player say these words. Won't be the last.

But it's the first time I've heard a player say these

words when I've used *our schedules conflict* as one of the reasons we can't be together.

Which is a very specific situation that has only happened this one time in my life.

"I'm old," he adds, quieter.

I swallow hard, again. Today is making me entirely too emotional. All of it. "You *feel* old, or the numbers say you're old?"

His knees touch the seat in front of him. He's in shorts. Bare knees. Strong knees. One with a scar suggesting knee surgery at some point in his career. His arms rest on his thighs as he inhales deeply.

"I wouldn't have overheated ten years ago."

"You don't play hockey in summer weather."

"It's been two years since I broke my personal speed record, and I've had fewer minutes on the ice every season for the past three."

"Being a team player is about more than one or two personal stats."

"There are more guys on the team now who didn't win our first cup with the team than there are guys who did."

"It's been a lot of years since then. Trades happen. Teams slip and rebuild." Why am I doing this? Why am I trying to talk him out of retiring?

"Ares Berger retired at the end of last season. Wants to spend more time with his wife and kids. Manning Frey retired season before last. Wanted to spend more time with his wife and kids and visit his home country more. Murphy's been retired for a couple years now. Spends his time mostly with his wife and kids, with a few hours a week devoted to the Thrusters' front office."

Heat prickles over my arms.

My pulse is still trying to prove it can outrace a cheetah. "You want that."

"I always wanted it." He stares out over the field, where the grounds crew is still cleaning up after the commercial shoot. "You marry your college sweetheart two years into your career, you think you're gonna have it. And then it falls apart and you think you'll get a second chance, but the closest you come, you're more into it than she is."

I flinch, and I know he notices.

He lifts one shoulder. "Not saying either of us was right or wrong. Just how it was. You didn't—*don't* owe me anything. Sometimes things just don't work. People are in different spaces, and we don't always recognize that about each other. People have different histories and different goals and different lifestyles. It just is."

And this is my biggest problem with Duncan Lavoie.

When he's not pissed that I need to be independent, he says all of the right things.

You don't have to pick me. I'd pick you, but I understand you're under no obligation to pick me back. You don't need me. I get it.

I want to press about what he meant yesterday

when he said he'd reached acceptance with having me back in his life. If this is him treating me the same way he'd treat any other friendly colleague, or if this is his way of trying to prove to me that we could be good together again. How much of it has to do with the text that I'm pretending I didn't send him Saturday night.

But I'm not ready for that conversation.

"So what does retirement look like for you now?" I say instead.

That's what players usually want to talk about when they toss around the R-word.

This is what I've always done. I know I can't do it forever, but I don't know what comes next.

I had the conversation with Cooper as he was starting to pursue dating Waverly while he was standing in the batting cages. *You ever think you'll leave baseball one day, Coach?*

Everyone leaves baseball sometime. How soon depends on when you find the next thing that will make your life more fulfilling.

All while knowing that I'm never leaving baseball.

I fucking love this sport.

"I have one year left on my contract." He scuffs his shoe over the concrete floor. "Got time to figure it out. *All* of it. Not just the parts I already know."

"Gonna start your own band?"

He lifts his head and looks at me.

Just looks at me.

Doesn't say yes.

Doesn't say no.

Heat builds under my sternum as those bright green eyes bore into mine.

This man wants something.

He wants something from me.

Maybe not *something from me* though.

More like *all of me*.

"Duncan—"

He smirks.

He smirks, and my belly drops, my nipples shiver, and my mouth goes dry.

I shake my head, but it only makes the smirk grow bigger.

"Duncan," I start again, but I have to pause.

And that's when I realize I'm licking my lips.

My body drifting closer to his.

My breath getting shallower.

This isn't happening.

Those are the words I'm supposed to say.

Because this *isn't* happening.

Our lives aren't compatible, and even if they were—even when he retires—I don't do relationships.

Baseball is my one true love. The thing I can depend on while knowing the sport itself will never take anything from me.

It doesn't matter what team I'm playing for.

Not when I'm on the field. Rain or shine. Hot or cold. Breathing in the fresh-cut grass or dirty infield. Through the bad calls and hard losses and brutal injuries. Soaking in the game-winning go-ahead homers and stolen bases and acrobatic fielding.

And if I think I'm busy now, I'll be even busier when I take over Santiago's job.

And if that isn't next year, it *will* be another year. The other coaches are older than I am. They have more experience.

But they don't have the same finely-honed instincts and they don't have my drive.

They can't. They haven't had to fight as hard for it as I have.

I know I might not get the job.

But I'll do everything in my power to win it. And I meant what I told Tripp yesterday. So long as the Fireballs treat me well, I'll stay here.

I'll put the team first.

So me not doing relationships isn't only because I don't think a man exists who can supplement my life instead of sucking it away. It's also that I don't think I can be an equal partner.

My job isn't a job. It's a lifestyle.

Duncan's staring at my mouth.

I bolt to my feet, my thighs unexpectedly shaky. "I have to get back to work. I hope you find what you're looking for in retirement. And I'm glad you're okay."

His gaze lifts back to my eyes. "I'll find it," he says.

My brain hears *I've already found you.*

This is when I should walk out of this stadium,

cross the street to the admin building, hit the elevator for the top floor, and go tell Tripp *absolutely not.*

That I'm done with this specific Fireballs-Thrusters community outreach program.

"Do you need help finding your way out?" I ask Duncan.

He leans back in the stadium seat, then stretches his long legs out and crosses his ankles over the seat in front of him. "I can manage."

"Do you need more water?"

He lifts the bottle of sports drink and shakes it. "All good."

"You're just going to stay here?"

"Pretty day to stare at a ball field."

I blow out a short breath.

He's up to something.

I don't dislike it as much as I need to. "I'll let security know you're still here so they don't freak out on you. And they'll want to escort you to your car. Liability. That's all."

"You really have work to do, or are you running away?"

I'm running away, but I'm calling it a strategic retreat to evaluate and regroup. "I always have work to do."

"No game two weeks from this coming Thursday," he says.

I blink.

"Great day for *Croaking Creatures,*" he adds.

Fuck me.

I owe him a date.

"Fantastic," I say.

"Looking forward to it."

"Same."

He studies me, lips barely twitched up, the tilt of his brows telling me the man has ulterior motives.

And that's not as irritating as it should be.

11

Duncan

THERE ARE several places I could be this morning.

I could wake up Paisley with a bribe of breakfast if she'll keep me company.

I could drop by any of my teammates' or former teammates' places to say hi.

I could hit a golf course. Leave town and head into the Blue Ridge Mountains for some hiking. Take a float trip.

Instead, I'm knocking on Addie's apartment door.

Am I obsessed?

Yes.

But also, she saved me yesterday at the stadium. I owe her a thank you that's more than dropping a hint-laden bomb that I'm hanging up my skates soon.

That definitive decision isn't giving me the anxiety I'd expect.

Maybe because what I want to do after hockey is so crystal clear. Not all of it, but enough of it.

There's a chance she won't answer. Might not be home. Could be showering. I doubt she's still sleeping.

She's a morning person.

Being a morning person is a pain in the ass when your team plays until ten or eleven nearly every night, especially at the end of road trips when you get home after a red-eye.

If she were a player, her coaches and trainers would have something to say about her 6:00 a.m. wake-up every morning.

But since she *is* a coach, nobody questions her early bird habits that sometimes require extra coffee.

My coffee-adoring and early morning-loving ass flipped her off a few times back in the day when she'd indulge in both while I was supposed to be sleeping later before or after a game.

And I do mean only a few times.

Weren't many nights either of us stayed over with the other when baseball and hockey were both in season.

The lock clicks, and the door opens just wide enough for me to see two-thirds of Addie's face.

Suspicious doesn't touch the raw wariness lurking in her pretty brown eyes. Determination flows through my veins.

I will win this woman over.

I'll prove to her that I can fit in her life.

And if I can't, then I'll know I gave it everything I had and I'm just supposed to be alone for the rest of my own life.

"Duncan," she says.

Her hair is tied back in a ponytail that has me wondering how she managed it. Light makeup on her face—there's something about her eyes and lips that pops. Not as much as at the auction, but she's definitely wearing something. She's in a black Fireballs polo, and I wonder if she had help getting that on too.

If she did, I'm jealous of whoever got to help. I want to be the one making sure she gets everything she needs.

I lift the insulated to-go coffee mug that I filled with a special order at what used to be her favorite coffee shop around the corner on my way over.

Since I threw out a couple disposable cups stamped with the shop's logo while I was here the other morning, I figure there's a good chance it's still her favorite.

"Gratitude coffee. Thank you for not letting me die of heat exhaustion yesterday."

The suspicion doesn't fade while she drops her eyes to the mug.

It's a Thrusters mug decorated with Thrusty, our rocket-powered bratwurst mascot. He has a bit of a cult following. There've been times when people have put stickers of him on all of the lampposts all around the city. Other times when plush versions of him have been found in weird places, like lined up around the fountain in Reynolds Park or overflowing every locker in the other local sports teams' dressing rooms. Copper Valley's mayor once found a three-foot-tall stuffed Thrusty sitting in the driver's seat of his car. Someone even made a *Thrusty Bratwurst* filter on SnapChat.

I blame Zeus Berger for most of the Thrusty mischief, but I suspect his identical twin Ares is equally responsible, just quieter about it.

"If this was true gratitude coffee, Ash would be on that mug," Addie says.

Can't blame her for loyalty to the Fireballs' baby dragon mascot, who's technically growing up now, but everyone still loves the baby merch the best.

Also, I didn't grab the Ash mug I have at home purely because I knew it would look like I was trying too hard.

I'm determined and patient, not stupid and reckless. "Superior mascot for superior coffee."

"Did you make it?"

"Peppermint mocha from the place down the street."

"It's not peppermint mocha season."

"Barista's a Thrusters fans."

"Which one? Jenny? Or Nikki?"

"The one with the pink hair."

She gasps. "That's Nikki, and she's a Fireballs fan first."

"Lucky you, she made your coffee. Unless you don't want it?"

It's not hard to see the conflict in her face. Take the coffee and shut the door in my face, reject both me and the coffee, or let us both in?

I know I'm in when her eyes narrow. "This is me saying thank you and you're welcome and that's it."

"Of course."

She opens the door wider, and I step inside her apartment.

The living room blinds are open, showing off her view of Reynolds Park. She's just high enough to see the tops of the oak and maple and elm trees, but not high enough to get a full view of the expansive park and its sports fields, walking trails, and the fountain that's basically the centerpiece of the city. Her walls are painted peach, and the soft gray furniture with the pastel throw pillows feel so very *Addie* to me in a way that I doubt most people in her life would recognize.

More tissues litter the end table next to her plush recliner, which is draped with a quilt featuring cartoon sloths that match one of her throw pillows. An open container of cantaloupe is sitting on her countertop next to her tablet, which I take to mean she's having breakfast and catching up on sports news. The sink's full of dishes again.

"I have twenty minutes before I have to leave," she tells me as she heads toward the kitchen. "Thank you for the coffee."

"My pleasure. How's your shoulder?"

"Annoying as fuck."

I shouldn't grin, but it's hard not to appreciate her blunt honesty. "How much longer in the sling?"

"Only until my doctor appointment in a few days. I hope. Still have to wait on the scans, but I'm reasonably certain I won't need surgery. Just PT."

"First thing you'll do when you have full use of both arms. Go."

"Cut a cantaloupe myself. This precut stuff isn't always fresh. Or cut small enough."

"Huh. I thought the first thing you'd do would be to give a double middle finger to the sling."

"I can do that already."

She demonstrates, and I grin again as I step into the kitchen with her.

"Do not do my dishes," she says.

"Housekeeper coming to do them?" I ask.

"No. I'll do them—*Duncan*."

I sidestep her attempt at stealing the clean plate out of my hand as I start unloading her dishwasher. "Sorry. Can't help myself. It's an illness. I'm seeing a therapist, but we're not making much progress yet on breaking my dishwasher obsession."

The heat coming off her glare is a fraction of what it should be, and she doesn't stop me when I grab the next clean plate out of the dishwasher.

Addie's way of taking help.

I have a fuckton of admiration for her independence and strength until she lets it work against her.

Everyone needs help sometimes.

Look at me yesterday.

"You didn't call your sister-in-law, did you?" I say as I put the full stack of plates away with the others.

"It's just a few more days," she grumbles.

"Paisley's looking for a job. She has the same sickness as me. It's genetic. We have to clean. Family theory is that one of our ancestors must've drowned in a mud pit and we're carrying the trauma in our genes. It makes us clean obsessively."

Addie stares at me over the rim of the to-go mug as she takes a sip of coffee, giving me the same badass stare that she'll be using on her players when they get back to work after their break.

She knows I'm making shit up.

But after her first sip, her eyes drift shut, her expression relaxes, and her whole body sags against the counter. "Why do they only serve this a few months of the year?"

"They'd serve it to you year-round if you asked."

She wrinkles her nose. "They'd serve it to you."

"I told Nikki it was for you. Actually, I don't get any more unless I have picture proof of you drinking it."

I get another stare that says she doesn't know if she believes me or not.

"They all saw the articles," I tell her.

It's the truth.

And it's enough of the truth that I can feel my face turning pink, which doesn't happen often.

But it's also not often that I'm referred to as *the boy-half of Daddie* to my face.

Addie studies me another moment, her eyes darting across my features, her own cheeks going a shade of pink.

And then she goes back to eating her cantaloupe quietly while I finish unloading and reloading her dishwasher. Anytime I glance at her, she's watching me.

Just watching.

And occasionally sipping her coffee and drifting off into bliss-land, her complexion back under control.

"Do you have plans today?" she asks as I'm rearranging the top rack to get the last bowl in.

"Nope."

"Would you like to make some young athletes' days?"

"With you, or in your place?"

Her cheeks do that pink thing again. "With me."

Yes. "I could think of worse things to do."

"This isn't a date."

"Didn't think it was."

"Didn't you?"

"I know where we stand." For now.

And *for now* has me driving Addie to a softball diamond in the Mulvaney Hill district of the city with a bagful of stuffed Baby Ash mascots in the rear of the Sin Bin, which is what I call my SUV.

I'm the muscle. Not her date.

Her *partner* in community outreach.

But it's clear when we arrive at the practice diamond that Addie's the real show.

"Coach Addie!" the first baseperson yells, and that's it.

Practice pauses as the teenage girls in softball-practice gear dash to the sidelines.

"Sorry for the disruption, Coach," she says to an older woman who's wearing a sun visor and a whistle and standing at the edge of the field.

"For being late or for interrupting practice?"

"Yes."

The older woman smiles at her as the team crowds around. "Practice was supposed to be over fifteen minutes ago, and they know it."

"We hit traffic."

The older woman's gaze slides to me, but her silent questions are swept away by the tight crowd of players.

"Morning, Stingrays," Addie says to the team. The difference in her at this exact moment is remarkable.

When I catch sight of her on TV during games, she's always straight-faced. Holds herself rigid. Doesn't let a single muscle or joint out of place. All business.

But this morning, she's smiling at the team as they chorus back an enthusiastic, "Hi, Coach Addie."

"I can't throw well today, so I brought you a target instead," she says to the team.

Two dozen young women roughly my niece's age, maybe a little younger, turn to stare at me.

"He looks familiar," says the one holding a catcher's glove with her mask pushed back on her head.

"Were you in a constipation commercial?" someone in the middle of the group wants to know.

"Guys, he plays baseball," a shorter woman holding a bat tells them.

"No, I know all of the Fireballs. He's not one of them."

"In the minors."

"He's too old to be in the minors."

Addie's grin keeps growing. "Ladies, this is Duncan Lavoie. He plays hockey for the Thrusters."

A chorus of *Oooohs* erupts around us.

"Oh, shit, that's the dude who tried to buy you," someone in the middle of the group says.

Half the girls shush her and one tells her not to say *shit*. One or two squeal, but no more than that.

"Duncan and I are old friends," she tells the group. "And you shouldn't believe anything you read in the sports pages when they're trying to be gossip pages."

"If you need us to take him out, we're here for you," a girl in pink-rimmed sunglasses says as she pumps a fist into her glove.

Addie's visibly fighting a bigger smile. I swear she's biting the inside of her cheek. "Thank you, but I don't need any of you provoking the Thrusters fans."

"We can be subtle."

"They'll never know it was us."

"Besties, I think Coach Addie can handle him. I mean, look at him. She can definitely take him out if she needs to."

"Okay, okay. I know I said we can use him as a target, but I was joking. We're going to be kind to Duncan today," Addie says.

Mumbles of *fine* and *if we have to* go up amongst the group.

I glance at their coach.

She's also smirking. "Not your usual welcome, is it?"

"Did hockey players hurt them all?" I deadpan.

"Enough of them."

Well, fuck. Aren't they too young for that? "Here?"

"We handled it," Addie says to me. She turns back to the team. "Who's ready for breakfast?"

We didn't bring breakfast.

We brought plush mascots. Unless the mascots are hiding food.

But the team whoops and heads to the bleachers like the question is code.

When I turn to watch, I spot a rideshare delivery car in the parking lot next to the Sin Bin.

"You ordered breakfast?" I ask Addie.

She doesn't look at me as she follows the women, their coach on her other side. "I bring some kind of meal every few weeks to different teams in the summer league, listen to the gossip, answer questions, hang out...it's good."

"For you or them?"

"Yes."

"Fireballs sponsor this?"

"No."

"Huh."

She slides a look at me. "This is the sort of thing you can do in retirement too."

I don't hold back a smile. "You've been thinking about me."

"You make it very hard not to. Don't let the plushies fall out of that bag. The team has plans for those."

"Addie Bloom, are you encouraging pranks with stuffed mascots?"

"I'm a role model, not an instigator."

She's absolutely an enabler though.

The team is passing around bags of what looks like breakfast burritos and containers of fruits and muffins, plus juice boxes.

I stay off to the side while the team pulls Addie in, not hesitating to pepper her with questions and fill her in on things in their personal lives. I wonder how many other teams she hits regularly enough for them to know her this way.

"She's been a great asset to the city," the coach says to me as she, too, lingers on the side. "But I think she's been an even greater asset to us. A lot of our players want to play ball in college and then follow her lead into professional sports."

"Best role model to have."

The coach studies me. "And what are your intentions?"

"Make sure she knows she's awesome."

"You and your teammates play pranks."

"Harmless fun."

"Don't test what these players will do to support Addie if those pranks are ever aimed at her."

"Zeus Berger once told me he would never prank a locker room of women because he's good, but they're better," I tell her. "He's not wrong."

"I hope that's not lip service."

"Too much to lose for that to be lip service."

She's not smiling while she keeps watching me.

But I smile to myself.

Not lying.

I want Addie in my life. And I'm willing to do whatever it takes to earn her and deserve her.

12

Addie

I'M PLAYING WITH FIRE.

Dating? I don't do it.

Flinging? Hooking up? Yes.

But *dating*? No.

However, *dating* is exactly what it feels like when Duncan asks if I want to hit a bar for the best smothered fries in Copper Valley before he drops me back at my place.

"Is this a trick to get me to eat poutine?" I ask when I should tell him I have things I need to do.

Which wouldn't exactly be a lie.

The things I need to do are to not spend the afternoon with him when he's so damn likeable.

My mother used to tell me my father was *so damn*

likeable when they first met too.

And then she spent thirty-five years losing herself to try to make him happy when the truth was that nothing would make him happy.

He didn't *want* to be happy.

But he certainly seemed to enjoy the power he had over her to make her try.

"You'd love poutine," Duncan says as he steers his SUV around a corner. "But this isn't a trick to get you to eat it. These are your typical American loaded fries. Cheddar, onions, bacon, and you can even smother it in ranch dressing if you want. They're delicious."

"Hmm."

"Is that a no, or is that an *I'll be the judge of how good these fries are?*"

"I can spare an hour for loaded fries."

"The Stingrays will appreciate it when you order this next time for breakfast."

I actually laugh at that.

"You ever order breakfast for the Fireballs?" he asks.

"No."

"No Coach Addie question-and-answer time with the starting lineup?"

"Pro baseball players don't need the same thing as college athletes on the women's teams."

He *hmms* back at me.

"*Hmm* what?"

He shakes his head.

"No, really," I say. "What?"

He opens his mouth. Closes it. Wash, rinse, repeat. For a whole block.

I twist sideways in my seat and stare at him, and he finally shrugs. "You looked happy."

Not what I was expecting him to say.

I thought I'd get *you'd be surprised how dumb rookies can be* or *even veteran players need to know they're heard sometimes.*

And I *do* hear my players.

All of them.

It's why Cooper Rock asked for my advice before he retired. Why Diego Estevez sometimes pops in with relationship questions. Why Brooks Elliott and Luca Rossi ambushed me two weeks ago to talk about concerns they have about the batting order we've been using.

It's why my brain has been swimming since Tripp's comment that the guys had noticed a change in me this year, when I know I've clammed back up.

And I know I need to fix how I'm presenting myself if I'm going to get Santiago's job.

Mostly, I need to come to terms with the paranoia that my history before the Fireballs brings out in me.

And I had all of those arguments ready to go, then Duncan hits me with *you looked happy.*

"I enjoy mentoring young women," I say.

"It shows."

I tilt my head, watching him. It feels like there's

something more he wants to say, something more on his mind, but he doesn't elaborate.

Nor do I goad him into saying it. What would be the point?

It's not a discussion I'm ready to have. Not with him.

That would be too personal. Too close. And I'm still feeling out what this friendship between us means.

After another block, he switches on the radio. We ride the rest of the way to the bar with him quietly humming along to the music.

Once we're inside, it's clear he's a regular. The hostess greets him by name with a warm smile that she extends to me as well. "You playing today?" she adds, which is weird, since it's not hockey season.

His cheeks take on that ruddy hue again. "Nah, not today. Just hungry."

"Barry'll comp your order if you play."

"I brought a sugar mama. She's paying today."

It's so unexpected that I crack up.

"I hope you're as loaded as our fries," she says, taking him completely seriously. "I've seen this guy put some food down."

"I think I can afford him," I tell her.

He's getting ruddier in the cheeks, which is pinging my *something's off* meter.

And when we're seated in a booth along the wall, I kick him lightly under the table to pull his attention away from the menu. "When they say play…"

He nods toward the stage set up along the closest wall.

And it clicks. "They don't know who you are here, do they?"

He shakes his head.

You'd think that wasn't possible, but while Copper Valley is a sports town, it's so much more than *just* a sports town. Go out to eat near the arena or the ballpark, and yes, it's inevitable that someone will recognize the players. Sometimes me too. But I've also been out with the whole Fireballs team before and seen the looks of people around us who clearly realize the team is a big deal but couldn't name a single person on it.

Outside the city, we're known more for being the birthplace of Bro Code, the boy band that Tripp, Levi, and three of their friends played in for years before I met any of them.

"Think our PSA will blow your cover?" I ask Duncan.

He grins. "Only if I ever walk in here in a helmet and skates."

"You like being anonymous?"

"Sometimes. I get a high off of playing for a crowd that isn't predisposed to telling me I'm awesome." He winks at me. "Sort of like I'm more inclined to go home with a woman who clearly doesn't know I'm the shit for other reasons than how well I play a guitar."

"I'm not touching that."

"Suit yourself."

"Hey, Duncan. You both know what you want, or should I give you a minute?" Our server is a smiling young man with a ponytail and a scruffy beard. He takes our drink orders along with Duncan's request for loaded fries, then slips away.

"How often do you come here?" I ask him.

"Few times a month. It's my new regular spot. Switch it up every summer."

"Because you *do* get recognized."

"Eventually."

"And then it gets weird."

"Yep."

"Do your teammates know you come here?"

He shakes his head.

"Retired teammates?"

He shakes his head again. "Can you imagine Ares or Zeus showing up here and not blowing it?"

I smile. "Ares would be quiet." It took a few years, but I eventually had reason to meet a few of the Thrusters through various opportunities. I'm still shocked I was in the city for over a year before I saw Duncan again. But I was pretty focused on baseball and only baseball those first two years.

"Felicity wouldn't be quiet," he says.

I haven't met Felicity Berger in person, but I've seen clips of her using her ventriloquism skills between periods at Thrusters games before.

She'd out him in a hot second.

He half smirks, then shakes his head.

I lift a brow.

"Don't tell her brother, but I dated her for a hot minute the season I got here."

A shocked "*No*" slips out of my mouth.

A heavy dose of something green floods my vision.

Not my business. Not my business. Not my business.

"Just kissing," Duncan says. "Nothing more. Long time ago."

"Isn't her brother—"

"Nick Murphy. Yeah. Dude does vengeance like the Berger twins do pranks."

It's disturbing how much I want to have helped Nick Murphy teach Duncan a lesson for kissing his sister.

I should've had Duncan take me home.

He snorts with what looks like absolute glee.

"What?" I say.

"You look mad."

"I'm not mad."

"I didn't say you *are* mad. I said you *look* mad."

"I have resting bitch face."

"You have resting pretty face."

I frown at him.

He leans back in his seat and glances at our server, who's arrived with our drinks. "Chuck, my dude, does my companion have resting bitch face?"

"No way." He jerks his head toward the small stage in the corner of the room. "Those three guys over there asked if you're brother and sister. They want to give her their phone numbers."

"That's a them problem," I say. "Also, I don't believe you."

Regret sinks in immediately as hurt flashes through Chuck's brown eyes, then disappears like he's used to being abused at work.

"I'm sorry," I say quickly. "I didn't mean to imply you're a liar. I believe you. Mostly. Kind of. I—I'm going to stop talking."

"She's not used to believing she's pretty," Duncan adds. "It's like her mirrors don't work."

I'm blushing.

Furiously.

"Suppose it's not likely the Fireballs are telling her she's pretty every day," Chuck says to Duncan. "Probably crosses lines with their coach."

My lips part.

Duncan's brows hit his hairline.

Chuck slides my iced tea in front of me on the smooth black table, his long sleeve pulling up just enough to show off a Baby Ash tattoo on his wrist. "Don't worry. I won't let your secret out."

"Thank you," I breathe.

"Also, I think you can do better than an unemployed guy who hangs out playing bars for free. No offense, Duncan."

I choke on air.

Duncan's grinning widely. "None taken."

Chuck leaves Duncan's bottle of sparkling water on the table too, then slips away.

"I can't decide if I'm mortified or amused," I whisper.

It's obvious which one Duncan is. He's barely holding in a laugh. "You're more famous than I am."

"He was joking about you being unemployed, right?"

"Nope. I told them I was living in my parents' basement, waiting for my musical career to take off."

"Long commute from Calgary every day."

He laughs again. "Very draining."

"You think you'll stay in the US when you retire?"

I cringe and wish I could take it back the minute the question leaves my mouth.

But if he reads into it, he doesn't show it.

Just shrugs instead. "Dunno. I'd like to be local as long as Paisley's in college here. After that, suppose it'll depend on what my life looks like then."

"Think you'll stay in hockey?"

"Maybe. Just as likely to be a real unemployed guy playing bars for fun though. Sometimes...sometimes I'm ready to slow down."

I feel that.

Being a professional athlete—or coach—means long hours, lots of travel, being *on* when you're spotted in public. Sometimes the break between seasons isn't enough.

Especially if you're using it to get in better shape

before the next season. Or showing up as the conditioning coach the guys want to work with in the offseason.

I've done that most winters, usually up in Shipwreck, Cooper's hometown in the mountains just outside the city. It's easy to relax there. The entire Rock family is genuinely kind, and the locals are used to having baseball players and sometimes bigger celebrities coming around.

"Just a break or a forever slow down?" I ask.

His green eyes land on me, and my stomach dips.

"Either," he says. "Depends on what my life looks like then."

Depends on if you want a lazy-ass retired hockey player in your life.

That's what I hear.

Not that I'd ever call Duncan *lazy-ass*. Far from it. If he takes a break when he retires, he's earned it.

But I can hear him calling himself that.

And I can see him washing dishes in his house. Studying cooking videos and whipping up ever-more-delicious masterpieces. Folding laundry. Getting a dog. Spending his evenings eating popcorn at Duggan Field or nachos at Mink Arena.

Dammit, why are my eyes getting hot?

"I don't do long-term relationships," I tell him, which shouldn't be news to him. And if I'm reading this wrong, I'm calling a ride and leaving all of the mortification of the past fifteen minutes behind me.

But Duncan takes the statement in stride, like he's expecting me to go there. "Why?"

"That's none of your business."

He leans forward. "You ever talk to anyone about it?"

"Again, none of your business."

"My sister's first husband was the biggest dick in the history of dicks. They were high school sweethearts. Got married their final year of college when she got pregnant with Paisley. He started telling her she needed to lose weight faster after she gave birth. That since he made ten percent more than she did, it was her job to do the cooking, cleaning, shopping, bill-paying, laundry, taking sick days when the baby was sick…"

I flinch.

Cannot help myself.

Because that was my mom, but instead of one baby, she had five.

Duncan's still watching me. "She left his worthless ass before Paisley was two, and she swore she was never dating again. It was easier being a single mom than it was depending on him for anything. Or taking care of two kids instead of one, since he was a big baby himself. And then Jordan happened."

"Who's Jordan?"

"He's the guy who earned the privilege of being in her life by being a partner and not a leech. And I've never seen my sister happier."

I reach for my tea and pretend to sip it.

"I know you like your life," he says quietly. "I like my life. Doesn't mean it can't get better though. And you never know where *better* will come from when you quit standing in your own way."

"Are you saying *you're* supposed to be my *better*?"

"I'd let you take me for a test drive."

"We've already done that."

"Between the two of us, that was a bunch of championships ago."

"Duncan—"

"I don't want to just *like* my life. I want to *love* my life. So I'm going to open myself up to whatever the world wants to throw at me and look at every moment as an opportunity. This? Us? Here? This is an opportunity. Life put me in that dress shop last week because I was supposed to be there. Because I'm getting a second chance to do this right, at whatever pace you need."

He shifts in his seat, making it squeak. "If you don't see it that way, I can't make you, just like I can't go back four years and make you feel like we were as serious as I thought we were. But I know this much—there will always be another chance for me to find what I'm supposed to do. Who I'm supposed to be. Who I'm supposed to be with. And I'm not afraid of what happens on the way."

My hand is shaking so badly that the ice in my cup rattles. My heart is pounding and there's this thick sensation of being in a cloud all around me.

But it's not a stifling cloud.

Not a dense fog that's too thick to drive through.

This cloud is all lust.

Why is it so damn attractive when a man—no, when *this man*—tells me he'll leave me in the dust and find someone even better?

That shouldn't be attractive.

But he's activated something deep inside of me.

Something that wants to know if he's right. If he truly gets it. If he *could* be the one man in the world who could make my life better instead of sapping away the essence of who I am and what brings me happiness.

I liked him four years ago.

I liked him so much it scared me, much like I've retreated into badass, take-no-prisoners Addie recently at work because it terrifies me to think that being myself will keep me from the biggest professional dream I've ever had.

It's easy to like him again. To forgive him—and myself—for how we ended.

But I don't know what that means for our future.

Beyond absolute terror.

It definitely means absolute terror.

A large oval plate filled to the brim with cheesy fries appears between us. "You're not unemployed," Chuck says to Duncan with a frown.

We both jerk back, and it takes me a breath to catch up to the fact that we're not alone. We're out in public. Both of us, moments ago, leaning in closer and closer.

Or maybe that was just me.

Drawn in by the hypnotic attractiveness of a man not afraid to tell me he likes me, and it's on me to decide what to do with that information.

"She's paying," Duncan says with an easy grin. "You didn't have to run my credit report."

"Those guys say you play hockey."

Duncan winces. "Might've picked up a stick a time or two."

I wince for him too. That was a weak denial.

"For the Thrusters," Chuck says.

"Can this be our secret?" Duncan asks.

"Not up to me anymore, friend." Chuck looks back at the table of guys who were offering to give me their numbers. "They're Barry's cousins. Already texted him. He just called and told us to get you booked for Friday night."

Duncan shakes his head and holds his hands up. "I don't do bookings."

"I get it. Enjoy your fries. This one's on the house, so slip out anytime you feel like it. Nice knowing you, my unemployed friend." Once again, Chuck steps away from our table.

I stare at Duncan. "What just happened?"

He stares forlornly at the fries. "My good friend Chuck recognizes that I'm not coming back. Barry's the owner. He'll put my name on posters if I agree to show up on Friday, and then I might as well be playing Chester Green's."

Oh.

The hockey bar near Mink Arena.

He'd be recognized there instantly.

And apparently, he'd be instantly recognized here too now.

He slides the plate my way. "Here. Try these. You need a baseline if you ever go hunting for the best loaded fries in Copper Valley."

I'm not going hunting for the best loaded fries in Copper Valley.

Not when it'll make me think of Duncan every time.

13

Duncan

"My dude, you have a problem."

I don't have to look up to know who's talking.

One, because I invited him to join me today. Two, because only Nick Murphy, former star goaltender for the Thrusters, would be cackling exactly that way at any of the rest of us having a problem.

"Going to a baseball game isn't generally considered a problem," I say, lifting my head to look at the row of seats behind me, where Nick and his wife, Kami, are getting settled. Also approaching in the same row are Ares and Felicity Berger. Ares is massive enough that he doesn't fit easily in stadium seats, and he's newly retired from the Thrusters. Felicity is Nick's hilarious sister whom I was not supposed to date.

She's much happier with Ares than she ever would've been with me.

Bonus, Ares might be relatively silent, but he can out-prank and outmaneuver anything Nick would ever consider doing.

"The gates haven't even opened yet," Nick says. "People without problems don't make arrangements to get into the ballpark before the gates are opened."

"More room to breathe before we're squished in." Fireballs games have a tendency to sell out these days.

It took some work to find seats where I can see the dugout *and* where I could have some friends join me. Got pretty lucky in that we're only about eight rows back from the infield.

"Who's *Bloom*?" Kami asks. "I don't remember a player named Bloom. Is he new?"

I can't tell you exactly the first time I met Kami. Been a lot of years. She was always around whenever Felicity would show up, either at the arena or at bars after the games. Where Felicity was exactly as loud, fun, and hilarious as you'd expect of anyone in that family—but more so, given how she taught herself to be a ventriloquist in her spare time—Kami was the epitome of the quiet, sweet BFF.

But there's mischief dancing in her brown eyes as she slides a smile at Felicity and Ares.

"You know Addie Bloom," Nick says to her. "She's the Fireballs' batting coach."

"*That* Addie Bloom?" Felicity says. "The Addie that

Duncan paid out the nose for in that bachelorette auction?"

"It wasn't a bachelorette auction," Kami says. "At least, it wasn't billed as one. But it does seem like he was trying to buy some pussy."

Assholes rehearsed this. You can tell by the way Kami said *buy some pussy*. She'd never say that on purpose.

I glance at Ares to see if he's having any reactions.

Dude's pretty stoic. Tends to speak mostly in grunts.

He pulls out his phone and hits play on a video without searching for it.

"Adults deserve fun too," a voice announces from his phone.

The opening of the PSA that we shot last week.

It went live yesterday.

"Ooooh, she *is* the woman you bid like a million dollars on at the auction," Kami says.

"A hundred and ten thousand, Kam," Nick says. "Just over ten percent of a full million."

"Silly me getting my numbers confused again."

She's a veterinarian. She doesn't get her numbers confused.

"How're the kids?" I ask all four of them.

"Awesome," Nick says.

"A handful," Felicity reports.

"A fun handful," Kami corrects.

A half smile crosses Ares's face. "Perfect." He hands

me his phone, now open to a picture of all of their combined munchkins climbing inside the fencing around Nick and Kami's massive chicken coop.

"They're with their grandparents," Nick says.

"My parents *and* Nick and Felicity's parents," Kami adds. "We thought four grandparents to five grandkids would be best. They're getting more…let's call it *courageous* with the youngest walking and the oldest able to read now."

"You need sunscreen, Duncan?" Felicity asks me as she slathers it on her own arms. "Little more UV exposure here than in a hockey rink."

"Already got it, thanks."

"Did Addie help?" Kami asks.

"No."

"But you're wearing her name on the back of your Fireballs jersey."

Proudly.

And not for them.

No, it's all for the woman who's standing behind the protective fencing that goes up immediately behind home plate during batting warm-ups for the team.

She's saying something to Brooks Elliott, a power hitter for the team who's in the batter's box, and he's grinning back at her. His "you got it, Coach" carries into the stands as he gets into position to hit the next ball.

"Did someone pay you to wear Addie's name?" Kami asks.

"*No.*"

"So is this like some extra publicity stunt? Was the auction a setup too? Did the Fireballs and Thrusters fund it so all the local sports fans would be talking about *Daddie?*"

I look back at her again.

"Legit questions," she says with a grin.

I jerk a thumb toward Nick. "You've been with this guy too long."

She laughs while he plays with her hair, smiling that completely smitten smile that's always on his face when they're together.

"Not nearly long enough," she says. "I'm still having too much fun."

You know that feeling when you're happy for someone but you also want what they have so hard that your entire body aches with it?

That's me in this moment.

If you'd told me ten years ago that Nick Murphy would retire in his prime because he wanted to spend more time with his wife and kids, I would've laughed until I threw up.

And I've never laughed that hard in my life.

Nick was the epitome of *free-living hockey bachelor.*

Liked killing it on the ice, aiming for a shutout every single night. Hitting the bars afterwards. Having fun with the women.

But he hung up his pads and skates a year and a half

after he married Kami because he hated road trips away from her and their baby.

They have three kids now, and I've never seen him happier.

Ares hung up his skates this year too to be home more with Felicity and their two kids. That's massive for a guy who led people to believe he intended to play until he was fifty. Told me once it's the only thing he's ever been or will ever be good at.

But now he's spending his days with his own little family, and frequently with Zeus, his identical twin, and Joey and their quadruplets.

Being even better at being a dad and a father than he is—*was*—at playing hockey.

And he looks pretty content as he's sitting there with an arm draped around the back of Felicity's seat.

They have something bigger to live for.

Something I always assumed I would've had by now too.

"Hey, Uncle Dunc," Paisley says as she steps into the row. She's decked out in Fireballs gear and carrying a bag of popcorn. "Little early, aren't we?"

It's easy to shift a smile to my niece. "More time to enjoy the weather."

And it's gorgeous today.

Lots of sunshine. Puffy white clouds hanging around merely for decoration. Cool breeze.

Perfect day for baseball.

Paisley takes the seat next to me, and when she leans forward, I can't stop the noise that comes out of my mouth at the sight of the name on the back of her jersey. "*McBride? Are you fucking kidding? He's a disaster.*"

She grins at me. "I like 'em that way. More fun to watch."

Rory McBride was brought in as a rookie to take Cooper Rock's place at second base this year, but he's spent half his time being sent back to the minors.

"Just to watch," I say.

The kid's only a couple years older than she is.

I know this story.

Hockey player's niece uses his connections to get to know baseball players who are nothing but trouble and then gets her heart broken.

Not on my watch.

She rolls her eyes. "Don't be like Mom."

"Paisley, do you know why your uncle is wearing the batting coach's name on his jersey?" Kami asks. My friends and niece have met before. Several times over the years, in fact.

"Because he's got a thing for her and won't admit it any other way," Paisley answers.

I make a buzzer noise. "Wrong."

"And yet, it seems so likely," Nick muses.

I peer back at him. "You're too simple of a man to understand the nuance of my fit."

Kami chokes on her beer.

Nick grins at me. "You need help, my dude."

"Why does Duncan need help?" a semi-familiar voice asks on my other side.

I turn and do a double take.

Shit.

Tillie Jean Rock-Cole.

Cooper's sister. Married to a retired Fireballs star pitcher. Doesn't come around the city often—she's mayor of their hometown about an hour away in the mountains now.

Kami squeals her name and steps over Nick to give her a hug. Felicity shuffles around Nick to hug TJ too.

"Who's that?" Paisley whispers.

"Someone who knows her way around a glitter bomb," I whisper back. "Tread lightly."

"Just when I swear I'm never believing another word Cooper says, I show up and Duncan's wearing an Addie jersey," Tillie Jean says.

I'm holding in a wince while she plops into the seat beside me.

"That one's taken," I tell her.

"I'm sitting up in the owners' box with Waverly," she replies. "But I heard a rumor there were old hockey players hanging out and wanted to say hi. Now I feel like I should be offering advice."

"I've tried. It's hopeless," Felicity says.

"If razzing me counts as offering advice," I say.

"It does if you're smart enough to recognize it," Nick says.

"Also, I'm not old," I tell Tillie Jean.

"You kinda are," Paisley says. "But I'm allowed to say that since you've been old to me since the day I was born."

"I like you," Tillie Jean says to her.

"I've been told I'm not allowed to talk to you for fear of glitter bombs," Paisley replies.

"My first act as mayor of Shipwreck was to outlaw glitter in all forms in the town and surrounding areas that are serviced by town utilities."

Paisley whistles. "That's hardcore."

"When your sister-in-law can afford a helicopter to glitter-bomb your brother's entire house to prove who's top dog, you have to take drastic measures. Sometimes the wind still blows leftover glitter down his mountain and all around town." Tillie Jean looks at me, clearly intent on leaving out her own history of launching glitter bombs. "So are you here to hit on Addie, or is this a PR stunt before the pickleball league sign-ups?"

"Addie and I are friends." And one of us—me— wants more. And I'm willing to play the long game to get it.

The very long game if necessary.

I wouldn't if I didn't think I had a chance.

But the way she looks at me—the way she let her

guard down when I showed up the morning after the auction, the way she sat with me when I overheated, then sat with me while I told her I'm retiring, the way her eyes went dark while I told her I was taking advantage of this second chance over loaded cheese fries—she knows what I want.

And she hasn't told me no.

Implied she doesn't think I can earn her, yes.

Reiterated that she doesn't do *relationships*.

But told me no to being her friend? To being in her life?

Nope.

She invited *me* to take breakfast to the Stingrays softball team. She didn't argue about grabbing a bite to eat, just the two of us, afterward. And the way she lingered when we got back to her apartment, saying so much with what she didn't say—she still likes me.

She simply doesn't know how to handle it yet.

Fine by me.

I have time.

"Are you *friends*-friends, or *just* friends?" Kami asks.

"I don't know the difference between those two." Which one means friends with benefits and which one means *we're honestly friends*?

Never mind.

Doesn't matter.

Neither fits.

"Uncle Duncan's seen her naked," Paisley supplies.

"I've seen Duncan naked," Nick says. "Happens in

sportsing. Sometimes in cross-sportsing. Like when we forget we're not at our own home arena and walk into a different sport's locker room. You smell that locker room smell, and *boom*. Clothes come off."

Just when I'd started to give up on him, he comes through with the support.

We bump fists.

"When does baseball season end?" Kami asks.

"October," Nick tells her. "Maybe early November, depending on playoffs."

"And when does it start?"

"February," Tillie Jean says. "Spring training. Kiss 'em all goodbye at that point if you're not going with them."

All four of them look at me.

I look at the field.

Addie's staring up at us.

I lift a hand to wave at her.

"Hey, hockey boy, quit looking at my coach," Brooks yells.

The few other people who are in the stadium before the gates officially open look our way.

I stand up.

Turn around.

Stretch.

Show off her name on my back.

"And quit wearing her name," Brooks calls as I turn back around and take my seat again.

"We appreciate real talent and recognize where your skill's coming from," Nick yells back.

Brooks gives him a *what the fuck?* look.

Tillie Jean and Kami both crack up.

Addie's wearing her sunglasses, but I can feel her staring at me too long before snapping her attention quickly back to Brooks. Whatever she says to him makes him crack up.

To my absolute shock, her lips stretch in a smile too.

So maybe she didn't say *get your ass back in the dugout, I don't need you defending my honor to puckheads in the stands.*

She got to ditch her sling, but you can tell by the way she moves that she's being extra cautious with her left arm. I got a single text message. *No surgery. I'll be fine again very soon. PT is about to be my bitch.*

About to be, but clearly not yet.

The Addie I knew four years ago would be crossing her arms and widening her stance.

Instead, it's just the widened stance with her right hand resting on her hip.

"Good to see you, Murphy," Brooks calls.

"Good for you to see me too," Nick calls back.

"He means play good today," Kami calls. "Tell Mackenzie we said hi."

"Don't strike out," Tillie Jean adds.

Addie's voice comes through clearer as she tilts her

head at him. "Still think you can keep up with that level of heckling?"

"Almost as many older brothers as you, Coach. These puckers don't bother me."

"I can see why you like her," Paisley says. "And I like her a lot more than I ever liked Lena."

It takes a full two seconds for me to register who *Lena* is.

Paisley watches me while she shoves a handful of popcorn in her mouth, and then she slowly starts grinning.

Like she knows my ex-wife is finally so far in the rearview mirror that the way she left me doesn't hurt anymore.

Tillie Jean's staring at me from my other side.

"What?" I say to her.

"Addie's been with the team for five and a half years. She's spent most off-seasons up in Shipwreck for conditioning training with at least a half dozen guys on the team."

"And?"

"And she doesn't date."

"And?"

"And you paid over a hundred grand for a date with her."

Paisley leans forward and looks around me. "He didn't like how the old dude at the next table was looking at her. The old dude who was super creepy and bidding more and more too."

Tillie Jean looks between us. "Have you *met* Addie?"

"Just because a woman *can* handle her own business doesn't mean her squad should leave her hanging when things get crazy," Paisley replies.

"She ate." Ares smirks like he's enjoying the shocked looks from all of us at the man who never speaks keeping up with the lingo. Then he rubs my head. "Good job."

Addie's talking to Diego Estevez behind home plate now.

And she keeps glancing toward the stands.

Toward us.

Unlike Tillie Jean, who's still frowning at me, Addie seems happy.

Possibly amused.

Two other coaches join her, and they both look my way.

"Oooh, they're talking about you," Kami says. "What do you think they're saying?"

"*Is that Duncan guy looking at you wrong?*" Felicity says in one of her grumpy-guy puppet voices. Don't have to look at her to know she's not moving her lips. It's freaky and cool at the same time.

But it's better when she's surrounded by people who don't know she's a ventriloquist and she makes pets and inanimate objects talk than it is when she's mocking me.

"*Don't worry, fellow coaches. I know how to punch a guy in the nuts!*" she says back in a cheerful feminine voice.

"*Not sure a nut-punch will be enough for someone who tried to buy your pussy at auction*," the grumpy voice says.

"*You haven't felt the strength of my nut-punch!*" the happy lady voice says.

I look back at her.

Nick's cracking up.

Kami's trying to keep a straight face as she says, "All in good fun, Duncan."

Felicity's grinning proudly.

So is Ares.

"I can't decide if you scare me or if you're the coolest person I've ever met," Paisley says to her.

"That's the same thing Ares's pet monkey said the first time he met Felicity too," Nick says, which actually makes Ares crack a real laugh with the rest of us.

He's a harder nut to crack than Addie is.

I suspect he laughs more at home than he does out in public.

Just like Addie.

Tillie Jean sighs on my other side, half smiling as she rises. "I'm going back to the suite. But Duncan, seriously—if you're planning on trying something with Addie, just...just don't, okay?"

Nothing's funny anymore. This is giving *someone hurt Addie* vibes, and I don't like it. "Why?"

"Because no one gets as tough as Addie is without going through shit. And she doesn't deserve more shit. From anyone."

"What kind of shit?" I ask.

"Don't know, and I wouldn't tell you even if I did. But I stand by what I said. You don't get that tough without going through shit. She deserves to be happy."

"Tell Max we said hi," Nick says.

"And that we're sorry for what Zeus and Ares did to him at the game bar last week," Felicity adds.

"No worries," Tillie Jean says. "Glitter bombs are only outlawed in Shipwreck. They're fair game in Copper Valley. And it turns out Waverly and Max are really great prank partners, so it'll all work out in the end."

Felicity freezes and glances at Ares.

Not often you see the big guy look guilty. Or worried.

But he's definitely both right now.

He should be.

I hear Max Cole is a quiet pranker.

And Waverly Sweet has basically unlimited funds.

She could buy the Thrusters if she wanted to.

I'm smirking as I glance back at the field again.

Addie's two fellow coaches are still looking our way.

She's demonstrating a batting stance for Francisco Lopez. Still not using her left arm though.

I'll see her again tomorrow.

We're making a guest appearance at a pickleball league sign-up.

And I can't wait.

Plus, we have our *Croaking Creatures* date in two

weeks. After this home series, she has a road trip and then a day off.

She's giving me her day off.

Nick pokes me after Tillie Jean leaves. "If you ever want to talk to someone about retirement and what happens when you hang up your skates, I have a really great life coach recommendation."

"Who said anything about retirement?"

I've told Addie.

That's it.

As far as the Thrusters know, my agent is in talks with me about what we'd want in another contract when mine expires at the end of the year.

"You have the look," Ares says.

"Well-spoken, my friend," Nick says.

Ares doesn't waste words.

Ever.

I look between my two former teammates.

Ares is poker-faced.

Nick's unusually sober. He shrugs at me. "We all know where your contract stands. And she's breaking barriers. That shit matters more. You're not the kind of asshole who'll pretend you can make it work when your seasons overlap on both sides."

They're not wrong.

I want a shot with Addie. A real shot with the possibility of forever. And I'm willing to do whatever it takes to get it.

And this time, I'm not telling my friends I'm seeing

someone but it's not serious enough to introduce them, the way she more or less asked me to.

This time, I'm letting myself get their support.

Or listen to their objections.

"She was my secret hookup four years ago," I say.

All four of them look back at the field.

Nick whistles low and soft.

Ares grunts.

"Are you serious?" Kami whispers.

"Oh, Duncan, no," Felicity says. "She broke you."

"I broke myself. And I got through it. With help. I realized that last time, I didn't listen. That's on me. This time, I'm listening. I know what I'm getting into."

Paisley's the only one who smiles at me. "Good. I like her."

"Me too." Feels so damn good to say it out loud. "Enough to see if she's willing to let me help her work through her shit. And if she doesn't...then at least I'll have real closure this time."

Paisley nudges my shoulder with hers. "Aww, look at you being mature. I'm so proud."

"I'm worried," Kami says.

"Same," Felicity agrees.

"Got your back," Ares says, rubbing my head again.

I fist bump him too. "Thanks, my dude."

He nods.

His eyes say *you're in for a hell of a ride*, but that nod reiterates that he's on my side.

"Who started this party without us?" Zeus asks as

he and Joey enter my row on the other side. "And who's taking bets on who makes the biggest scene on the kiss cam?" he adds with a look at the familiar couple following him.

"We're literally the reason all sports arenas and stadiums quit doing the kiss cam," the Berger twins' little sister answers while her husband smirks.

He turns just right, and there's glitter sparkling in the dude's chin dimple.

People think Zeus and Ares are the reason we're known for glitter wars.

Wrong.

It all started with their sister.

Who also doesn't get the credit she deserves.

Just like Addie before she came here to Copper Valley.

"Somebody start this party without us?" Tyler Jaeger asks. He and his wife, Muffy, have also arrived. Tyler's one of few guys still active on the team who hasn't retired yet, but I suspect it won't be many more years before he's done too.

"Do you think the people sitting around us have any idea what they're in for?" Kami muses as she and Muffy hug each other.

"Nope," we all answer for her.

I know what I'm in for.

A fun game with good friends where the woman I want to date knows I'm wearing her jersey.

And then patience.

And then—well.

Guess we'll see what's *then*.

I know what I want it to be.

I want it to be with Addie wearing *my* jersey in *her* off-season.

It'll take time, but I believe it'll happen.

I have to.

14

Addie

IT'S a terrible day for pickleball sign-ups.

A wall of thick, dark gray clouds are making a slow roll our way from the horizon. It's hot enough here in a corner of Reynolds Park near the pickleball courts that the mascots have had to take breaks inside the concrete restroom building. And every fifth person who's approached the table has asked if Duncan and I are dating.

"She deserves someone way better than me," Duncan's saying to a seventy-year-old woman who's here to sign up for the *seasoned citizens* bracket, and who has asked *the question*.

He's in a maroon Thrusters polo and a tan bucket hat that hides his curly hair. If you didn't know who he was, you'd think he was any random admin person who sat in the back office for the Thrusters instead of the team's captain who has four championship rings and celebrated a thousand career games played two seasons ago.

"It's nice to see a young man who'll recognize that," the woman says. "So you know, though, you don't get credit for lip service. You have to prove you mean it."

"Would you like a Fireballs water bottle, ma'am?" I interject.

"Honey, when you get to be my age, you have so many water bottles that you forget which ones have water and which ones have vodka in them. Don't fall for any sweet words from cute young men. Make them earn you. Don't call him *Daddy* like those articles say you do."

"The articles gave us that nickname because of how it sounds when you smush our names together." It's not the first time Duncan has said this today. "We didn't ask for it. We're not using it."

"I'm unattached and planning to stay that way," I tell her. The statement is lacking its normal conviction, and it doesn't slide off my tongue the way it used to.

Freaking Duncan.

The man is in my head. And I'm not as mad about it as I would've expected.

She leans across the table and lowers her voice. "If he gets you knocked up, you call me. I can help with whatever you need. My number's right there on the sheet, and I'm here for you anytime. For anything. Understand?"

"Thank you, ma'am. Denise down the way has your shirt. And she slipped me pepper spray before we started in case he gets too forward."

While she takes the hint and heads over to the T-shirt table, Duncan grabs his own hydration bottle from under the table and takes a long drink, then offers it to me.

"I have my own, thank you."

He grins. "Don't want to get pictured sharing drinks?"

"On the same day you're front-page sports headline news for wearing a jersey with my name on it to a Fireballs game? Which revived the *Daddie* thing? No."

"Won't do it again. But only because it was clearly bad luck for the team with that loss. I know you're a superstitious lot."

I lift my brows at him. "*Who's* superstitious?"

"Afternoon, ma'am," he says to the next woman in line. "You ready to sign up for some pickleball?"

"How likely are you to get hurt playing pickleball?" she asks him. She's middle-aged, wearing an oversize T-shirt featuring the Pounders rugby team logo and leggings criss-crossed with a bright mishmash of all of the colors in the rainbow.

This question's my domain. "There are inherent risks in any sport, but you can play at the level you're comfortable, and we have protective gear available, like goggles and kneepads."

"Is this league coed?"

"Yes, ma'am."

"How many men have signed up who look like him?"

While my brain trips over itself trying to figure out that answer, Duncan steps in. "They're all far more attractive than me, ma'am. But we don't know who's single and who's in a relationship, so tread lightly as you hit on them, eh?"

Her cheeks turn into beets. "Oh, no, I can't hit on them. I want to know if I'll feel...out of place. With attractive people."

"What's your name?" Duncan asks her.

"Mary," she stutters back.

"Mary, it's nice to meet you. Now let me tell you a few things about Pickleball Club. The first rule of Pickleball Club is that you don't let anyone make you feel like you don't belong here. The second rule of Pickleball Club is that you don't make anyone else feel like they don't belong here. And the third rule of Pickleball Club is that you have to do your best to have fun. Think you can handle those?"

She shifts her weight back and forth. "My husband just left me for a twenty-two-year-old," she whispers.

"Is he a Thrusters fan?"

"Yes, but he likes the Berger twins more than you. Only because he's a complete twatwaffle and thinks genetics are more important than character. No offense to the Berger twins."

Duncan whips out his phone, thumbs over the screen, and sets it upside down on the table. "Takes a lot to offend those two," he says. "You signing up, or you want more information first?"

"What happens if I sign up but I get hurt and can't play anymore?"

"You can come watch," Duncan says.

"The league will try to get someone to fill your spot if you can't find anyone," I add.

"So there are spare players?" she asks.

I shake my head. "No spare players, but some people like to play more often and will happily step in if someone's missing a partner, or if you're playing singles and your opponent still wants to play."

"Oh, good. Good. I don't want to let anyone down if I can't do this. But I want to do something fun. For me. I haven't done something fun in *years*."

That sentiment from a middle-aged woman will never not hit me right in the gut. This is exactly the sort of thing my mom would've done if she were still here. I try to smile at Mary, but it's a wobbly smile.

"I'm proud of you." Shit. My voice is wobbling too. "You deserve this."

We make full eye contact, and hers go shiny. "It's hard," she whispers.

"I know," I whisper back. "But you can do it. And

you'll be so glad you did. New friends. New hobby. New life."

"You've started over?"

I shake my head. "My mom did."

"Is she happy now?"

"Yes," I lie, ignoring the way Duncan's head whips around toward me.

I want to believe she would've been.

That she would've signed up for a pickleball league and made new friends that she had dinners with and traveled with and celebrated weddings and grandbabies with. Maybe taken art classes with.

That she would've kept living the life she'd finally given herself permission to have if it hadn't been cut short.

"Okay," Mary says. "If your mom can do this, I can do this. Where do I sign up?"

Duncan passes her a clipboard. "Waiver and sign-up form here. If you want to be added to the Thrusters or Fireballs email lists, you can add your name here, or scan the QR codes and sign up online."

"Do I bring it back here when I'm done?"

"Yep."

She half jogs to the bench under a tree that people have been using to fill out their forms.

Duncan looks at me. "I thought your mom passed away."

I don't look back at him. "Can't exactly tell people she finally seized life by the balls only to have it ripped away by a freak accident a year later if we want to stay inspirational, can we? She *was* happy. For about ten months. Are the Berger twins coming for spite pictures?"

"Very likely. What made your mom finally seize life by the balls?"

"It's nice of you to ask them to come for a complete stranger." I wave the next person over with my good arm. He's already carrying a clipboard.

Duncan's still staring at me.

I can feel it.

"I'm all signed up. Can I get a picture?" the guy in line says to Duncan.

That gets him on his feet. "You betcha."

One of the Thrusters admins who have been hanging around steps in to snap the picture while I take a drink out of my own hydration bottle.

"How's it feel to be *Daddie?*" the guy asks Duncan.

"Coach Addie and I are professional friends," Duncan replies. "We aren't individually or together anyone's daddy."

We take the guy's form and send him on his way as quickly as possible. The wall of clouds is getting darker, thicker, and pressing closer to us, bringing in heavier winds that make us scramble to keep our stack of sign-up forms from flying away. Mary finishes her form and slips between the next two pickleball players to deliver them to us. Duncan tells her to stick around for a little bit. That it'll be worth her while.

I flag down Sadie from PR and point to the sky. "When are we calling it?"

"Fifteen to twenty minutes," she replies. "We're shutting down the line and directing people online for sign-ups after these last half dozen or so."

I nod and get back to sign-ups, roughly tracking that the mascots have returned from their break. Hard to miss when a commotion breaks out under the refreshments tent moments later though.

"Hundred grand says Zeus and Ares just got here," Duncan murmurs to me.

"Sucker's bet. If you wanted to put real money down, we'd be betting on what they're wearing or what they're carrying."

The mascots.

The answer is the mascots.

Zeus gets Thrusty the bratwurst up on his shoulders and Ares gets Ash the teenage dragon up on his, and the two sets line up against each other for a pool noodle sword fight.

Mary's laughter echoes over to our table as the giant former hockey players wave her over to get a picture with them.

"Thrusty's gonna kick your dragon's ass," Duncan says to me as we all pause to watch.

"Ash can breathe fire. She'll roast your bratwurst without hardly trying."

He laughs, but it's cut off by the first roll of thunder crossing the park.

We both look up at the sky.

"Time to close up," the Thrusters admin says to us as three more assistants fan out to speak with the remaining people in line. "Quick pictures if anyone wants them, and then take shelter."

Two people want pictures with me.

Seven get the fastest pictures I've ever seen with Duncan. I shouldn't linger helping the admins get the table picked up and the paperwork in bins, especially since I'm still favoring my shoulder and can't help as much as I want to, but it goes against my nature to not do whatever I can.

Which isn't the real reason I'm lingering as lightning flashes in a distant cloud, sending another low roll of thunder grumbling through the park moments later.

No, the real reason I'm lingering is because Duncan is a magnet and I'm a pile of iron flakes.

I shake myself out of it as he's doing the next to last picture. "I live across the street," I tell the admins. "Mind if I get out of here before it starts pouring?"

Rain is fine.

We get our fair share of drizzly games over the course of any given season.

But it's the thunder and lightning we need to take shelter from.

"Can you make it?" one asks me.

"Absolutely." I'm not as quick as I was before I dislocated my shoulder—running is still jarring for my joint and I've just started working on rebuilding my strength and range of motion—but I can speed walk.

"Go, then," they say. "We've got this."

"Later, Duncan," I say, just to not look like an asshole who can't say goodbye.

His gaze hits mine for a split second as he's posing for a picture, but I shift my attention toward the mascots, who are climbing into the back of vans that have been waiting. I wave to the Fireballs staff finishing up the rapid teardown of the shelter over the refreshment and swag tables, then head off at a fast clip toward my building.

Which is a little farther than just across the street.

Just farther enough that a fat raindrop plops down onto my head while I'm still roughly a block's length from my building.

That fat raindrop is followed by another, then another, and another, in rapid succession, beating the oak and elm leaves around me, until it's a full deluge only partially blocked by the trees.

"Addie!" an achingly familiar voice says behind me as my building comes into view.

A blinding flash of lightning rips through the sheets of rain pummeling us, nearly immediately followed by a crash of thunder.

"You should be headed to your car," I say to Duncan as he falls into step with me. I'm soaked. He's soaked. We need to get inside.

"I parked by your building."

"Is everything from sign-ups picked up?"

"Staff is cleared out completely. They're fast."

"Good. You should've parked closer to the courts."

We reach the street at a crosswalk. Duncan hits the button on a street post to flash the drivers an alert that pedestrians are crossing, and when we've made sure the traffic is slowing, we dash across, then three more buildings down, utilizing the overhangs to get out of the rain.

My shirt is clinging to me.

So are my pants.

I don't want to look at Duncan and see what his clothes are doing to his body.

"Where's your car?" I ask Duncan.

He jerks a thumb behind us. "About six blocks that way."

"That is not *close* to my building." I stop under my own overhang and finally fully look at him.

His curly hair is plastered to his head. Water drips down his strong nose and over his cheeks and into the scruff on his jaw. His Thrusters polo clings to his broad shoulders and the hard planes of his chest and his thick, corded arms as he wipes water droplets off his forehead. The wind blows rain into the sheltered area next to the door, and he visibly shivers.

"Good to see you today," he says. "Thanks for letting me walk you home. Still on for Thursday after next?"

Is he serious? "I don't need you to—"

"I know," he says quickly. "That's why I said thank you for letting me do it."

"You should've taken a ride with one of the staff." I shouldn't be cranky.

But I know why I am.

I'm mad at myself for telling him about my mom. When you know what's wrong with someone, you can give it lip service to try to make it go away.

I don't want Duncan giving me lip service.

I want him to mean it. I want him to prove it. I want to believe in him and not have him let me down.

Wanting him scares me.

He's watching me as cars drive past, splashing water over the curb but not close enough to get us.

We shouldn't be out here where we're visible to anyone.

"I have to get to the ballpark," I say.

"Yeah, game day."

"The storm will pass. We'll play tonight."

"Definitely."

"If you want to wait at my place until the storm blows over, that's fine."

He eyes me cautiously. "Addie, I'm not angling for an invitation in. I just wanted to make sure you got home safe."

And that makes me mad too, and I don't know why.

Fine.

Yes.

I know why.

It's because it's exactly what he'd say if he only wants me as a friend, *or* it's exactly what he'd say if he wants more but he's respecting all of the walls I've put between us. "You didn't cook up the fucking storm, Duncan. Just come in and get dry and don't get hit by lightning going back to your car, okay?"

He stares at me while thunder cracks the wet morning air.

"And don't do my dishes," I add.

He widens his stance and runs a hand over his head, slicking back his soaked hair. "When I do your dishes, I'm not looking for anything in return. You don't owe me. There's no tally board keeping score. It's what you do for a friend when they need help. And sometimes it's what you do for a friend even when they don't need help."

I squeeze my eyes shut and blow out a long breath. The wind blows more mist under the overhang, and this time, I shiver.

Get out of your own head, Addie. This is just about being safe during a storm. "I hear and acknowledge the words you're saying, but I have a lifetime of examples to the contrary."

"I can see where that makes trusting people hard."

"Where it makes trusting people not worth it." I hate sounding bitter. *Hate* it.

But if we're going to continue doing community events together, and if he's going to keep parking near me and walking me home and offering to do my dishes, and if I'm going to keep having this growing attraction to him again, and if he's going to keep giving me all of these signs and signals that he likes me too, then he needs to know where I stand.

That it's not him.

It's me.

I have issues. They might be insurmountable.

And I like my life. I don't feel like anything's missing.

But lately, I want more.

Lately, I want *him*.

He squeezes my good arm. "Good luck at the game today. I promise I won't wear your jersey. Clearly bad luck."

"It's thunderstorming, Duncan."

"I'll hang out in the lobby until it passes."

And now I'm getting pissed. "Is this a game? Are you playing mind games with me right now?"

He shakes his head. "I'm just trying to respect what you want. I don't think you want me in your apartment, and you don't want me walking six blocks in a thunderstorm, so I'm fine hanging out in the lobby until it's safe for me to go. That's it. That's my whole agenda right now."

I want him in my apartment.

And that's why I'm mad.

Duncan Lavoie has once again made me like him, and that scares the ever-loving fuck out of me.

Especially after talking to a woman today who put my mom back at the forefront of my mind.

I unclench both of my fists and suck in a deep breath.

I *want* him in my apartment.

But I *need* space to figure out if that's a good idea.

"Okay," I say stiffly. "Thank you."

"You betcha."

I push into the lobby as a long grumble of thunder rattles the glass in the door and walk straight into a wall of cold air that hits my wet clothing and skin with enough force to instantly pucker my nipples and make goosebumps erupt over every inch of my skin.

Duncan follows but stops beside the door.

I growl softly to myself.

This is stupid.

Him hanging out in the lobby is ridiculous.

My neighbors will see him.

And I can be a goddamn adult and work out my issues on my own.

"Will you *please* come up to my apartment until this passes?" I mutter as I jam the elevator up button with my finger.

I'm not looking at him.

But he's watching me. The hairs standing up on the back of my neck tell me so.

There's a soft ding in the lobby with every floor that the elevator drops on its way to pick me up. As the number clicks down to three, then two, then one, Duncan steps beside me.

"You're sure?"

"Do *not* do my dishes."

"I won't touch your dishes."

"I probably have some T-shirts and sweatpants that are big enough for you. So you can get dry."

"Appreciate it. I'll bring them back clean."

"They might be pink."

"Then I might not bring them back. I don't have much pink in my wardrobe yet."

The elevator doors open, and we step onto it. I don't look at him. I don't think he's looking at me.

He doesn't try to hit the button to my floor, so I take care of it myself.

The doors close, and the elevator begins its ascent.

"I'm not trying to be an asshole," I mutter.

"I don't think you're an asshole. I think—"

The elevator jerks. I reach out with both arms to steady myself, banging into Duncan with my good arm and smacking my bad arm against the wall as everything plunges into pitch blackness.

Shit.

Goddammit.

Don't ride elevators in thunderstorms.

"Addie?" Duncan says in the darkness.

"Fucking *fuck*," I reply on a sigh, gingerly rubbing my left shoulder.

"Does this happen often?"

"No. At least, I don't think so." Aren't there emergency lights? Shouldn't some battery-powered backup lights be on?

"So it should be quick?" his voice is getting quieter.

And new alarm bells start ringing in my head. "Should be. Are you—are you okay in the dark?"

"Yeah."

It's a short *yeah*.

"But?" I ask softly.

"I'm fine."

He's not fine.

He's stuck in an elevator with me in the pitch black.

Soaking wet.

And there's no telling how long we'll be in here.

Fuck.

15

Duncan

I WILL NOT LOSE my shit in this elevator.

Nope. Nope nope. Not thinking about *where* I am.

In the dark.

In a small room held up by just a cable.

Who knows how many stories up.

In the dark.

I squeeze my eyes shut.

Still the same dark, but I'm in control of dark-behind-my-eyelids dark.

I'm in control. I'm in control. I'm in control.

Do we have enough oxygen? Does anyone know we're stuck? Will they help us? How can they help us? Are we between floors? How long will we be here?

Nope, not in control.

Breathe. Breathe. Breathe.

Is Addie afraid of elevators?

Addie.

I will not lose my shit in front of Addie.

Better.

I *cannot* lose my shit in front of Addie.

That would be mortifying.

But also, I still give it a fifty-fifty chance.

A light flips on.

Her phone. Duh. Of course. Get light from the phone.

Her fingers touch my wrist as I lean against the wall and let my eyes close again. My pulse is hammering. I'm starting to sweat. And I'm pissed and embarrassed too.

"Wanna sit down? Get comfortable?" she says. "Could be a few minutes."

"I'm good." I'm not good.

The worst part, though, is how quickly I'm panicking.

That's what it is.

Panic.

We're alone, but I feel hot bodies crowded tight around us. I hear a baby crying. My mom grips my shoulder harder and harder while my dad tells her not to worry. The scent of onions lingers in the air while the minutes drag on and on and on. Someone had onions on their lunch and got in an elevator and now we're all stuck here.

"I want to sit." Addie's voice is a lifeline pulling me out of the memory, bringing me back to where it's just the two of us. "Will you sit with me?"

Shit. My thighs are shaking and I still smell onions. "Yeah."

I don't move.

Not even when her fingers move on my wrist, reminding me she's here and that she's moving.

"Duncan?"

"Yeah."

"I'm texting building support to let them know we're in here."

A shiver wrenches through my body with the same force of the thunder making its presence known outside. "No signal—in—metal boxes."

"I have a strong signal. Sit with me. Since the power hasn't come right back on, it might be a few more minutes."

Right. I'm still standing. I press my back against the wall and let myself slide down it.

Addie slides down next to me, then squeezes my thigh. "Better, yeah?"

"I got stuck in an elevator at the CN Tower in Toronto on a family vacation in high school. Full elevator. Crush of people. Near the top. It dropped a little when the power went out. I'm fine. Long time ago."

"Is that the last time you were stuck in an elevator?"

I'm definitely sweating.

It's fucking cold, my clothes are soaked with rain,

my hair is dripping, it's the temperature of a refrigerator in here, and I'm sweating.

I'm definitely not *fine*. "Yeah."

"First place your brain went just now?"

"Yeah."

"We're okay. We're barely a floor up. Super close to the ground."

I make myself suck in a breath. Ignore the fireflies dancing in my vision. Concentrate on Addie's voice.

"Management is usually very quick to respond," she's saying. "They're ridiculous. They pitched in and got me a champagne basket the first time the Fireballs went all the way. Gift certificates for restaurants around the neighborhood too, though I'm pretty sure the restaurants donated those. They act like I'm some kind of celebrity."

The sound of her voice is pulling me back from the edge. "Say more."

"We're playing Minnesota this week. First series on our road trip. That's always hard. They were my team when I was growing up, and now my job is to crush them. Well, to encourage the guys to crush them. My first season, I got completely tongue-tied when I realized I was standing on the same field as guys in Minnesota uniforms. Luca Rossi caught me taking a selfie with the other team in the background and offered to introduce me to some of the guys. He played for Minnesota for a year. I declined. I didn't want any of the guys to know I was freaking out on the inside. Embarrassing, eh?"

My breathing is evening out. My eyes are still closed. Easier to not think about where I am this way. "*This* is embarrassing."

"Human intelligence has advanced world technologies much faster in the past two hundred years than the evolution of our brains can keep up with. Normal fight-or-flight response to an unnatural situation. Rooms aren't supposed to go up and down."

This isn't fight or flight. It's *freeze*. "I hate MRIs too."

She tucks her arm through mine.

Her good arm. I'm on her right.

It's warm.

She's warm.

I shiver, then huddle closer to her.

"Same," she says quietly. "And I'd be lying if I said it's because MRIs mean I'm hurt. They're...just as bad as being stuck in a dress."

"You know what's dumb?"

"The price of ice cream these days?"

I huff out a surprised half laugh. Maybe a quarter laugh. But more of a laugh than I expected to have in me right now. "Airplanes don't bother me. Not even when we hit turbulence."

"That's because you have a solid understanding of aerodynamics."

More shivers ripple through me. We're both soaked.

She has to be cold too, despite the warmth radiating off of her.

And now I'm remembering giving her a presentation on how airplanes work when we were hooking up a few years ago.

In another place, in a different situation, the reminder would make me laugh again.

I geeked out hard.

"Should've taken the stairs," I mutter.

"Next time."

"Every time."

"I took the stairs when we got back to the hotel after a game in the middle of a long road trip a few years ago. The team was all lined up around the elevators, and I didn't want to wait. Or be stuck in a small space with them when their body washes don't always work well together. It was a hike. Something like fourteen stories. Halfway up, I started smelling something weird. Like, worse than their body washes combined. Skunky, but not normal skunky."

I don't remember any stories about any of the Fireballs being suspended for weed, but that's where my brain goes at *skunky*. "What was it?"

"We were staying in the same hotel as a bunch of music fans who met on the internet and decided to go on vacation together for a nineties band tour. Apparently they didn't get along as well in person as they did online though, so there was a group of them that kept going to the stairwell to smoke."

"Plain pot."

"Pot and burning human hair."

My chest is loosening. I pry my eyes open and look at her, illuminated by only her phone's flashlight. She's staring straight ahead, not looking at me, but she's still gripping my arm.

"Burning human hair?" I repeat.

"Someone got careless with a lighter, someone else thought it was intentional, and all of these fifty-something white dudes were trying to light each other's hair on fire while high."

"No."

"All I wanted was to get to my room. I always preorder my room service because I know once the team gets back to any hotel, the kitchen is getting backed up. I had a hamburger on the way, and I hadn't had a hamburger in weeks. And instead of eating my burger in peace and quiet, I'm calling the front desk and helping put out hair fires and getting a contact high. By the time I called Santiago to tell him to have the boys lock down in their rooms until the drama was over, I sounded like a Smurf."

"That the only time you've ever been high?"

"I did gummies with my brothers a few years ago at the holidays."

"And?"

"And now I know what it's like, and I don't need to do it again."

"What happened?"

"My sister-in-law put *Frozen* on the TV, and I cried my eyes out from the first note to the end of the credits."

"That's it?"

"That's it."

I stare at my legs, sticking straight out in front of us. Breathing is easier. Panic's mostly receded. I'm okay.

I'm okay.

"Was it at least a fun cry?" I ask her.

"No."

"Do you cry often?"

She makes a noise that I interpret as *that's a stupid question, of course not*.

Most of my body is cold, but it's warm where our arms are touching. I lean closer to her. "No shame in crying."

"The day the rest of the coaching staff cries, I'll cry with them."

"You were good with Mary today."

She stiffens.

I lift my free arm and reach across my body to grip her forearm. "You were. And with the Stingrays too."

"It matters to me that women know they can reach for their dreams."

"You let them in."

She's quiet for a long moment while I wonder if I've overstepped again. I'll blame the panic if I did.

It's true enough.

"I'm not the marble statue I used to be," she says quietly. "At least, I wasn't. Until I found out Santiago's retiring."

I angle a look at her.

"I can't—I don't—when people take advantage of you and watch for every mistake to try to prove you don't belong, it's hard to not put up walls so they can't hurt you. My longest gig before coming here was about eight months. I spent the first two years here waiting for that call into the office to be told that someone had complained that I'd looked at them wrong, or I'd crossed a line that a female coach shouldn't cross with a male player, or that I wasn't living up to expectations."

I squeeze her arm again. "You kick ass, and the Fireballs know it."

"I started to believe that. We won the whole damn thing, and I started to relax. The team, the coaching staff, management—they made—*make* me feel like I belong. Like we're family. *Good* family. And I was still scared, but I wanted to trust it. So I started to loosen up. Be more *me*. And it felt good. But going through the process of thinking about applying for the manager position, telling the Fireballs staff to put my name on the list, thinking about how I can level up as a coach— it's put my brain back to all of the interviews I went on after college, when I was switching jobs every four to six months and feeling like I didn't belong anymore."

"You smiled before the game yesterday."

"My boss asked me why I was being an asshole to the players."

I jerk my head up. "Seriously?"

"Not quite those words, but he did say I'd seemed *stressed* and the players had noticed. So I—I'm trying to remember to be more *me*."

"Believe in what the universe has planned for you," I muse.

Yeah, I'm better.

Because she's here.

I'm not alone.

She makes me okay.

"I really love working for the Fireballs," she whispers. "Before coming here, I was starting to doubt I could make it. They made me believe in me too."

"Good. I don't have to secretly hate them."

"I just don't want to cross a line that I don't even realize I shouldn't cross and lose it all. I'm *really* happy here."

"Favorite coach I ever had was the one who pulled me into his office to chew me out when my game was shit right after my divorce," I tell her. "But he didn't chew me out. He sat me down, said, *son, you're gonna get through this just like I did*. Told me about his wife leaving him. About drinking too much after. About having to find what was good in the rest of his life to live for again. Told me to call him day or night, no matter what."

Her arm tenses under my hand. "I'm glad you had good support."

"Wasn't just me. He talked to the whole team about the shit we'd all been through. Sometimes privately. Sometimes to all of us. First team I played with to win the cup."

"I was fired once for giving a player a hug right after he lost a parent," she whispers.

"That's complete bullshit. I hug my teammates all the time. Coaches too. Don't tell me baseball dudes don't hug. I've seen them."

"I know. But knowing it and getting over it are different."

I scoot lower on the floor so I can lay my head on her shoulder. "I feel better. Thank you."

She checks her phone. "Management says the power's out on the whole block. Crews are working on it. Should be up in half an hour to an hour. They can call the fire department if we need out *now*."

"I'm okay."

"I have to get to the ballpark. No one has to know you hate elevators."

"I do hate elevators. But I don't mind being stuck with you."

Her shoulder lifts, then settles back as a heavy breath leaves her nose. I watch as she replies to the text from the building's management.

We're okay for the moment. I'll text my boss and let him know I might be late.

She switches to Jimmy Santiago's contact info and types out a quick *stuck in an elevator* update.

His near-instant response of *I told you to move into a building with backup generators* makes her snort. She gives it a thumbs-up emoji, then closes her text messages.

We sit in silence for a few minutes, just the sound of our breathing filling the dimly lit space between us.

My skin is starting to itch from being wet. Hers can't feel too good either.

"I'm debating withdrawing my name for the manager position," she whispers.

I lift my head and look at her. "What? Why?"

"I got into coaching baseball because I love it. I love the game. I love the weather. I love living every day in the presence of the idols I had when I was growing up, playing baseball with my brothers and going to games with them and teaching myself to read with the sports pages."

She's playing with her hands. "I love *coaching* the men I would've idolized as a girl, even knowing that my idolatry was likely misplaced. It's about the player, not about the man, and believe me, that's a lesson I learned the hardest of hard ways. I love being part of an organization that believes in growth and that believes in putting resources into continuously getting better as a team. I don't love that I have to be better and stronger and more professional than everyone else on the coaching staff, but I do love that I *am*. No one can take that knowledge from me."

Her clothes have to be itching like mine, but she doesn't so much as twitch as she keeps talking. "My job is hard. It's demanding. But it's so damn fulfilling to watch the growth and see this team that used to suck donkey eggs *be* something. I want to keep being a part of the Fireballs being something no matter my own title. And I want to keep being better than everyone else at the same time."

That.

That right there is why Addie Bloom is fucking irresistible.

Her passion. Her belief. Her drive. Her acknowledgement of why things are harder and her refusal to let it stand in her way.

There's this fire inside her that makes her shine brighter than every other person I've ever met. She tears down roadblocks and she makes her own path. I wonder if she realizes the impact she has on the world is so much bigger than the lives she touches directly with all of her volunteer work on top of her job.

"You're fucking incredible, you know that?" My voice is husky, and her shiver in response to it is nearly instantaneous.

"I'm just a girl with a dream."

"And the determination to get it. That's hot as hell. *You're* hot as hell."

"I'm a pain in the ass."

"I don't want anything from you, Addie. I don't want your job. I don't want your connections. I don't want your championship rings. I just want *you*."

"You wouldn't if we weren't stuck here."

"I've never stopped wanting you. Not when you told me we weren't serious. Not when I was a massive dumbass who blew up over it instead of listening to what you were saying. Not when I thought of you every time I played a set onstage the past few years. Not when I saw the footage of you celebrating all of your wins with the team. Not when I saw your tattoo in the dress shop. Not when I watched you walk onto that stage at the auction. Not when I see you being a mentor to the next generation of coaches and players. Not when I watch you encourage other women who are doing the scary things. I haven't ever stopped wanting you."

"You scare me." Her voice is so soft, I wouldn't be able to hear her if the elevator were running. "The *idea* of you scares me. The idea of *us* scares me."

The Addie she shows the world isn't afraid of anything.

But I know better.

"I fucking hate blacked-out, stuck elevators, but I'm okay. Because I'm with you. If you want to face your fears with me too, I'm here. Ready and willing to be your lifeline."

"You are so damn infuriating."

I suppress a smile.

She's not mad at me.

She's mad at herself for liking me. And maybe she's mad at me for getting past her fences.

But I don't care if she's mad. Why she's mad. Who she's mad at.

I truly don't.

Not when she's angling her body and her head exactly right to brush her lips against mine.

"So fucking infuriating," she repeats.

I love you too, Addie Bloom.

But I don't say it.

I know better.

She doesn't know yet that love is what this is. And this time, I'll give her the time to figure it out.

In the meantime, I take advantage of her lips on mine, and I twist my body into hers. Let myself lick those delicious lips. Curl my fingers into her wet ponytail. Drown in the soft sounds of her surrender as she parts her lips and sinks deeper into kissing me.

Fuck yes.

I could be trapped anywhere, anytime, and I'll be fine if I'm kissing Addie.

And fuck me, I've missed this.

Her.

I've missed her.

She doesn't half-ass anything in her life. Not coaching. Not volunteering. Even when I was just a fling to her, she didn't hold back when we were alone together.

And she's not holding back now either.

She crawls into my lap and pushes my wet shirt up over my abs, over my chest, until I have no choice but to lift my arms and take the damn thing off.

Her hands roam over my still-wet skin, hot against the chilly air that's giving me goosebumps.

Her touch is giving me goosebumps too.

"Shouldn't be doing this," she says against my mouth.

"Why not?"

"Always ends poorly." She nips at my lower lip.

"Problem for later."

Much later.

Definitely not a problem when she's straddling my hips, rubbing her sweet pussy against my rock-hard cock while I stroke my hands down her thighs.

I love the power in her body. Her curves. Her muscles. Her buttery-soft skin. Her plump lips caressing mine.

She could be right. This could end poorly. Again.

But if it doesn't—if it doesn't, we could be magnificent.

Her tongue touches mine, and my balls tighten.

Fuck, I've missed her.

"Should…not…do…this," she says as she grinds her pelvis harder against my aching cock, dipping her head to bite my shoulder.

"No regrets here." I lick her neck and stroke up her legs again, my thumbs dipping into her inner thighs, close to her pussy.

And I officially hate her pants.

Loathe them.

If it were up to me, she'd never wear pants again.

Except baseball pants.

She's fucking hot in baseball pants.

I wonder if she took home any of the see-through pants from that uniform snafu. If she'd model them for me.

Without underwear.

And my dick just grew an inch.

She rakes her fingers down my chest. "Why do you feel so good?"

"Because *we're* good."

"Dammit, Duncan."

"So fucking good, Addie. Only gets better."

"*I know.*"

"I want you naked. I want you naked and exposed and I want to lick every inch of your body. I want to eat your pussy until you come so hard you can't remember your own name. I want to fuck you into blissful oblivion until you see stars. The next time I'm in the shower with you, I want to take you against the wall and then wash you clean and then do it all over again."

"Oh, god, Duncan." She's jerking hard against my cock, her breath getting shallower, her head thrown back, exposing her neck for me to lick just above her collar.

Fucking collar.

I hate all of her clothes.

I want to see her breasts.

I want—

The world shudders around me and sunshine erupts, blinding me, while something *whoosh*es nearby.

"Oh, god, I'm coming," she pants. "Duncan, I'm—"

"Afternoon, ma—ah, hi," a voice says.

Addie shrieks.

I grab her and hold her head in the crook of my neck while I gape at the sight before me.

I'm not seeing blinding sunshine because I'm coming too.

I'm seeing blinding sunshine because the elevator doors are open and there are six firefighters gaping at us.

Six fucking firefighters.

"Holy shit, you're Duncan Lavoie," one of them says.

Fuuuuuuuck. "Nope," I say.

Six grins greet my denial.

Addie makes a muffled noise that could be her riding out an orgasm while she's frozen on top of me, or it could be all of her mortification leaving her body.

Or maybe it's both.

"Power on?" I ask.

The firefighter who recognized me nods. "Yep."

"Can you hit the button for the seventh floor and go away?"

Chortles of laughter greet my request.

None of them are coming from Addie, but she definitely makes another noise.

"Ma'am, you okay?" one of the other firefighters says.

"Hit seven, please," she says into my neck.

"Are you being held against your will?" a third firefighter asks.

"Only by extreme humiliation."

"If you need us to hold this guy until the cops get here—"

"I'm on top of him, you dolt," she replies.

"He looks strong."

"That's why this was enjoyable. Please hit seven."

"It's wrong to tell him he has to give us his autograph before we let him go, isn't it?" the guy who recognized me says.

"Usually, but these are unusual circumstances," his buddy replies.

He tilts his head sideways, frowning. "Aren't we supposed to be getting a baseball coach out of here so the Fireballs can win today?"

Addie makes another strangled noise.

"Thanks for your service, guys," I say. "Seven, please."

"Seven, please," Addie echoes.

"If that's the female coach, she could lay him out flat if she wanted to," a fourth firefighter says. "I saw an interview with her a couple years ago. She's *fit*."

"Don't you have an oath of privacy or something?" I say.

"Usually, but this is funny shit," one of the guys in front says.

Another one pokes him. "Don't make him mad or he won't get us tickets."

The lights flicker.

All of us look up at the elevator's ceiling.

Except Addie. She groans again, and then starts shaking.

And she follows it with a little piggy snort.

Thank *fuck*.

I know that piggy snort.

She's laughing. And it's a real laugh, or she wouldn't have let the piggy snort out.

"Stairs," she says in a strangled voice.

"I like stairs," I agree.

"You need an escort?" one of the firefighters asks.

She peels herself off of me, and just when I think she won't make eye contact, she hits me with a shy smile.

Addie.

Shy.

My heart flops over and offers itself to her.

But then she's all motion.

"Gentlemen," she says to the firefighters, "thank you for your assistance. And your discretion. Am I clear?"

All six of them straighten as if she's said more than

a dozen words on the matter and they know they're never setting foot inside of Duggan Field to watch another Fireballs game in their lives if they breathe a word of this to anyone.

"We would never, ma'am," one says.

"Not with your names attached," another adds. "Or identifying occupations."

"I'll never forget the way you dead-eye stared at Brooks Elliott when he walked onto that practice field wearing a thong and a cape," a third says reverently. "That's serious facial muscle control."

A fourth pulls his cap off and watches her with wary eyes. "You're scary. In the good way."

The fifth and sixth guys don't add anything, but they stare at me with significantly more respect as I pull my soaked shirt back on and follow Addie off the elevator.

"Thank you again," she says to all six of them, as dead-ass serious as she's known to be on the baseball field.

I trail her to the stairwell.

The firefighters don't follow.

She's silent for two flights.

And then she stops on a landing, looks back at me, and doubles over laughing.

Fuck, yes.

This Addie.

I like this Addie. The one she hides from the world.

The *real* Addie under all of the layers of expectations that she thinks she has to live up to.

And I'll do everything in my power to make sure I get to keep seeing her.

16

Addie

IT'S BEEN ALMOST a week since the elevator incident, and I can't decide if Duncan texting me GIFs every other day or so is a good thing or a bad thing.

It'd be easier to make up my mind if I'd let myself decide if I want to like him or not.

And possibly if one of us would actually talk about what happened in the elevator.

I haven't. Not then, and not since.

Once I finished laughing my ass off, I told him I needed to get ready for work, including packing for a long road trip.

He checked the weather, said the thunder was past us and he was going to head home.

He didn't even make it up to my apartment.

And now, I'm traveling with the team. We're in LA, finishing the first three-game away series of our road trip tonight. We get a day off for travel tomorrow, then two more series to go after this one before we're done and head home again.

Then I owe Duncan his *Croaking Creatures* date.

I step out of the makeshift locker room set up for me in the visiting team's quarters after a hard-fought win and find Dusty and Hugo, the team's fielding and conditioning coaches, waiting for me.

"Cooper and Waverly invited us over for drinks," Dusty says. "You in?"

Yes. "They're home?"

"She's got a show in Seattle this weekend, but they're not leaving for it until tomorrow."

"Yeah, I'm in. Thanks."

One of Waverly's security agents is waiting for us at the team entrance, and he hustles us into a black SUV. Despite the late hour, lights are ablaze at Waverly's place when we arrive. The security guy shows us out back to the pool deck, where Cooper's entertaining several of the older players and their wives and partners already.

And by *entertaining*, I mean he's swaying back and forth, baby in a sling, while he chats with his former teammates and friends.

Dusty and Hugo head over to join them.

"Alcohol or not?" Waverly asks behind me.

I turn, finding exactly the woman I was looking for

standing behind me with a can in each hand. Bubble water or hard cider.

I glance at the players again. "If I say alcohol, can we hide somewhere else for a while?"

She grins at me. "Girl talk?"

"You'll think it's dumb, but my sisters-in-law don't get it, and I can't talk to my ladies pro coach group because—just because." Because the Thrusters just hired a woman conditioning coach who joined my professional group, and I *cannot* talk about Duncan in there now.

Not that I would've before, but I would've been tempted.

"I won't think it's dumb," Waverly tells me. She hooks her head to the left. "They can't hear a thing if we're on the other side of the pool. I'll turn on the hot tub jets."

"You're a goddess."

"Aww, usually only my husband calls me that."

I laugh. Half the world thinks Waverly Sweet is a goddess, and I have zero doubt she hears it regularly.

And that's why I feel like a complete dumbass for wanting to talk to her over every other woman in my life.

She's mountains more successful than I am.

But I'm as successful as I want to be, and I get more public attention than I would if I weren't in pro baseball.

Also, that feeling is all on my side of our friendship,

and I know it. She's never treated me like anything other than an equal as a woman in a man's world.

So when we reach the other side of the pool, I just spit it out. "How do you get brave enough to date a guy when your career is all you've ever wanted and your schedules don't line up at all but he makes you happy except you don't trust happy in relationships because you've been so screwed before, but he's giving you all of the right signs and signals that he's willing to be patient until you work out all of your own shit because he likes you that much and he knows the good and the bad and *still likes you that much?*"

Her lips briefly plump out in an O before she grins at me. "Normally I'd tell someone to breathe after a sentence like that, but I think I need to tell you to drink instead."

I don't disagree with her assessment, so I pop the lid and take a swig of cider.

"That enough?" she asks me.

"Unlikely."

"One more, and then Dr. Waverly is at your service."

I crack up, but sober quickly. "I've never had good relationships or good relationship examples," I say quietly. "I don't believe they exist. I don't know *how* to believe they exist."

"Even when you're surrounded with that every day?" she says, nodding to the group across the pool.

Luca Rossi has one arm tucked around his long-time girlfriend's waist. They have two babies together, and I suspect a third on the way, though it hasn't been confirmed yet, and Luca's mom is traveling with them to help watch the adorable little minions.

Brooks Elliott is wearing his *I'm not listening to a word you're saying* face—and yes, I'm *very* familiar with that expression from him, which is fine so long as he keeps hitting the ball.

And why is he wearing that face?

Because he's staring at Mackenzie, his wife, across the group as she baby-talks Cooper and Waverly's baby girl.

Emilio Torres is joining the party, carrying a fresh wine cooler for Marisol, his wife.

And Max Cole, who's retired now, but married to Cooper's sister, Tillie Jean, is standing behind her with his arms looped around her waist. They show up frequently at home games, but less frequently at away games.

Harder to travel with their two little ones as well.

I'm guessing the fact that Cooper and Waverly are here is the biggest reason they showed up. Uncle Cooper's a good babysitter, and odds are high at least one of the Rock parents are here too.

Especially since the last couple in the group is Cooper and Tillie Jean's oldest brother, Grady, and his wife.

"I wasn't around when *any* of them met," Waverly says quietly, "but Cooper's told me about them. You'd know better than me, clearly, but can you point out which one believed in love when you met them?"

"Emilio," I say without hesitation, even though we both know that's a cheating answer. He and Marisol were practically engaged already when I started with the team.

"And?" Waverly says.

"And Cooper."

"Cooper's a unicorn who believed in love but not necessarily for himself. Who else?"

That's it.

That's it.

Brooks was pissed as hell at being traded to the Fireballs because the team historically sucked. He didn't want forever. He wanted to lose his virginity and catch up for all of the years he didn't sleep around because of a superstition that his bat would go to hell if he got laid.

And yes, I do regularly wish I didn't know that about him.

Luca didn't do relationships. Between his own very relatable family issues and the fact that he was more or less the most-traded player in the game when he landed with the Fireballs the first season that I was with the team, he was a dedicated bachelor who would've rather spent his free time renovating his house than having anything to do with a woman. Especially a woman who believed so strongly in love that she writes paranormal romance novels for her day job and who often has to do interesting research that leads to more pets—of all varieties—entering his life.

The only guy on the team who had him beat for never wanting to be involved in a relationship was Max. He was battling mental health demons and had no intentions of ever settling down.

And yet here they all are, completely and madly in love with partners they've all sworn to love forever, whether they've made it legally binding or not.

As for the last couple, after spending several winters in Shipwreck, where Grady runs a bakery, I've heard stories about how he and Annika reconnected years after being secret best friends in high school. Not the easiest romance, but they made it work, and I've never seen them anything but happy together.

"If you asked any one of them what they'd do if their ladies ever left them, do you know what they'd say?" Waverly asks softly.

I squeeze my cider can too tightly and feel it in my still-recovering shoulder. "Are you calling me a chicken?"

"No. It's completely normal to be afraid of getting hurt. It's a risk. It's a massive risk. And when you feel like you'll have to choose between a man and your career…" She shrugs. "Do you know how many people told me I'd never go back to recording and touring when I announced I was taking time off to support Cooper while he finished his baseball career?"

"All of them." I was there. I saw it firsthand. Cooper

quit doing media availability for a while because even Mr. *My life is awesome because Fireballs Forever!* got tired of being asked nearly daily if Waverly was recording or if he'd tanked her career forever. "But it bothered him more than it bothered you. Unless you hid it well."

She smiles across the pool. "He promised me he'd retire, and I believed him. I didn't have any reason for the questions to bother me."

"He played an extra year."

"I told him to."

"Why?"

"I wasn't ready to go back out on tour, and I just felt like he wasn't done. Now? No regrets. He finished his time playing on his terms, and he went out on the highest high you can go out on. Was it hard? Sometimes, yeah. But worth it. And the thing is…I don't regret any of the guys I dated before Cooper. Including the ones who completely destroyed me. Including Cooper the first time. Because those experiences made me who I am today. They taught me so much about who I am and what I do and don't want. What I will and won't tolerate. What I can and can't sacrifice for love." She nudges me. "Sounds like you have a very firm grip on what you won't sacrifice. But if you could be that happy?"

I watch the group across the pool too. Hugo's stepped away from them and is smiling as he has a conversation on his phone.

Talking to his wife, I'm nearly positive.

Brooks has slipped around the group to stand closer to Mackenzie.

Darren Greene and his wife, Tanesha, step onto the patio from the house and head to the little group too. Darren's also retired from the Fireballs, and he and Tanesha have two kids as well.

"What if it's not in your genes to be happy in love?"

"Don't you have four married older brothers?"

"*Married* and *happy* don't necessarily go hand in hand."

"They're unhappy?"

I wince. "I don't ask. I don't want to know. Especially when I don't think they saw our parents' relationship the same way I did. I don't think they can. Being the only girl and the youngest... It was just different for me."

Waverly leans closer. "You know who makes the best partners in life?"

"Who?"

"The people who understand all the ways relationships can go wrong and choose to actively be part of them anyway. Who choose to do their best with all of the lessons they've learned from their own experience and from watching others."

Duncan's already told me about his sister and what he learned from watching her first marriage. Plus he's been through a divorce himself. And he's an athlete. Doesn't matter that it's a different sport. He's seen his teammates struggle and triumph in relationships the same as I've watched my players struggle and triumph in relationships. He knows the ups and downs. The good and the bad.

"He says he's retiring at the end of his next season." I say it so quietly, I'm not sure the words are actually coming out of my mouth.

Waverly doesn't squeal *I knew it!* or bounce in her seat or clap at the hint. Instead, she asks back, just as quietly, "For you? Or for himself?"

"He says his body's giving him signs."

"What does he want to do after?"

"What does he *say*? That he has a year to figure it out. What did I *hear*? That he wants to do whatever's best so that he can be part of my life."

She smiles. "Do you want him to be part of your life?"

I blow out a long breath. "The man he is right now? I like that man. I feel like I can be me with that man, like he appreciates me for me, not for who he thinks he can make me be. But how do I know that that's *him* and not the him that he wants me to see? How do I know that this isn't best behavior rather than standard behavior?"

"You give him a chance."

You give him a chance.

You take the risk.

You quit being a chicken.

You do the brave thing and face your fears to see if

what you *want*—and I do *want*—can turn out to be better than it's been before.

I swallow hard. "I've never wanted a relationship, but he makes me want to give it a real chance. Not because something's missing. But because he makes everything better."

"Will you regret it if you don't?"

"Yes," I whisper, unable to squash the truth from coming out.

"Then go for it. And call me if you need anything. *Please*. My friend Aspen is about the only person in my life who believes me when I say that, but I mean it. You, Addie Bloom, are freaking awesome, and I like being your friend. Okay?"

I've trained myself not to be a hugger, but I hug Waverly.

She squeezes me back.

And I realize how much I miss hugging.

How much I say I love my job, but how much of myself I'm sacrificing for it every day too.

And that's why I like Duncan so much.

He caught me with my defenses down, but he's never used it against me. At my request, he kept our situationship a secret four years ago. He's reading all of the silent cues I didn't even realize I was giving him that have him moving slowly as he's working his way back into my life. The man *washed my hair* with a raging hard-on, *hugged me*, and didn't make a single innuendo.

I know the sex is good.

He knows the sex is good.

And he's waiting for me to tell him I'm ready.

Who does that?

Someone who loves you.

That's who does that. Someone who loves you.

"I have to go," I tell Waverly. "I need to send a text message."

"Calls are better."

"Text is where I'm at."

"Good luck then." She smiles. "And I hope you hit *phone call* level soon. Those are way more fun."

17

Duncan

It's two in the morning when my phone dings with a text message notification. I lunge for it since I know Paisley's at a party and I told her I'd come get her, no questions asked, if she needs me.

But it's not Paisley.

It's Addie.

My heart trips, then races even harder than when I thought my niece was in trouble.

And that's before I read the message.

I'm withdrawing my name from consideration for the team manager position.

I sit straight up.

Blink a few times.

Get up and take a piss to verify I'm actually awake and not having a whacked-out dream.

When my toilet looks like my toilet and I don't struggle to relieve myself, I know I'm truly awake and not dreaming or hallucinating.

So I head back to bed. Sit up. Read Addie's message again.

And then I call her.

When she doesn't answer, I call her again.

This time, she answers on the fifth ring, sounding mildly out of breath. "You're not supposed to call me."

"Why not?"

"Because we're only at the texting each other stage of this…thing. Hang up and text me back."

"*Look at this funny hockey GIF* is texting stage. *I'm making a massive career decision that I texted you about at two in the morning* is phone stage."

"Oh, fuck, it's two a.m. on the East Coast."

"It's past your bedtime in LA too."

"Cooper and Waverly had a party."

I hear distant laughter, and I realize she's still there. "You went? Good on you."

"Waverly's my friend. And I wanted to talk to a friend."

"About your job?"

"About you. But that's for text. Not for phone."

I almost smile while I rub my hand over my heart that's pounding in my chest. My pulse is still hammering, but it's starting to slow down. "How about you tell me what you were going to text to save your hands the trouble?"

She blows out a breath. I wonder if she's working up her *I'm a badass* expression, or if she's scrunching her face up in frustration that I'm not cooperating. "You should go back to sleep."

"Paisley's at a party. I'm sleeping like shit while I worry some fucker's plying her with alcohol or getting pissed that she's whomping him in pool or...worse."

"Is she alone?"

"No. She made a few friends at her new job and apparently she's doing some Greek life thing too."

"Are they the good kind of friends?"

"If I knew they were the good kind of friends, I'd be sleeping a lot better."

"Oh."

"She's never made bad friends before, so she's probably fine. But I'm not, which is a me problem." No matter how much work I've done to remind myself that I'm not responsible for everything that happens to everyone in my life, I'm still likely not sleeping the rest of the night. "What's with this change in job idea?"

When she doesn't answer right away, I settle deeper into my bed and switch the call to speakerphone. "Addie?"

"I deserve to be *me* at my job," she says quietly. "The professional me, I mean. And the professional me is too hard still. I can't lead a team if I'm afraid to connect with the players."

"You scared?"

"Yes," she whispers.

"Don't be. You've got this."

"I don't. Not…not right now. But I *want* to."

"What's the plan? How can I help?"

"I think…I think I need to picture them all as women."

I bark out a laugh in the darkness, then sober quickly. "Sorry. Sorry. Didn't mean that."

"No, it's okay. It's an unorthodox approach, but I think it'll help me relax. I know where the lines are. I know where the boundaries are. I know what's professional. I don't worry at all when I'm volunteering with the women's and girls' teams around the city. So if I can picture my players as women, I can be more effective. And if it turns out that *relaxed Addie* makes a bad batting coach, then this job isn't for me, and the manager position *especially* isn't for me."

"It's all you've ever wanted."

"It's what I've wanted to *prove*." She inhales again. "Like my independence is what I've wanted to prove."

"Your independence is sexy as hell."

"It's really, really nice when you do my dishes."

You can hear how hard it is for her to say that out loud.

And that's what's making hope grow in my chest.

She's trying.

She wouldn't try if she didn't want me in her life.

"I've done my own dishes for about fifteen years

now," I tell her. "Cooking too. I don't grocery shop and I don't do laundry. Spoiled myself hiring those out during one of my early seasons, and I can afford it, so I keep paying for them instead."

"I know."

"That doesn't change when I'm involved with someone."

"I wouldn't expect it would. Not with you."

I love the sound of her voice. It's a soft melody tickling my ears and making me want to write poetry. An ode to Addie and her voice.

"You know the problem was always me and not you, right?" she says.

"*You* are not and never were a problem. You're a human being who's been hurt and who's been through things that make you wary. That's life. *I* am not a problem now, and I wasn't a problem then either. But my refusal to acknowledge that you needed to go slower than I did was a problem. My *action* was a problem. Not me. And you needing to go slow isn't a problem."

She's quiet on the other end of the line, like she needs a minute to process.

"I spent a couple years seeing a therapist," I say. "It...helped."

"I should do that."

"Highly recommend it."

"It scares me how much I like you."

The way I want to book tickets across the country

to meet this woman at her next city so I can look her in the eye and promise her she's safe with me is almost unbearable.

But if I truly mean she's safe with me, then I have to let *her want* me there.

Not leap because *I want* to be there.

"I'm proud of you for doing the scary things." I'm *proud of her*. That's not what I want to tell her.

I want to tell her so much more.

You're the sexiest woman I've ever met.

I fantasize about you hourly.

Shampooing your hair is my favorite memory.

I want you back in my bed, every night, for eternity, and I want to make you coffee and breakfast every morning.

"What if it takes me years to fully get there?" she says.

"Can we hang out during those years?"

"Yes."

"Is there any chance you'll let me kiss you during those years?"

Her "yes" is softer this time, with a hint of longing that makes me hard so fast my balls ache.

"I would enjoy kissing you again." My voice is softer too. Husky. Raw. I don't want to scare her. But *fuck*, I miss kissing her. Holding her. Having sex with her. Telling her stories and listening to all of her stories too. Laughing with her.

I adjust my cock, which is hard as granite just from hearing her voice.

I miss this woman.

I *want* this woman.

"When I texted you after I saw you throw out the first pitch—it wasn't about hooking up again," she says. "I just wanted to ask you to be discreet about that night after my interview. But you're so damn irresistible and you don't even try. You're so easy to be with, and *that* is the scariest thing about you."

Don't be scared, Addie. Don't be scared. Easy means it's right. "I'll work on that."

She doesn't laugh. "I'm not easy to be with, Duncan."

"Yes, you are."

Her breath hitches. "No, I—"

"You are to me."

She huffs a soft laugh. "Who have you been dating to make me look easy?"

"It's you, Addie. Not in comparison to anybody. Just you. You get the drive and passion I have for playing hockey because you have the same drive and passion for coaching baseball. I like that. I *need* that. Even after hockey, there'll be something. I don't go halfway. I can't. You get that."

She makes a soft noise that makes me want to physically be with her so badly, it hurts.

I swallow. "When you get home and kick your shoes off and let your hair down, you're as big of a marshmallow as any of us in downtime. When we're with family and friends. With the people we let in. When we don't worry about how we'll look if we get a little too tipsy or too competitive or too honest. I've always felt the obligation to go overboard taking care of the people in my life, and you—you don't need me to take care of you. You just need me to stand next to you. It's nice. I like it. I like *you*."

She's quiet again. I hear more distant laughter. I'd ask if I'm keeping her from the party, but she's not there for a party. She's there because she needed to see her friend.

If she wanted to go talk to everyone else, she would.

"I don't know if anyone has ever liked me…for me," she finally whispers.

Her confession is a sucker punch to the heart and a call to ride at dawn.

Someone hurt her.

Likely multiple someones.

I want to end them all.

But not as much as I want to hug her and kiss her and show her how much *this guy* likes her for exactly who she is.

All of her.

"From this moment forward," I say, "you can go to bed every night knowing someone likes you for you. All of you. Your drive. Your intelligence. Your passion. Your independence. Your body. Your heart. *All* of you. And I will destroy anyone who makes you feel like you don't deserve that. Understand?"

When she doesn't reply right away, I mentally punch myself.

Too much, dummy.

We're going slow.

We're not scaring her away with *I am obsessed with you and I will defend your honor to the end of time.*

Except that's what I just did.

"Duncan?" she whispers.

"Sorry," I mutter. "I'm going slow. I promise I'm being patient."

"Thank you for liking me enough to want to destroy my enemies."

"I know you can do it yourself."

"I—I think I understand now how that turns women on." Her voice is throaty.

And there goes my dick getting harder. "Yeah?"

"Yeah."

I swallow hard. Adjust myself again. Let my eyes fall shut while I imagine Addie's hands on me. "Let me know if you ever want me to tell you that again."

"I'll try."

My phone buzzes in the middle of the call, and I lunge for it. But I smack the water bottle on my nightstand too, and it goes crashing to the floor.

"All okay?" Addie asks.

I scan my text message. "Paisley's home safe. Had a good time."

"So you can sleep now."

Not with this hard-on. "That's the theory."

"Great. Good. You need your sleep. I'll—I'll see you next week. For *Croaking Creatures*. Thank you for calling."

"I don't have to go."

"I think I do."

"Okay. Call or text anytime. I'll be here."

I don't hang up.

I don't want to hang up.

I want to wait for her to hang up.

But she doesn't either.

Instead, there's a very long pause, and then—

"Thank you," she whispers.

Anything for you, Addie. "My pleasure."

The line goes dead.

I pull up our text messages and scroll back.

I wish you hadn't gotten attached. Then we could've hung out forever.

I'm attached, Addie. I'm attached, and we'll still hang out forever.

But in the meantime, I have a boner to rub out and some upgrades to our *Croaking Creatures* date to plan.

18

Addie

MY NERVES ARE ON FIRE.

It's Thursday.

That Thursday.

Croaking Creatures date day.

What, exactly, does an athletic lady baseball coach wear to a date that's supposed to be platonic per auction rules but definitely is *not* based on the text messages Duncan and I have been exchanging since our phone call when I was in LA?

You wear what makes you happy.

Is it weird that I hear Duncan's voice telling me that?

Probably not.

He's pro-*do what makes you happy*.

Should I order a burger or a salad from room service?

Do what makes you happy.

Should I get tickets for my family to come to the Fireballs' next home game against Minnesota?

Do what makes you happy.

Should I tell this guy I've been talking to that he's making me feel like an absolute queen?

Do what makes you happy.

What would make me happy right now is to have this date in my apartment instead of in public, where it's likely everyone will be staring at us.

But also, if we *don't* do this date in public, then people will question if I carried through with what I offered at the auction, and that will suck.

I delay deciding what to wear by doing my physical therapy exercises on my arm, and then I text Waverly.

What should I wear?

I don't expect an immediate response, but I get one anyway. *For the tea shop? Send pictures. What are you considering?*

I lay out the four choices on my bed, snap a picture, and send it to her.

There's zero chance she'll tell me to wear the ripped jean shorts and Led Zeppelin T-shirt that I bought at a thrift store in college. Very little chance she'll tell me to wear the jeans and Fireballs polo either.

So will she suggest the black or the tan slacks? And the peach or the green blouse?

My phone rings.

Why am I friends with people who think texts require phone call answers?

Or, in this case, video calls?

I answer, watching my own face wincing on my phone screen. "None of them?" I ask Waverly.

She's makeup-free with her hair pulled up in a ponytail, moving up and down as she apparently jogs on a treadmill. "Do you have a sundress?"

I make a face.

She laughs. "I thought you secretly loved dresses."

"I do, but this is a professional transaction between someone offering an experience and a man who paid over a hundred grand for that experience. There will be pictures."

"Ignore the pictures. Ignore the auction. If you and I were going to tea, what would you wear?"

I mumble an answer.

There's zero chance she understood what I said, but her grin says she knows what the answer was anyway. "So go pick a sundress."

"My favorite one has spaghetti straps and it might be cold in the teahouse."

"Do you have a light cardigan?"

"It's pink."

"You look fabulous in pink."

"*I know.*"

"Do you feel good in pink?"

"Yes," I grumble.

"Wear your hair down. Go light on the makeup. Pick your favorite sundress. Add the pink cardigan. And then sit in that teahouse with both of you on your devices, playing that game where you'll both be shrieking about eyeballs getting poked out and sticks up each other's butts, and have a great time."

"My creature died yesterday when my boat ride to another island was attacked by sharks."

"This is *exactly* what I'm talking about. People will be so busy talking about how weird you are, they won't even notice you and Duncan making eyes at each other all afternoon."

She has such a good point that I do, in fact, pick my favorite sundress, strappy sandals, and the pink cardigan. I add tiny diamond stud earrings and the barest coat of makeup, and then I take her advice and leave my hair down.

And there she is.

Girly Addie, staring at me in the mirror.

I smile at her.

She smirks back.

My reflection is clearly not suffering from smoldering nerve endings.

There's a knock at my apartment door as I'm hooking the clasp of my mom's favorite jade necklace. My fingers tremble through finishing, and then I hustle to the door.

I haven't seen Duncan in close to two weeks.

And he looks even better than I remember.

A soft "Wow" slips from his lips as he takes in my outfit.

My cheeks burn hotter than my nerves. "Hi. Are you ready? You look nice. I mean, you always look nice. You just look nicer. Is that the same suit you wear before games?"

He's not wearing a coat, just the slacks and a white button-down shirt with the top button open. Casual fancy.

I'm glad I didn't wear slacks.

Am I saying that out loud? I hope I'm not saying any of that out loud.

He quirks a half smile, popping a single dimple, then puts one hand to my hip while he brushes his lips to my cheek. "You're gorgeous. I'm ready. You?"

And then he has his hands back to himself, straightening like he didn't just send a jolt of lightning from my cheek to my clit via my nipples merely by brushing a kiss to my cheek.

I have it bad.

I have it *so* bad.

"Yeah. Yeah, just let me grab my keys and phone."

We take the stairs. My heart is pounding like I'm running away from a charging wildebeest rather than casually making the same trip down the same stairs that I regularly do.

"Am I driving or are we walking?" I ask as we reach the main floor. The tea house isn't far.

"I got us a car."

I blink at him.

His cheeks go the barest shade of ruddy.

"Are we going to argue about who's paying for what after you already paid over a hundred grand to go on this date today?" I ask.

He hits me with a full-force smile. "Yep."

It's impossible to not smile back.

His gaze dips to my lips.

My stomach dips to put all of the pressure on my ovaries and vagina.

I missed you.

I don't let the sentiment slip out of my mouth, but I do hook my hand around his elbow and lean in to him while we walk to the door.

A suited driver is waiting beside a shiny black SUV. He greets me with a smile and a nod as he holds the rear passenger door.

I climb in and slide across the smooth leather seat.

Fascinating.

I would've expected two bucket seats.

Instead, we're set up for sitting right next to each other.

Duncan joins me, and soon, we're on our way. Thighs touching. Shoulders touching. Auras touching.

"Good road trip?" he asks me.

"Won more than we lost."

"Always a bonus."

"It's been a harder year."

"Losing the heart of a team will do that."

He's not wrong, and it's nothing we're not aware of on the coaching staff. Especially when we're asked questions constantly during our media availability times about how missing Cooper is affecting the team. "It's a team sport but it's so critical to have the right blend of personalities and skillsets. Missing just one..."

"It's a big one."

"We have a new heart."

He lifts his brows.

"He doesn't *know* he's our new heart, but I think everyone around him is starting to recognize it."

Duncan shifts closer. "Think that was intentional?"

"A good leader trains their replacement."

It's supposed to be a hint for Mr. Captain, but if he picks up on it, he doesn't let on.

Instead, he hits me with a hard question right back. "You being trained?"

I shake my head.

It's better for me to stay where I am and work on improving my relationship with the team itself than it is for my ego to lead me into fucking up the head coach position for the team. *Especially* in a year when we've just lost one of our biggest and most consistent stars.

"You're sure," he says quietly.

"More sure by the day." The more I've thought about it, the more I know it's not my time yet. *Yet.* "I make a difference where I am. And I still have some work to do on me."

He holds my gaze.

I want to kiss him.

I want to slide into his lap and kiss him until I can't breathe. I want to feel his arms around me, feel his erection poking me, taste his mouth, feel his freshly shaved face, and lose myself in letting go.

In trusting him with my body.

The way I used to.

But if I kiss him—if we do this—I'm committed.

We won't be secret this time.

It won't be casual.

It will be very, very real, with the intention of finding out if we're truly compatible as a couple.

I glance at the driver, who's staring studiously ahead as we make our way through traffic. Then back at Duncan.

He doesn't say a word. Just smiles at me like he has so many things he wants to say, but doesn't want to push it.

I grip his hand. "I do not want to hurt you again," I whisper. "It's not just me I'm afraid for. It's you too."

He blinks quickly, then squeezes my hand back. "I trust you."

Other men I've known would've smirked. *I can take it.*

Not Duncan.

There's no ego. No *honey, you'll want me so badly, you'll never think of leaving me.* Or *psh, you can't hurt me, I'm made of lead.*

273

With Duncan, it's *I acknowledge your fear and I'm here to tell you I believe in you.*

I swallow the lump forming in my throat. "I don't think you'll be saying that after I kick your ass in *Croaking Creatures* this afternoon."

His answering smile is all tenderness and light. "You know the fun thing about a *Croaking Creatures* date with me?"

"How easy it will be to kick your ass?"

"How much I'm willing to pay the creators to give me an advantage with new ways to croak that you don't know about yet."

I gasp.

He wiggles his eyebrows.

I know I told my boss that a bid as high as Duncan's didn't come with blowjobs.

Duncan might've just convinced me otherwise without even trying.

19

Duncan

ADDIE'S GLOWING when we pull up to the teahouse. She's been trying to guess what new ways to die I managed to get put into the game, and I'm refusing to tell her if she's hot or cold.

But I do tell her to update the app on her phone.

It's possible things will glitch.

Rush jobs sometimes do.

But that'll make it all the more fun.

When we reach the hostess stand, we're immediately taken to our table.

And that's when I realize there's something worse that could happen here than our pictures being taken and leaked to the sports gossip pages.

I looked up the teahouse so I'd be ready for this part

of our afternoon. The website was plastered with pictures of groups of women, of daddies and daughters on afternoon teddy bear dates, of families with little kids.

Made sense. I used to take Paisley for experiences like this when I'd go home for visits in the summer, before she outgrew teddy bear tea dates.

What I didn't anticipate was how many Fireballs baseball players and their significant others would be sitting at every one of the tables surrounding us.

Addie's steps slow as she glances around the room, obviously seeing what I'm seeing too.

"Hey, Coach." One of the guys lifts his chin at her and goes back to his menu like this is completely normal.

Her shoulders bunch at the second *Hey, Coach* from deeper in the room.

By the third greeting, she stops and spins in a circle.

There are twelve tables in this room of the teahouse.

Eleven of them are occupied by her players. If it's not one of her players and their significant other, it's two players together.

Practically the entire team is here.

"What's going on?" she asks the room at large while the hostess fiddles with the menus.

"We're here having tea," Luca Rossi says. His partner gives Addie a pained but supportive smile.

"Tea is delicious," Brooks Elliott adds from another table.

"Good for your superstitions," his wife pipes up.

"We should have tea in the Gatorade coolers, Coach," Diego Estevez says. He's sitting with Rory McBride.

The young guy whose name Paisley wore on her jersey.

The young guy who better never, ever, ever, ever look at my niece wrong.

Addie spins in a slow circle again, staring at all of her players.

Half the tables have the team's roster of pitchers, who aren't really her players, since they don't bat.

They all grin at her.

"Enjoy your tea, Coach." Francisco Lopez lifts a teacup toward her in a mock toast while his girlfriend whispers for him to behave himself.

"And your table is here." Our hostess points to the lone empty table with forced cheer. "Have you had tea with us before?"

"Yes," Addie says.

"Not here, but I've been to tea," I say.

Our hostess's forced cheer doesn't waver. "Wonderful."

I pull out Addie's seat.

"Did they pay you to do this?" Addie whispers to our server as she takes her spot on the floral cushioned dining chair.

"There was an arrangement with management," the server whispers back. "I have no idea how much money was involved."

"Look at her wrong and you'll have broken laces for a year," Robinson Simmons says on a cough.

Relatively impressive to get that much out on a cough.

His date's clearly impressed too. She giggles and leans in and tells him to say it again.

Addie looks back at him. "Gentlemen, it's your one day off."

"We wanted tea," Francisco says.

"And to keep an eye on this guy," Robinson adds.

"I don't need babysitters," Addie says dryly to the room at large as I take my seat across from her and accept a menu from the hostess.

"Here's the deal," Luca replies. "You're like our mom. We don't like it when men pay over a hundred grand to go on a single date with our mom. It makes us suspicious. Especially since he's also showing up to games wearing our mom's name. So we're going to be good kids who make sure the big bad hockey player isn't trying to convince our mom that she has to do more than she agreed to do, given the price he paid and the ideas that he might have gotten."

"I'm your *mom*?" Addie repeats.

"It's more accurate than sister," Diego says.

"I thought we should call you our aunt," Francisco

chimes in. "I got voted down because we listen to you like we'd listen to our moms."

"And we protect you like we protect our moms," Brooks says.

I lift my hands. "Are you all serious? How long have we known each other?"

"Long enough that you should've told us you were messing around with her four years ago," Brooks mutters.

Addie spins all the way in her seat to look at him.

Uh-oh.

Coach Addie has entered the chat. "And that's none of your business."

"It's our business if he hurts you," Brooks's wife, Mackenzie, says. "Not because it's bad for the team. But because we care."

"We'd do this for Coach Dusty too, but he seems to like his dating life being a disaster," Rory says.

Addie squeezes her eyes shut.

And then the funniest thing happens.

Her mouth twitches.

It's the tiniest twitch. You have to watch closely to see it.

But I am, and I do.

"All right," she says, her exasperation quickly morphing into amusement. "You can stay. But only if you all let me kick your asses in *Croaking Creatures*."

"We weren't leaving," Luca says.

"I could let you duke that out with the Berger twins

and half the Thrusters," Addie replies. "Or you can all behave yourselves and load up *Croaking Creatures* on your phones."

Most of the guys and their dates follow orders.

"I've known the Berger twins longer than you and I have been with the Fireballs," Brooks says. "They'd take my side."

"Duncan, whose side are the Berger twins on?"

"Whoever's side is most fun," I reply without hesitation. "If it's equal fun, they default to hockey loyalty."

"They're afraid of my sister-in-law," Brooks says.

"Everyone's afraid of your sister-in-law." Luca's response is met with a chorus of agreement.

Even Addie briefly seems to acknowledge that as fact. "Is your sister-in-law here?"

"No."

"Does she write the story or the code for *Croaking Creatures?*"

"No."

"So you're willing to just use her name to threaten a very nice man who made a large donation to charity while knowing he'd appreciate this experience more than the other guy who was twice my age and had— what did you call it, Duncan?"

"Nefarious intentions," I supply.

All of the players and their significant others look at me.

I fold my hands together on the table and let them.

Now that I know why they're here, I'm honestly

enjoying this. It's good for Addie to see how much her players care about her.

Calling her *mom* might've crossed a line, but their objective in being here seems to be respectable.

"Do you have nefarious intentions?" Luca asks me.

"Have you *met* Duncan?" Addie replies for me. "He's incapable of having nefarious intentions."

"Aww, thank you," I murmur.

She blushes. "It's the truth."

"You never know what's in the darkest corners of people's souls, Coach," Robinson says.

"What's in the darkest corner of your soul?" his date whispers.

"I can't tell you here," he whispers back.

"So what are your intentions?" Brooks asks me.

I grin. "It *was* to kick Addie's ass in *Croaking Creatures* this afternoon, but now it's to kick all of your asses."

"That's *Coach Addie* to you," one of the pitchers says.

"Are you all up on the game or not?" Addie asks.

"We're up," another of the pitchers says.

"Almost all of us," another agrees. "We're only missing Luca and Brooks. And you and Lavoie."

Addie looks at the last two, who are at tables next to each other. "Are you in?"

The two men share a look. Their significant others share a more amused look.

"Yeah, we're in." Luca shifts his attention to me. "But I can see your feet from here. No footsie."

"Or handsy," Brooks adds.

"Or kissy-kissy," Diego says.

Addie looks at the ceiling and blows out a breath. "Are you all twelve today?"

"If you're our mom, that would be about right," Robinson says.

Everyone cracks up.

Even Addie after a beat.

I lean across the table and open her menu for her, which gets me some approving nods and a few more suspicious looks.

Just for fun, I rise, shake out her napkin, and put it in her lap too. "Here. Let me."

That earns me a warning eyeball that has me suppressing a snicker.

By the time I've sat back down, she's smiling too. "You did that on purpose to annoy them," she whispers.

"It's the nefarious in me."

She laughs.

I get more warning eyeballs.

A server approaches our table. "Welcome. You've been here before? Can I answer any questions?"

I gesture to the room at large. "I'm on a date with their mom, so that means I'm paying for the room."

"You can't buy our love, step-Daddie," Diego says.

Addie pinches her lips together and presses a fist to them. Her cheeks are glowing pink. And her brown eyes are absolutely sparkling with amusement.

If she doesn't realize yet how much this team likes

her and wants the best for her, I hope she's closer after today.

Would they do this for one of their guy coaches?

No idea.

But if she were coaching a women's team, they'd show up for her like this.

Zero doubt.

Paisley's played softball her whole life. I've heard her talk about baby shower presents for coaches and the whole team showing up for a funeral when one of her coaches lost a parent.

"There's not enough money in the world to buy their love," I tell our server, "but I can pay for their tea. If I don't, they'll call me a cheapskate."

"One test down, three hundred to go," Brooks says to Luca.

They bump fists.

"The last time I was here, you had a raspberry lemon tea, but I don't remember the exact name," Addie says to our server.

The woman nods. "Still do. You want a pot?"

"Yes, please."

They look at me. "Same," I say.

"You want to share it? And then try another kind when you're done?" our server asks.

"Yes," Addie and I answer together.

"We could even share a teacup," she adds.

Objections rise around the room, and the most beautiful thing *ever* happens.

Addie Bloom, Ms. Straight-faced Badass, doubles over laughing in front of her players.

I nudge her foot with mine. "Nice job, Coach."

"*Footsie!*" Robinson shrieks.

"Can we also get a tray of the traditional English sandwiches too, but swap the salmon spread for extra egg salad?" I ask our server.

She nods and slips away.

Addie's still chuckling, but she straightens and looks at me. "You remembered."

"Of course I remembered. Remember why too."

She hates salmon.

Had the canned version too many times in salmon patties as a kid.

She's smiling at me, but it's a softer smile. A *thank you* smile. An *I like you* smile.

And the grumbles going up at the tables around us tell me I'm not the only one noticing.

She shakes her head. "Game time," she announces. "And anyone who only targets Duncan's creatures is getting extra treadmill time for a week."

We both know we'll have to set up a special island for all of us to play on. But I suspect at least one of the Fireballs—or their significant others—know it, and I'm not surprised when someone calls out the code for us to get to the island to join them.

Nor am I surprised when I've been gifted poison, a splinter-handled axe, and a kitten of death within the first three minutes of my character arriving on the group island.

"I said, be nice to Duncan," Addie says loudly as she stares at her phone.

Snickers go up around the room.

"It's okay, I know where their lockers are," I whisper to her. I don't tell her I know someone who got a 3D printer who's been stockpiling 3D-printed thrusting Thrusties in case we ever need them for a prank, because that's need to know and she doesn't need to know.

Yet.

And in the next moment, she's squealing with joy. "You got them to make Doc Rover's evil twin!"

Doc Rover is the keeper of all islands.

He usually plays dumb and is horrified to hear the creatures have died.

But today, Sock Grover is in the house, offering "better tools" from inside his trench coat.

"Better tools" are not, in fact, better.

They're worse.

Which, for the purposes of the game, *is* better.

"Congratulations," I tell Addie. "You've found surprise number one."

"How many more surprises are there?"

"Can't tell you. That would ruin the surprise."

"*A flying squid?*" Diego shrieks. "That wasn't there yesterday!"

"Your kids are ruining the surprises," I tell her.

She cracks up and bends over her phone again. "Then I better play faster. You stay right there, Sock Grover. I'll be back for you later."

I bend over my phone and get back to work trying to plant boobytraps for the Fireballs while saving my favorite murder weapons to gift to Addie.

Having most of her team show up to crash our date wasn't how I would've planned it.

But it's fun.

And putting Addie in a position where she's relaxing with her team is good.

"You stole my black hole, Brooks Elliott!" she shrieks. "You are *so* paying for this at practice tomorrow."

Everyone cracks up. Pretty sure no one believes her.

It's like watching her with the teenage softball team.

I don't know what she'll be like with them tomorrow on the ball field.

But I'm glad she's getting this opportunity today.

20

Addie

IF YOU'D TOLD me the best date of my life would be crashed by all of my players while the man I'm sort of seeing took it all in stride like he had no idea that my heart was pounding in equal parts joy and terror for most of the afternoon, I wouldn't have believed you.

I taught myself over a decade ago to not rely on a man for happiness, and when I slipped and let Duncan in only to have him walk away four years ago, I thought I'd learned my lesson.

But every moment I spend with him now, every moment I talk with him on the phone or text him while I'm gone, I'm falling harder and harder.

And I don't want to be afraid anymore.

What's the very worst thing that happens if you let him in again? Waverly asked me when we were in LA.

I can think of a thousand terrible things.

He breaks my heart again.

We adopt a dog together and he takes the dog when we break up.

We decide to have kids together and things are hard when we break up.

But every single answer to *what's the very worst thing that happens* is *we break up and I move on.*

It's not *I sacrifice my happiness for his in the hopes of making it last.*

I hurt for a little bit, and then I move on. I remember the good times. I regret the bad times. And I move on.

And what's the best thing that can happen? she asked me.

He makes me see the world in brighter colors and takes me to new highs and is there holding my hand during my lowest lows. And I make his world brighter and take him to new highs and I'm there holding his hand during his lowest lows.

Inviting him up to my apartment after our date is the most natural thing in the world.

Even though it's gorgeous outside—no risk of thunderstorms breaking the elevator—we take the stairs.

"I'm getting a dog when I retire," Duncan tells me as we climb.

"Like Doc Rover?" I ask.

"Like something that can devour the kitten of death."

I slip my hand into his and squeeze. "I meant it when I said I'd make my players run extra on the treadmill. I'd absolutely do that for you. Four kittens of death for a guy who was eaten alive by his housecats in a former life is extreme."

"You had fun?"

"I pretended they were all women."

His laughter echoes through the stairwell.

I squeeze his hand again. "I had fun. Thank you. Did *you* have fun?"

"I was with you."

"I've lived with myself for over thirty years, and I can assure you, that does not sound like the regular definition of *fun* to me."

"You clearly don't know yourself very well."

I can be fun. But I can be *not* fun too. "Thank you for being such a good sport about my players crashing the entire room."

"I don't count the pitchers as your players. So they only crashed half the room."

That cracks me up. "Fair enough."

"The rest of them were fine. Besides, I know something they don't."

"Oh, god, what kind of horrible Thrusty prank did you set up?"

"Sorry, Coach. That one's confidential."

And it will likely be hilarious. "Probably for the best."

"But that's not what I know that they don't," Duncan adds.

I peer up at him, silently telling him to go on.

"They don't know I still get you to myself for a few more minutes."

A few more minutes. More like hours. I hope. "You have plans tonight?"

It's his turn to watch me as we push through the doorway onto my floor. "Do you?"

"I didn't."

"You do now?"

My door is close to the stairwell. I pull out my key and unlock it before I answer.

And I don't so much answer as I grab him by the shirt and haul him into my apartment. "Stay," I whisper. "I want more plans with you tonight."

His pupils dilate and his gaze dips to my mouth for the briefest moment before returning to my eyes. "To kick my ass some more in *Croaking Creatures*, or did you want me to do your dishes, or—"

I wrap my arms around his neck and lift myself the barest amount on my toes to press my mouth to his.

And beyond a soft "Fuck, Addie, yes," he stops talking.

Settles those big hands on my hips and pulls me closer. Angles his mouth to take charge of the kiss.

I don't know if I'm pulling him deeper into my

apartment or if he's pushing me. The backs of my knees hit the couch, and I wrap myself tighter around him.

My shoulder hitches.

I adjust it but ignore the pain.

What is pain when Duncan's tongue is slipping between my lips and touching mine?

My *god*.

I've missed this.

I've missed *him*.

He smells faintly like English breakfast tea, and his shirt is still crisp and smooth under my fingers. His five o'clock shadow is the finest sandpaper against my mouth, and the wall of muscles pressed against my chest is everything.

He makes me feel safe.

He makes me feel sexy.

He makes me feel loved.

It should be the most terrifying thought, but there's nothing terrifying about trusting Duncan.

"Are you sure?" he says against my mouth.

"Only with you."

His erection pulses against my belly while he tugs on my hair, pulling my head to one side. "I love being your only."

His lips trace a line down the tendon in my exposed neck while his hands explore my ass. My heart is pounding. My nerves are buzzing. My clit aches.

I want him.

I want him naked and sweaty and talking dirty to me in my bed.

I want him quiet and relaxed with his head in my lap while we watch movies after a long day.

I want him smiling and laughing while we trade our favorite stories about pranks and mischief and our childhoods and families.

I don't need him.

But I *want* him.

He peels the left side of my cardigan off my shoulder, following the fabric with his mouth while I make quick work of unbuttoning his shirt. His body radiates heat. I shiver at the skim of his fingertips against my arm as he gently pulls my cardigan all the way off, letting it drop to the floor, taking extra care with my left shoulder.

"Much better," he murmurs. "I love your arms. They're fucking gorgeous."

Addie's so big. It's not feminine to have such broad shoulders. She should play the Beast.

"Say it again," I whisper.

His fingers stroke down both of my arms, leaving a trail of goosebumps in their wake. "You have the most incredible arms and I fucking adore them. And these collarbones... They drive me fucking mad."

He nips at my right collarbone.

My breasts swell while my nipples tighten.

I believe him.

He thinks I'm sexy. Attractive. Beautiful, even.

My eyes burn. I distract myself by tugging his shirt out of his pants, then discard it the same way he removed my cardigan. Off one shoulder, then the other, until it falls to the ground. "You're not half bad yourself."

God, Addie.

The man makes me feel like the most stunning woman in the world, and my response is *you're not half bad?*

"*You're a sexy beast, Duncan,*" he intones into my neck.

I shiver. "You're a s—sexy beast, Duncan."

"*With the best ass in hockey.*"

I squeeze his ass. "That was never a question."

"Say it."

I rub my face against his as he continues kissing and licking and sucking at my neck. "You have the best ass in hockey."

"Mm-hmm."

"And I love the way you make me feel delicate when you're holding me," I whisper.

He's bunching my dress in his hands, tugging it up inch by inch as he moves his mouth to my ear. "You're goddamn perfect, Addie. Your strong parts and your soft parts and your stubborn parts and your vulnerable parts. So goddamn perfect."

No, he is.

I don't have the words, but I have something else. I can show him.

I tug at his undershirt, pulling it out of his pants, and then I tackle his belt.

He lifts my dress faster. "Slow and careful," he says as I pause in stripping him to lift my arms.

The sundress comes off easier than the gown did a few weeks ago, and he's so gentle, there's no pain at all in my shoulder.

Once he has my dress on the floor, he strips out of his undershirt. I kiss him while he circles my ribcage with his large hands and I reach for his belt again.

"Mm, lace," he whispers as he unhooks my bra. "I love your underwear."

"I hate your pants."

Though I do love the stiff hard-on behind them.

And I love the way he's kissing me. Teasing my lips with his tongue. Being so very *Duncan*.

He's smiling.

I can feel it against my mouth.

I win the battle with the belt, and the button and his zipper give way easily. I push his pants off his hips, boxers too, and then I have that thick, hot, hard cock in my hands.

"Fuck, Addie," he groans as I squeeze and stroke.

"I missed you."

His heavy-lidded gaze connects with mine. He doesn't say anything, but he doesn't have to.

You'll never have to miss me again.

I want you.

I won't give up on you again.

I'm all yours.

This time, my shiver comes from deep inside my soul.

But it's not fear.

It's anticipation.

"Duncan, I lied," I whisper.

His gaze doesn't waver. "About what?"

"Dates this good do come with blow jobs."

His cock pulses in my hand while his eyes go impossibly darker. "Addie—" he starts, but I'm already on my knees.

"No arguing." I lick the bead of moisture at his tip.

"*Fuuuuuck,*" he groans.

I swirl my tongue around his plump head, and he makes an incoherent noise while his fingers grip my hair.

My breasts ache. My clit is hot and heavy. My vagina swells.

I cradle his balls while I seal my lips around his tip, then suck him deeper, my tongue rubbing the underside of his thick hard-on.

His incoherent noises make me want to stroke my own pussy. Driving him wild is driving *me* wild.

I suck and lick and take him deeper, then nearly slide off him, adjust and take him deeper again, until he grips my hair to the point of pain.

"Addie—" he pants.

I know what he's going to say.

I'm about to come.

I suck him even deeper, until he hits the back of my throat. If he's coming, then I—

He grunts out a noise and pulls harder on my hair. "Not this time, baby."

No other man in the world would get away with calling me *baby*.

But he follows it with, "When I come, I'm coming inside your pretty pussy," and my clit tingles so hard at the order that I let his dick slide out of my mouth with a soft *pop*.

"Fuck me," he pants.

"I'm trying to."

He's gorgeous. Neck straining, eyes squeezed shut, his rapid breath making that broad chest rise and fall, his thick, straining cock glistening with my saliva. He lifts me off my knees with one arm wrapped around my ribs and kisses me, swiping his tongue into my mouth for a deep, soul-searing kiss that has me lifting one leg around his hips, trying to feel that thick cock against my clit.

"Fuck, Addie," he says again, gripping my ass and guiding my other leg around his hips until he's holding me while I rub my clit against his erection.

He shuffles, and I freeze.

I'm too heavy.

I'm—

"Fucking shoes," he mutters.

Negligent.

I'm negligent in failing to remove his shoes so he could step out of his pants.

He shuffles three more steps, and then the world shifts as he bends, pressing me into the couch.

His mouth leaves mine.

My panties leave my body.

And then he's on top of me, all hard planes and thick muscles. "Tell me when your arm hurts."

"It doesn't hurt." I'm gasping for breath. My vagina is empty and I don't like it. My breasts ache.

He used to love to worship my breasts.

"Tell me if it does," he orders.

"'Kay."

"Good girl. Now spread your legs, because I cannot hold out one more second."

I wrap my legs around his hips, and *oh my god*, how have I lived without this man?

He glides his thick length inside me, and my nerves erupt with joy with every inch, his cock parting my inner walls and rubbing my sensitive flesh and making me feel whole.

I wrap my left arm around him while he thrusts into me, fast and hard and deeper and deeper and *so fucking good* while I tilt my pelvis to ride along with him.

"You—heaven," he gasps, holding me captive with his gaze.

"Missed—you," I gasp back.

"God, Addie."

"Don't stop."

"Best—ever. Fucking—gorgeous."

The tears sting as my body clenches around his, a precursor to the massive wave of my climax that hits a moment later.

I squeeze my eyes shut and tighten my legs around his hips.

He groans and dips his head to the crook of my neck, stilling while his cock pulses hard inside me.

This.

This is what I want.

Ecstasy. Wild, frenzied, desperate ecstasy with a man who makes me feel *more*.

With a man I could love.

If I let myself.

If I take the leap.

"My god, you're sexy," he murmurs as his body sags against mine.

My vagina is still pulsating with the lingering after-shocks of my own orgasm, but my limbs are starting to relax too.

The tears, though?

Those aren't going anywhere. "Thank you," I manage to choke out.

He lifts his head.

I squeeze my eyes shut.

A single tear escapes and trickles down the side of my face.

He shifts, and then I feel his lips against the tear

streak. "I've got you, Addie," he whispers. "You're safe. I swear to you, I won't hurt you like that again."

I believe him.

And it scares me, but what if he's right?

What if he won't hurt me?

I can't speak, so instead, I nod.

He settles his head back into the crook of my neck. "I've got you," he says again.

I suck in a shaky breath and lift a heavy arm to run my fingers through his short, thick, curly hair.

Tomorrow, I can say it back.

Today though, I'll be the one who lets him take care of me.

21

Duncan

I'M SPLAYED across Addie's bed Friday morning, buck naked, watching her get ready for the day. She's wrapped in a towel, and I can barely see her flipping through her hangers. "You don't have a game day uniform?" I ask her.

"I do, but I—hold just a minute." Her phone's ringing. When she picks it up, it's clear she knows the person on the other end. "This did not require a phone call. I'm not trying to take all of your time."

Whatever the other person says, it's obviously not what Addie wants to hear. She makes a noise that I know very well.

It's her *you're stepping on my independence* grunt. "Thank you. You could've said that in a text…. I would too have listened. You have a very authoritative text style when you want to."

A soft blue sundress comes flying out of the closet, followed by a short-sleeve white cover-up thingy.

I forget what Paisley calls those. She has a couple though.

The motion in the closet stills. "Are you asking because you don't know, or are you asking because you want to know if my version lines up with the version Cooper told you after Luca and Brooks texted him the rundown?"

I lift my head off the pillow and try to get a clear view of Addie, but she's moved deeper into the closet.

It's a walk-in, but it's on the smaller side. There's not far for her to go.

"Absolutely not. I—*no!* No. Okay. *Fine.* Hold on." She leans out of the closet, still wrapped in a towel, her hair hanging wet at her shoulders, her cheeks nearly burgundy. "Will you please tell Waverly she doesn't have to put one of her security agents up to following you to make sure you're behaving?"

She holds her phone out.

It's just a phone call—no video—which is good, since my ass is on display.

While I'm not all that modest, none of us need one of the world's biggest pop stars telling her husband she saw my ass in bed.

He'd enjoy the pranks he'd play as a result too much.

"I'm not behaving," I call to Waverly. "You should definitely have one of your security people trail me to give a full report to you and Addie at the end of every day. Especially if they can help me with my golf swing."

Addie squeezes her eyes shut, but I see the glimmer of a smile tilting her lips at the corners.

I like glimmers of smiles far more than I like tears.

Especially after the best orgasm of my life.

Overwhelmed was all she said when we finally got off the couch. But she insisted she didn't want me to go.

And I was more than happy to stay.

"Okay," she says into the phone as she puts it back to her ear. "I'm outnumbered. Put one of your security guys on him. Kick ass this weekend. I can't wait to see the videos floating around social media. Thank you for the reassurance on the dress. And you don't have to— okay. *Okay*. I promise I'll call next time."

She hangs up, then looks at me.

Really looks at me.

Her gaze starts at my eyes, but soon it's trailing down my face to my lips. Then my chin. My neck. Shoulders. Side.

She bites her lower lip when her gaze gets approximately to my ass.

My dick presses into the mattress like we weren't screwing like rabbits in her shower twenty minutes ago.

"I've made a lot of smart financial moves since my first contract," I tell her. "We could both quit our jobs and just stay home and have sex every day for the rest of our lives. Even if I pay a hundred grand another few times for more dates with you."

Her eyes dart back to mine.

I grin. "I'm only joking if you don't like the idea."

She flips me off, but she's laughing as she bends over to retrieve the dress on the floor, giving me a view of her ass peeking out from under the towel.

Dammit.

I cannot get enough of this woman, and not just because this is the first night we've spent together in four years.

It's because I never could.

And that's why I fucked up and got pissed that she didn't want to take things to the next level.

And that's why I'm not at all offended at her play-fully flipping me off this morning.

She drops the towel entirely as she reaches her dresser.

I groan.

That pretty pussy gets covered with blue silk panties.

Those lush, pink-tipped breasts go into a matching blue silk bra.

I stifle a growl. "You're fucking sexy as hell."

The look she gives me takes my breath away. It's sexy and shy and vulnerable and it makes me want to jump out of bed, toss her over my shoulder, and haul her back here to stay all day long.

"You're the first man I've ever believed when you say things like that," she says quietly.

I stifle another growl.

I officially hate every single person in her life.

None of them are good enough for her. None of them are supportive enough. None of them see her.

Or possibly I'm overreacting. She did just have a pop star on the phone who clearly adores her and thinks she's fabulous.

As she fucking should.

"You should come back to bed," I say.

The blue dress goes over her head. "I've come back to bed three times since my alarm went off. And I need to be in early today. I have a meeting with the big bosses."

"Twice," I say. "The shower wasn't bed."

She has no idea how gorgeous she is when she smiles like that.

Absolutely none.

If she did, she wouldn't be leaning over the bed to press a kiss to my lips. She'd be out finding someone much better than me.

"Do you have any idea how much I appreciate that you have nothing to gain from liking me?" she says.

Is she fucking kidding? "You mean beyond getting to enjoy your personality, your body, your heart, your intelligence, your sense of humor, your—"

"*Professionally*. You don't want my job. You don't want to play baseball. You don't want my connections.

You're not threatened by me. You just…like me. And when you don't like me, it's because I don't like you enough."

I shift so I'm sitting on the bed and pull her into my lap.

She doesn't fight it, though she does squeal. "Duncan, I *have to go to work*," she says on a laugh.

I kiss her neck and breathe in the scent of her.

Lavender will forever be Addie to me. Forever and ever. "You deserve all of the people to like you for who you are and fuck what you can do for them."

"Will you come over again tonight?" She loops her right arm around my neck and kisses the top of my head while I trace the barest hint of cleavage at the edge of her dress.

"If you want me."

"I want you."

"Good. I need to talk to you about how I've been thinking I should try baseball after I retire."

She playfully shoves my head away as she climbs off my lap. "Don't do my dishes."

"I thought being an equal partner meant sharing the load."

She stops dead in her tracks as she's reaching for the white cover-up thingy. Her eyes meet mine, and they start to water again.

Fuck. "Addie—"

"No, you're right." She straightens slowly. "I—I've done everything for myself for so long, I've *insisted* on

305

doing everything for myself for so long, so I wouldn't put myself in the same situation that my mom put herself in, that I didn't even realize that's exactly what I'm doing, but for opposite reasons."

I scoot to the edge of the bed, watching her.

She shakes her head, slips her sweater thing on, and then bends over to kiss me once more. "*Thank you.*"

I catch her hands in mine and press a kiss to each of her palms. "I haven't done your dishes yet."

"And you don't have to. But if you do…thank you. And thank you for being patient with me. I…clearly have a lot more to figure out than I thought I did."

I don't want her to go.

But I know why she has a meeting with her bosses this morning. I know what she needs to tell them. Whether or not she's making the right decision, time will tell.

"We all have a lot more to figure out than we think we do," I tell her. "Don't be too hard on yourself, eh?"

"I really have to go," she says softly.

But I don't want to is the rest of the sentence she's not saying.

I can see it in the way her gaze lingers on my body and goes dark. In the way she's not making a mad dash for the door. "The game will probably go until ten, and then we have some things after…"

"I'm free all night. Text me if you want to come over to my place. Or if you want me to come here. Or if you change your mind and don't want to see me tonight."

I hope we hit a point where I'm not holding my breath every time we have this conversation.

But until she tells me to stop going slow, we'll keep having this conversation.

"I want to see you tonight," she says.

Relief floods my veins. "All of me, or just this guy?" I ask, pointing to my hard-on.

She smiles. "That'll depend on how my day goes."

"Fair enough."

She kisses me once more, and then she grunts out a frustrated noise. "I'm leaving. I *have to get to work*."

"Good luck today."

"With the meeting or the game?"

"Both."

"Thank you. Now *shh*. Or I won't leave."

I blow her a kiss.

She's blushing when she charges out of the bedroom.

Fucking perfect.

I like being in Addie's life.

And I hope this time it lasts.

22

Addie

THE DRESS MIGHT'VE BEEN a mistake.

By the time I reach the top floor of the Fireballs' headquarters across the street from Duggan Field, no fewer than a dozen people have either asked me what's wrong or did a double take before realizing it was me.

When I step into the lobby on the C-suite level, Denise spots me and gasps. "Oh, no. No, ma'am. You are *not* quitting today."

"I'm not quitting," I tell her.

She looks down at my dress. "Are you asking for a raise?"

"I have a ten o'clock with Lila and Tripp."

There's another look up and down my outfit. "Do you need backup?"

"Are they ready for me?"

"Knock first. They're in Lila's office. And if you need backup, the code word is *Ash is eating the flowers again.*"

I head down the hallway, knock, and wait for the "Come in" that follows after several long moments.

I give it one more deep breath before I let myself into the corner office where there's still a godawful orange couch against one wall, the lone remnant in the entire building from the time when Lila's uncle owned the team before we all got here. Otherwise, there are photos of the team celebrating various wins all over the walls. An obligatory plant in one corner. And a massive rug with the Fireballs logo on the floor.

Lila's behind her desk.

Tripp's sitting in a chair with his back to the wall of windows.

They both initially look at me like they're prepared to claim they weren't getting handsy with the door closed, but as one, their jaws drop.

"How much time do you need?" Lila asks while Tripp says, "Whatever it is, we've got your back."

In my head, I throw my hands in the air, march back to my apartment, and change into slacks and a polo.

But my imagination doesn't immediately solve the fact that both of my bosses *also* assume there's something wrong because of my clothing.

There *is*, but it's not *wrong*-wrong. It's more *not the right time* wrong.

"I wear dresses sometimes," I say dryly. "Everything's fine."

Lila straightens and folds her hands on her desk. "Of course."

Tripp clears his throat and nods.

I stride the rest of the way into the office, letting the door shut behind me, and take the seat opposite Lila.

"What's on your mind?" she asks.

Time to do this. "I'd like to withdraw my name from consideration for Santiago's position."

Lila stifles another noise.

Tripp drops the leg he's just hooked over one knee, and his foot hits the floor with a thump. "Come again?" he says.

"I would *love* to be a baseball manager one day, but this isn't my time." I nod to Tripp. "You were right. I've been…harder this year. I'm not in the right headspace to take over as the head coach for the entire team. I need to do some work on me first so that I'm everything I need to be when it's my time to lead."

I've startled them.

I get it.

I've startled myself, to a degree.

But since my conversation with Tripp the day after the auction, since Duncan came back into my life, since I've started letting people in more, I've realized I can't be effective as a head coach until I sort out everything that's holding me back.

Which means I have to not be afraid of other people stepping on me. Of being *all* of me.

Even if it costs me another opportunity one day.

Letting myself have fun with my players yesterday was good.

But it's not enough.

I need to practice letting the real me, *all* of me, shine through every day before I'm ready to be the leader the team needs.

"Addie, we don't need interviews to tell you that you're one of our top two candidates," Lila says. "Are you absolutely sure this is what you want to do?"

I order my ego to sit down and take a seat while I nod to my boss. "If I'm one of your top two now, wait until you see how good I am the next time the job opens up."

Missed the mark on stifling my ego on that one.

Lila smiles though. Some amused, some not. "It could be years."

This isn't a surprise.

I'm in my sixth season. So are Lila and Tripp. So is most of the coaching staff. We've had very little turnover, most of it happening in the first two years that they were in charge as they put together their dream team.

Loyalty runs deep in this organization they've built.

"I'm not going anywhere," I tell Lila and Tripp.

"You've made this feel like home. So I'm going to treat it like home, and I'll be here when the next opportunity opens up."

"Will you be ready then?" Lila asks me.

"If I'm not, then I never will be."

"Anything we can do to help?"

"Not right now. But if there is, I'll let you know." I'm reaching out to a therapist who's worked with a few of our players as soon as I'm out of this meeting. A life coach too.

Fear is weighing me down.

In all parts of my life.

It's time to let it go.

I chat with my bosses for a few more minutes about how our batting lineup is doing and what we have to do to make the playoffs this year. We're currently just outside of where we need to be for even the wild card race. Some injuries and missing Cooper are taking their toll.

And that's okay.

We're not last.

We're not anywhere *near* last.

Our fans are still with us. Even when we lose, we fight hard all the way to the end.

Some seasons are tough.

After our catch-up, I head across the street to the ballpark to get ready for game day.

"Morning, Coach Addie," Diego calls to me from the tunnel beneath the stadium.

He doesn't blink at my dress.

Neither do the half dozen other players I pass on my way to my office.

They don't say a thing about my date yesterday either. Or about interrupting it. Or make threats against Duncan or imply that I look like I have been thoroughly and completely railed in bed.

They're just *normal*.

Santiago's head snaps my way when I pass his office.

"Morning, Skipper," I say.

He clicks his jaw shut, lifts his gaze from my dress, and blurts, "Are you quitting?"

"Why does everyone keep asking me that? You've seen me in dresses before."

"At special events."

"Maybe today felt special just for being today."

"If we lose, you're not wearing that again."

I'm laughing as I head down the hallway to my own small office.

Once I'm inside, I text Duncan.

I told my bosses.

He responds with a GIF of Zeus Berger dancing with the words *I'm proud of you* flashing over the top.

Also, everyone's freaking out about me wearing a dress, I text.

They probably think it'll be bad luck, is his instant response.

I bark out another laugh, and as I do, I realize I feel about a million pounds lighter.

Waiting for the next opportunity to interview for the manager position is the right call. Being *me* here is the right call. As is setting up an appointment with that therapist.

My life is already pretty good.

But I'll make it even better.

23

Duncan

BREAKFASTS WITH ADDIE are my favorite.

Her place. My place. I don't care which. They're my favorite.

In the month since our *Croaking Creatures* date, we've spent about half of them together.

The other half, she's been traveling.

And then there are the days when we're together, in public, making official appearances at kickball league games and volleyball league sign-ups and softball league award ceremonies.

Getting asked if we're still *Daddie*.

Responding with blank stares in the moment and cracking up about it later in private.

This morning, she's at my place, debating with

Paisley about if big dogs or little dogs are better. My niece swung by for free food before class. Addie showed up around one a.m. after a road trip up to DC.

I missed you was all she said before she fell into my bed and passed out cold.

My heart is in a happy place.

"Big guys cannot have little dogs," Paisley says. "It just looks weird."

"Some people think it's adorable."

"They're wrong."

"My new life coach's boyfriend plays rugby, and he carries his little dog in a sling everywhere they go," I say as I slide an omelet in front of Paisley. Addie's already eating hers. She has to be at the field before Paisley has to be at class.

"*Life coach*, Uncle Dunc?"

"To help me figure out what I want to do when I retire."

Paisley looks at Addie. Then back at me.

Addie snickers, then shoves more omelet in her mouth. "This is really good, thank you," she says with her mouth full.

I fucking love this woman.

I still haven't told her so, but I do.

I love her laugh. I love how bloodthirsty she is when we're playing *Croaking Creatures*, whether in the same room or while on the phone before or after one of her games. I love the way she's letting me in a little more every day.

I love that she's wearing dresses to work more often before she changes into her uniform, and that the team wins nearly every time she does. I love the way she tears up seven minutes into *A League of Their Own*.

I love the way she smells. The noises she makes when I'm eating her pussy. The way she feels coming around my cock.

Paisley points her fork at me. "You always said you'd coach hockey when you couldn't play anymore."

"So did Nick. So did Zeus. So did Manning. Want me to go on?"

"Nick's still working for the Thrusters."

"Nick's a hobby farmer who needs a part-time day job to keep him busy enough that he doesn't think to buy an elephant for his hobby farm."

"Isn't buying an elephant for a hobby farm illegal?"

"I'm sorry—have you met Nick Murphy?"

Addie giggles.

"You can't sit around playing *Croaking Creatures* all day," Paisley says.

"Actually, I could. They've had a good response to my requested upgrades and want to know if I have more ideas."

"Ooh, I know," Addie says. "You could be a *Croaking Creatures* podcaster."

Paisley sits straighter. "And you could sing your commentary instead of saying it."

They take turns one-upping each other with increasingly funnier ideas while I start my own omelet.

By the time I take the stool next to Addie's to eat, she's done, and Paisley's close.

I've lost track of what they're laughing about, and that's absolutely fine.

The fact that they're both here, laughing together, has my heart in its happy place.

For today.

For now.

There's a part of me still worried that I'll fuck this up somehow. That I'll push too far. Too hard. Too fast.

That I'll push Addie away.

Training camp starts in a few days.

I'm about to get very busy. And I don't know how that will go.

The Fireballs are sitting right on the edge of the playoffs. Regular season ends about the time I start traveling, but they could play for another month or more after that if they make the postseason. And if they do, odds are pretty high Addie and I will be on opposite travel schedules.

But only for a month or so.

If they make it all the way to the World Series again, she'll still be done in early November.

She says she's staying in the city this winter. But come mid-February, she'll be headed to Florida for spring training for about six weeks.

And then sometime between late April and mid-June, depending on how far the Thrusters go this season, I'll be done with hockey.

Done done.

I'm ready. Ready for my last season. Ready for the next part of my life.

If we can make it through this next year.

Addie's phone buzzes against my countertop. She checks it quickly, smiles, and sends a fast message back to whoever pinged her.

"Was that seriously Waverly Sweet?" Paisley whispers.

"She's a very normal human being," Addie says.

"I'm sorry, Uncle Dunc, but there's zero chance this is going to work out between you two," Paisley says. "You're cool, but you're not *date people who are friends with Waverly Sweet* cool."

"She's a *very normal human being*," Addie repeats with a laugh. She runs a hand through my hair and kisses my cheek, using her left arm, as it's gotten stronger and stronger every day. No surprise. If Addie's told to do physical therapy, Addie does physical therapy. "I promise if I ever break up with you, it won't be because you're not cool enough for my friends."

"If you two get married, would she come to the wedding?" Paisley asks.

I give her the *stop talking now* look.

We don't say the M- or W- words in front of Addie.

"You know Luca Rossi?" Addie says to her. "Outfielder for the Fireballs?"

Paisley nods.

"He met his partner when she got jilted at what was her fifth attempt at a wedding."

"To the same guy?" Paisley asks.

Addie shakes her head. "Five different guys. Five different engagements. After that last one, she tracked Luca down and asked him to teach her how to not fall in love. That...didn't end exactly the way either one of them thought it would."

"*Five engagements?*"

"She writes paranormal romance novels. She likes to say she's in love with the idea of love."

"So they're never getting married because she has a wedding curse?"

Addie laughs. "They're never getting married. Luca would marry her in a heartbeat, but after planning five weddings, she says it's more important to prove to your partner that you want them for something other than a big party."

"I hope he has his legal paperwork in order so she gets his life insurance policy if he dies."

"Are you fucking kidding me?" I say. "His *life insurance policy?*"

"And his will," she adds. "He better have his will in order. Marriage is dumb in a lot of ways, but there are legal benefits."

"Who *are* you?" I ask my niece.

"My friend Audra's stepdad just died, but he and her mom weren't legally married, so it's making everything a nightmare. She might have to quit school because they can't afford it now since his siblings are claiming they're the rightful heirs to his assets."

"How long were they together?" Addie asks.

"Like fifteen years. He was practically the only dad she knew. They never got married because his ex-wife wrecked him so bad. Sort of like how Lena totally wrecked Uncle Duncan."

I stare at Paisley without comprehending what she's talking about long enough that she wrinkles her nose. "Your ex-wife?"

Huh.

Once again, no hurt there. "I forgot she existed."

Addie peers at me.

We haven't talked much about Lena.

Basically *at all*.

I know Addie knows I'm divorced, but that's about it.

"She left me to pursue a career in modeling, and it wrecked me, and then I moved on." I shrug. "That was…twelve years ago? Fifteen? What year is it again?"

"It was twelve years ago," Paisley says. "I remember because he hit on my Grade 1 teacher right after it happened, and Mom kept saying *your uncle's heart is hurting and he's trying to make it better with Ms. Allen's Band-Aids*."

Addie coughs. "That must've been an interesting thing to experience at five."

"I repeated it in fourth grade when our teacher

went through a divorce, and someone explained it to me in middle school terms."

"Did you really forget your ex-wife exists?" Addie asks me.

"No, but it quit hurting."

"Just like that?"

"No. I owe my therapist flowers."

"Therapy only works as hard as you do." Paisley slides off her stool. "I have to get to class."

Addie glances at her phone. "Ballpark time for me too." She switches her attention to me. "What are you doing today?"

"As little as possible."

She smiles. "Let me know if you want a ticket to the game. Should be gorgeous today."

I walk both of them out to their cars. Paisley gets a hug and an order to study good.

Addie gets a kiss after Paisley's left. And I'm well aware that my niece left early to give me a chance to kiss my girlfriend without witnesses. Or so she wouldn't have to see it.

Addie lingers outside her car, something clearly on her mind.

"What's up?" I ask her.

"Would you...forget me if this doesn't work out?" she asks.

"If this doesn't work out, I'm never dating again."

She rolls her eyes, a half smile teasing her lips. "Mm-hmm."

I loop my arms around her waist and settle my hands on her ass. "I spent years looking for someone to replace Lena, and I found plenty of options. And then I met you, and I fucked up, and I spent four more years looking for someone, but this time, I was looking for someone who could measure up to you. Not someone to replace you. And no one measures up to you."

She blinks, then sucks in a shaky breath. Her pulse flutters in the hollow of her neck.

"Oh," she whispers softly.

"You excite me. You challenge me. You comfort me. You get me. And you make me want to do bigger and better things, while helping me see that sometimes the bigger and the better things are the little things." I nuzzle her ear. "And you're sexy as hell."

She leans into me and hugs me tight. "You still scare me, but not as much."

It's not *I love you too*.

But I'll take it.

24

From the text messages of Addie and Duncan, aka The Daddie Chat

Duncan: Coaches are mean evil people and I hate them all (except you).

Addie: I take it your first day of training camp went well?

Duncan: I'm doing voice-to-text messages and I can barely open my mouth.

Addie: Are you home?

Duncan: Yesterday.

Addie: You haven't been home since yesterday?

Duncan: No yes. I'm home. Forking voice-to-text got it wrong.

Addie: Are you in bed?

Duncan: On the floor. Far as I got.

Addie: Do you need to phone a friend to help you move?

Duncan: I'll live. Too old for this.

Addie: Too much golf and not enough real cardio in your off-season, hmm?

Duncan: I wish you were here to kiss my boo-boos.

Addie: I hear one of the Berger twins is good for that. Should I have someone send them over?

Duncan: Send Addie a GIF of someone holding up a middle finger.

Addie: *laughing emoji* Message received.

Duncan: How was your game?

Addie: It starts in an hour.

Duncan: Why are you texting me?

Addie: Bathroom break.

Duncan: Are you sitting on a toilet?

Addie: You give the best sexy text talk.

Duncan: Mostly I like picturing you naked. Even half naked. I like you naked.

Addie: And now I'm thinking about YOU naked.

Duncan: You're welcome. I'm a sexy feast.

Addie: Cannot disagree.

Duncan: Yeast.

Addie: Did you get voice-to-text corrected?

Duncan: BEAST. Fucking phone made me pick it up and type and now I'm tired again.

Addie: Have you had enough to drink today?

Duncan: Unfortunately.

Addie: Was it good to be back on the ice?

Duncan: That's tomorrow.

Addie: Excited?

Duncan: Yes.

Addie: Nostalgic?

Duncan: So fucking much.

Addie: Dammit. Santiago just texted asking if I fell in. I have to go. Game's not over until about midnight your time. Text me proof you made it to bed okay and call me when you get up in the morning.

Duncan: Your phone will be unattended for the next several hours?

Addie: Yes.

Duncan: Excellent.

Addie: What does that mean?

Duncan: Let's just say I'm gonna help you sleep, and then you can tell me all about it when I call you in the morning.

Addie: Is that code for "don't let anyone else see your phone?"

Duncan: I'm fucking exhausted, but not too exhausted to stroke my cock while I think about sucking on your gorgeous nipples.

Addie: I have to get back to work.

Duncan: I want you to play with your clit and slide your fingers up into that tight pussy while thinking about me.

Addie: I needed to turn my phone off two messages ago. I'm turned on and I can smell myself.

Duncan: I love the way you smell. And taste. And look. And feel. And sound. Especially when you're coming for me.

Addie: We're one game from the wild card race. I have to get back to work.

Duncan: Do you remember the shower the other day? When you bent over and showed me that gorgeous ass and I took you from behind?

Addie: I'm sweating and my legs are shaking and my nipples hurt and I have to walk out onto the ball field like this.

Duncan: I miss you.

Addie: I miss you too. I'm shutting my phone off, and there better be at least twenty more dirty messages when I turn it back on at my hotel tonight.

Duncan: I'm picturing you naked, pinching your nipple with one hand while you finger fuck yourself with the other.

Duncan: Do you have any toys? We haven't talked about toys. I want to know what else you like besides me.

Duncan: My fist has nothing on your pussy. Or your mouth. Or your hands.

Duncan: Wear your baseball pants the next time you come over. Your ass is spectacular in baseball pants. It makes me hard as granite.

Duncan: I've jerked off three times since this game started. Every time they show you, I think about the way you went down on me after our first date, or that morning you slept in and I checked on you and found you completely naked, holding my guitar.

Duncan: Fuck me, they said line drive, and I thought

about driving, and I thought about driving you back to the ballpark when you forgot your keys and how we ended up in the backseat of the Sin Bin with me eating your pussy and now I don't remember how we got there, but I want to do that again.

Duncan: I miss the way your breasts fit in my hands.

Duncan: I miss cupping your ass.

Duncan: Fuck me, they just showed you bending over, and I have a hard-on again. When do you get home? I want to fall asleep with you holding my cock. That sounds so nice. Your hands are so much better than mine.

Duncan: I was just about to nod off and then I saw you in the background and you were laughing, and it's so fucking good to see you laughing. I'm glad you're having a good time. That's everything.

Duncan: I hope I don't regret these messages in the morning. I'm too tired to know right from wrong.

Addie: Game's over. I'm guessing you fell asleep. Call me when you wake up and I'll tell you all about me rubbing out my lady boner. Miss you. *kiss emoji*

25

Addie

IT'S HAPPENING AGAIN.

I'm falling head over heels for Duncan.

But this time, I know he's serious about me. This time, I know I'm in it because I'm serious about him.

This time, I'm not afraid.

This time, everything feels *right*.

We land back in Copper Valley late on a Sunday night after our final road trip of the season. We have one more home series, and we're still hanging on by a thread in hopes of getting into the wild card race to make the playoffs.

It's coming down to the wire this year.

Can't say we're not giving our fans all of the excitement.

And the more tense things get, the more relaxed I get.

My new therapist says it's because I'm facing my fears instead of treating them like strengths of their own. That sometimes, the act of choosing bravery is the biggest hurdle. Of admitting that I've told myself lies to keep myself safe, and in believing those lies, I've actually kept myself from living my best life.

She and I still have lots of work to do to fully conquer all of my fears—I'm in a honeymoon phase of believing in myself, and I know I'll have setbacks and doubts in this process—but I've never felt more connected to the team, to my fellow coaches, and to the baseball diamond itself.

And to Duncan.

I've let myself tell him things about my past, about my family, about friends and romantic relationships and professional failures and sabotage that I've admitted to so few people in my life.

He's in town for two nights before his first road trip for the preseason, and he's waiting at my apartment when I get there.

Since my place is closer to Mink Arena than his house, it's logical for us to stay there.

I let myself in quietly, expecting him to be asleep in my bedroom.

Instead, there's a grunt and a sharp inhale from my couch.

"Duncan?" I whisper.

"You're home."

"What are you doing?"

"Fell asleep watching the game."

A light flickers on, and he blinks at me with sleepy green eyes that take my breath away. His hair is mushed on one side and there's a line across his stubbled cheek from one of the throw pillows.

"You are too perfect for words," I whisper.

He rubs the line on his cheek and smiles at me. "Says the most gorgeous woman in the world."

I hold out a hand. "I'm going to bed. You coming?"

For a guy who's sounded exhausted every time I've seen him or talked to him on the phone for the past month, he's remarkably quick at tossing me over his shoulder and carrying me to my bedroom. He strips me out of my polo and slacks and bra and panties and shoes and socks—not in that order—while kissing and licking and stroking every exposed inch of my skin.

"I missed this nipple." He sucks on one of my breasts while I stand between his knees at the edge of the bed. "And this one too," he adds, switching to the other, while his hands roam my ass, tracing the line of my butt crack, teasing the curls hiding my pussy.

He pushes me onto my back on the bed, spreads my legs, and does new tricks with his tongue on my clit while sliding his fingers in and out of my vagina, making my hips buck off the bed when I come.

I see fireworks.

My heart nearly bursts.

And I push him onto his back, straddle him, and take his thick, hard cock deep inside of me, my swollen, satisfied flesh giving way to desperate need once again as I ride him.

"You're so fucking gorgeous." He keeps saying it.

And the tears are coming again.

Not from fear.

But from belief.

I believe him. He makes me feel beautiful. Cherished. Worshipped.

He rolls my nipples between his finger and thumb as that hot spiral of pending release builds inside me again.

"I love watching you come," he says while making love to me.

"You're so strong and it's fucking beautiful," he says.

"God, I love your breasts."

"Your pussy is so hot and slick and perfect."

"Ride me harder, Addie. Ride me harder."

"Yes, my angel. That's it, baby. Right there. Fuck, yes, right there."

His voice fills my soul, and that aching need between my thighs keeps growing, tighter and hotter and wetter, until he's panting through all of his praise, the cords in his neck straining.

"Come for me, Addie. Come for me now."

My body obeys, and if I thought my first orgasm was fireworks, this one is supernova.

My pussy clenches so hard around his cock that I

feel it all the way down my thighs and up into the pit of my stomach. The spasms overtake everything, and I strain into the feeling, sitting high on him while he grinds his pelvis into mine, groaning out his release with my name on his lips, his cock pulsating hard and thick inside me.

My toes curl.

My calves cramp.

My arms shake.

And I come hard and wet and messy all over his magnificent erection until I'm spent and collapse on top of him, gasping for breath.

He's panting beneath me too.

"So…much…better…than sexts," I gasp out.

He half chuckles, then loops one arm around my back. "Yes."

We lay together catching our breath, and eventually I shiver under the breeze of the ceiling fan. He helps me clean up in the bathroom, and then we return to bed.

Exhausted.

But so glad to be here.

He spoons me, murmuring soft questions about the game tonight, about when I have to leave in the morning, about if we can say screw the world and go get a little beach hut in Mexico and spend every day like this.

And just as I'm about to drift off with a smile on my face, he lifts his head.

"Mm?" I say.

He pulls away. "Thought I heard my phone."

"What's that?" I'm so tired, I'm loopy.

But I register the sag and shift of the mattress as he climbs out of bed. Hear the pad of his feet on the wood floor. Know that he's nearby and coming back.

I'm still smiling and nearly asleep when he sucks in a sharp breath and mutters a very strong, "*Fuck*."

I sit up. "Duncan?"

"Sorry. Sorry. I didn't hear my phone. Where are you? Are you okay? Shoot, Paisley, I'm sorry. I—yeah. Yeah. I'll be right there. Don't move."

My heart freezes in my chest.

Not sleepy anymore.

Something's wrong.

26

Duncan

FUCK.

Fuck.

I'm staying in Copper Valley so I can be here if my niece needs anything.

That's what I've told every fucking person who's asked for months.

And the one night she needs me, I didn't have my phone close enough. I wasn't paying attention.

Once we get to her, I know I'll be able to forgive myself.

But I don't know if Addie can.

"I'm coming with you," she tells me when I rush back into her bedroom, looking for clothes.

Her tone is so dead serious.

No-nonsense.

Badass.

Closed off.

"You don't have to—" I start, but she cuts me off with a curt, "Yes, I do."

Fuuuuuck.

Just *fuck.*

Is this it?

Is this when she tells me *we can't be together because we're bad for the other people in our lives?*

And why is that at the top of my head when Paisley's calling me in a panic, feeling unsafe somewhere?

I need to get her and make sure she's safe.

Then I'll handle everything else.

We're out the door and in the parking garage in record time.

She doesn't argue when I tell her I'm driving.

She doesn't say much of anything at all.

I'm white-knuckling the steering wheel with so much I want to say that I can't find a place to start.

None of it matters until I have Paisley safe and sound.

I break every traffic law known to man while following my GPS's instructions to the location Paisley gave me. When we arrive at the house a few blocks off campus, I barely get the SUV in park before I'm charging out of the car.

Addie leaps out too.

There's a party going on inside the house. Someone

in there scared the fuck out of my niece, and I'm going to fucking handle it. I'm halfway to the front door when Addie says my name.

She repeats it before I stop and look back, realizing she's not keeping up.

And she's not keeping up because she's stepped into the shadows and is crouched with an arm around my niece.

"I'm sorry," Paisley sobs quietly. "I'm so sorry."

"No, ma'am," Addie says, equally quiet but so very, very firm. "We do *not* apologize for needing help or for wanting to feel safe."

I suck in a breath.

"C'mon," she adds. "Let's get in the car."

Paisley doesn't hesitate. She's on her feet faster than Addie is. When she reaches my SUV, she climbs into the back seat, and Addie follows her.

I trail both of them, feeling abnormally useless, but still ready to charge back into that party and solve things.

As soon as I figure out what needs to be solved.

Who needs to be solved.

Then, nothing's stopping me from taking care of shit.

"What happened?" Addie's saying as I climb into the passenger seat.

Closer to the house if I need to find someone.

"He wouldn't quit dancing so close," Paisley whispers.

"Who?"

"This dumb jock."

"What sport?" I ask.

Addie shoots me a *shut up* look that sears my soul.

Not because I can't handle her taking care of Paisley.

More because that fear is sitting just underneath my heart. *This is it. This is her excuse to leave me. This is how it gets fucked up.*

I'll do something wrong.

She'll think this never would've happened if we hadn't been ignoring the rest of the world in favor of each other.

"Did he hurt you?" she asks Paisley.

My niece shakes her head. "He just...scared me. It's dumb. It's—"

"Your safety is not dumb," Addie says.

Paisley makes a noise.

"No, look at me. You get to feel safe. Okay?"

Paisley's chin wobbles as she stares at Addie.

"You deserve to feel safe," Addie repeats. "You get to take up space. You get to have needs. You deserve to be happy. And you do not ever, *ever* have to apologize for any of that, or minimize the bad things other people do to you."

It's the second time she's said it, and it hits me harder this time.

Addie's been through bad things. Likely things just like this. And I want to hide both of these two women away from the world so nothing can hurt them ever again.

But neither would let me.

And they shouldn't.

They shouldn't.

They deserve to experience the world and play ball and dance and party and have fun, and they deserve to do it safely.

And I want to be there for both of them, every minute, making sure nothing hurts them.

But I can't.

I can't.

So I have to trust that they're smart and strong enough to take care of themselves.

That they'll call for help when they need it.

Just like Paisley did tonight.

"He plays basketball." Paisley's breathing is ragged as she starts crying again. "And he wouldn't quit touching my friends either. He—he hooked up with one of them last weekend, but then he got weird, so she didn't want to see him again."

"Where are your friends?"

"They left. I didn't know they left. They brought me here. I didn't know how to get home. I'm sor—"

She cuts herself off and looks at Addie.

"Good job," Addie whispers. "I'm proud of you."

"Thank you for coming to get me."

Addie wraps her in a hug. "Absolutely any fucking time at all. I'm going to get you a list of backup numbers since Duncan and I both travel so much, okay? Safe people. Good people. You can share them with your friends too."

My heart starts beating again.

The night lies, my therapist used to tell me. *It tells you the scary things that you want to believe.*

The night is lying to me.

The night is telling me Addie will use this—will use us missing a call from Paisley—as an excuse to break up with me.

That she'll say *sure, we got to her safely this time, but what if we don't the next time?*

Except she's already solving that problem.

We'll get you other numbers to call if one of us doesn't answer.

One of us.

Fuck me.

I need to quit being scared too.

I need to quit being scared that I'm not enough. I need to quit being scared that I'll let her down. I need to quit being scared that she doesn't need me.

She shouldn't have to need me.

I just want her to *want* me.

"I was drinking," Paisley whispers.

Addie makes a noise. "You're in college. That's expected."

"I didn't drink much though. I didn't—I didn't want to be dumb."

Being involved with Addie is an exercise in feeling

useless.

She meets my eyes while she hugs my niece, and the sad smile that crosses her features almost makes my heart crack.

Paisley's safe.

Addie's a fucking goddess who clearly knows how to handle this better than I do.

At least the Paisley side.

I'll be having a talk with the basketball coach myself very, very, very soon.

Possibly within the next two hours. I don't give a fuck what time it is.

I'm having a talk with the hockey coach, football coach, baseball coach, soccer coach, and any other coach I can find on this campus too.

I can wait until the sun's up for those though.

Just like I'm sitting here hoping that that sad smile from Addie is all *I hate parts of this world* and not *we fucked up so badly that this is a sign we can't be together.*

It's *I hate parts of this world.*

It has to be.

The night is lying in trying to make me think otherwise.

"Can I stay with you tonight?" Paisley's voice is muffled against Addie's shoulder.

"Of course."

"I have a class at ten."

"We'll get you back to campus before then."

We. Again with the *we.*

She's not bailing on me. I hold onto that thought as hard as I can.

"I'm sor—thank you," Paisley says.

I look back at the house.

Party's still raging inside.

"Is he still there?" I ask.

She shakes her head. "He left with friends. I saw them right before you called me back. Uncle Duncan, please don't make a scene. I just—I just want to go home."

I glance at Addie.

She's still straight-faced, but there's a tic in her jaw.

Betting she doesn't like *don't make a scene* any more than I do.

She nods to me. "Let's go home."

I circle the SUV, climb into the driver's seat, and fire up the engine.

We're going to my house.

Paisley will get a bed.

Addie will have to call a ride if she wants to tell me this is a sign we can't be together.

But I hope she doesn't.

I hope this is all just my own irrational fears.

Guess we're about to find out.

27

Addie

I SIT in Duncan's guest room, watching over Paisley until she falls asleep.

You'd think it's odd for an eighteen-year-old girl to want someone to protect her from the monsters, but this is so far from the first time in my life I've done something like this.

And that makes me sad.

Sad, and angry, and fucking determined.

"You get to make mistakes and take up space and have needs and not be sorry for it," I whisper to her, hoping her brain hears it and absorbs it subconsciously.

I see so much of myself in Duncan's niece.

The independence. The drive. The hatred of asking for help.

Hers doesn't come from the same place mine does, but she has it. And so many of the young women and girl athletes that I volunteer with around town have it too.

Working with them, talking to their coaches, has made me recognize the link between the expectation of perfectionism for girls and their unwillingness to ask for help.

My hope in Paisley's case is that I can be a good enough influence on her in the next few years that she learns it's okay to ask for help so much sooner than I did. It'll be a journey, but I'm here for it, and I believe in both of us.

And I'm definitely still on my own journey.

If I'd worked through it all, I wouldn't have kept Duncan at arm's length. I wouldn't have withdrawn my name for consideration for Santiago's job. I'd probably spend more time with my brothers and their wives too.

There's still work to do for me to fully embrace the joy of being who I am without apology in all parts of my life. But it'll be worth it. And I won't have to do it alone.

Duncan will be there.

The Fireballs will get a front-row seat.

Waverly and Paisley will cheer me on every bit as much as I'll cheer them on.

It's three a.m.

Duncan has practice in a few hours, and tomorrow, he leaves for his first road trip.

But he's sitting at the top of the stairs, not sleeping. Waiting.

Watching me with the wariest of wary expressions in the dim light coming off of the hallway nightlight. His hair's disheveled. His jaw is tight. And his shirt is bunched at the neck like he's been tugging on it.

"She's asleep," I whisper to him.

"She wanted you."

I settle on the top step next to him. Something's off. Is this ego? Or hurt uncle? Or something else?

I'd say I was surprised Paisley wanted me instead of him, except I wasn't. Not entirely. "There are some things girls understand better than boys. Even when they have the best uncle in the world. It's not you. I promise there's nothing wrong with you."

He's still watching me like he's waiting for something awful to happen.

Or like *there are things girls understand* wasn't a good enough reason for me to take charge of handling his niece.

My pulse skitters sporadically.

Are we going to fight about this?

I don't want to fight about this. I didn't do anything wrong.

"I texted Santiago and let him know I had a personal matter I need to handle and might miss the game today." I speak softly in case Paisley isn't as asleep as she seemed to be, and also in the hopes that my sudden nerves don't come through my voice. "I'll get a meeting with the athletic director at CVU about inappropriate behavior from some of their players. It's never a bad idea for coaches to remind their players where the lines are and what the consequences are for crossing them. Or to remind the coaches and athletic director that the pro sports teams are watching how they handle problems."

"I'll come with you."

I don't ask if he'll get in trouble for missing practice.

He'll deal with that if he has to, but if I were his coach and heard the situation, I'd give him the day off to do what he needs to do.

So I nod like my heart isn't hammering harder and harder with every second. "We should get to bed. It's late, and tomorrow—*today* will be rough."

He doesn't move. Instead, he sits there, head cocked to one side, continuing to study me.

And I don't want this to be what I'm terrified it is.

Him, deciding I'm *too much* again. Too independent. Too *something*.

I wipe my mouth, then my nose, desperately hoping for any distraction so we don't have to do this. So we don't have to fight about any part of tonight.

"Do I have something on my face?"

"You're not freaking out," he says slowly.

It's my turn to stare blankly at him. "I'm pretty good

346

in a crisis. I'm pissed and I'd like to put my fist through something, but no, I'm not freaking out."

"About us," he says.

My heart lurches.

While I'm sitting here thinking he's stifling anger over how I handled Paisley's problems, he's sitting here worried about us.

Just like I'm worried about us.

We're both worried about us. "Am I supposed to be?" I whisper.

He opens his mouth, blinks a few times, then shakes his head. "No. But I thought—fuck. I was afraid you'd say we shouldn't keep seeing each other if it means we miss important calls like this one. And I wasn't going to say anything, except it's not fair to you to not tell you when I'm afraid too."

Oh. Oh, my heart.

He's not preparing to drop a breakup on me. He's waiting for me to find the next excuse to drop a breakup on him.

I scoot closer to him and slip my arm through his, then lay my head on his shoulder, my heart settling into a calmer rhythm. "I can see where you're coming from."

"I just—I like what we have, and I—I don't want to fuck it up."

"You're not fucking anything up. And all of that fear? That was the old Addie. This Addie's trying very, very hard to enjoy things like having a hot hockey player boyfriend with the patience of a monk."

He covers my hand with his and squeezes, then presses a kiss to my temple. "I love being with you."

I love you.

He's been telling me for weeks.

I love you.

It's what he's saying in so many different ways while intentionally not saying those three little words.

So he doesn't scare me.

Keeping his promise to go as slow as I need.

Proving he means it.

My pulse inches higher. My mouth goes dry. A shiver rips through my body.

He loves me.

He loves me.

And he deserves to know why it's always scared me.

"I was eighteen the last time I told a man I loved him," I whisper. "Barely started my freshman year. Just like Paisley. I thought he was everything, mostly because he told me he was everything, and I was dumb enough to believe him. But I told him I loved him, and the next day, it was all over campus that I'd gotten my spot on the softball team by giving the coach a blow job. The boy I said those three words to went home laughing that he had the power over me to make me fall in love with him, and he set up a rumor to destroy me just because he could."

Duncan's Adam's apple bobs. His hands have tightened into fists. "The only reason I'm not asking for a name is because I know you won't give it to me."

"I handled it." I squeeze his tight bicep harder. "You and your teammates and all of my players would've been proud. I pulled off the prank of the century and made it look like he did it, and he got expelled."

"That's my girl, and it's still not enough."

"Between watching the way my mom let everyone else rule her life, and then dating boys like that, I swore I wouldn't ever, *ever* let another man have any power over me. That I wouldn't love another man because loving is giving up your power. But when I'm with you —when I'm with you, I don't feel like I'm sacrificing my power. You make me feel stronger. You make me feel more confident. You keep showing me what real love is supposed to be, every day, and I want that. I want to love you. I *do* love you. And it's scary, but you're worth being scared for. I'm not afraid of you. I'm only afraid of me, and I'm working on that."

"Addie." His voice is hoarse, barely audible, and I hear so much in the way he says my name. *I love you. I will be your defender and protector and champion until the end of time. You are everything that's been missing in my life*.

He's said it in so many ways the past couple months. He says it when he brings me coffee. He says it when he gifts me the best weapons in *Croaking Creatures*. He says it when he does my dishes, when he watches a movie with me, when he helps me with physical therapy exercises, when he listens to me as I talk about my day.

And I hope I'm doing enough to show him that I love having him in my life too.

"I love you," I whisper again.

He shifts and pulls me onto his lap, burying his head in my neck while a shiver ripples through his body strong enough for me to feel it. "Addie, I love you so much that I can't hold it all in. I didn't know it was possible to love someone as much as I love you. I don't care what I do when I retire. Whatever it is, I want to do it with you."

I wrap my arms around him and run my fingers through his hair. "I'm still a work in progress."

"We all are."

"And I still worry we'll find out we want different things—"

"I always said I wanted kids. I wanted to coach hockey after my career ended and dote on my wife and family when I was home and get a dog and a cat and a few fish. And I don't care about any of that anymore. I don't want the labels. I don't want what's *expected*. I want a life with you. With or without kids. With or without a dog and a cat and a fish and a wedding. You are the basis of where the next part of my life begins. You're the sun that everything else revolves around. You are where I want to be, what I want to do, and how I want to live."

My eyes are getting wet again. I bury my face in his hair and breathe him in.

I believe him.

And it's *not* scary.

He knows my flaws. He knows my faults. He knows my imperfections.

And he loves me.

But more?

I know his flaws. I know his faults. I know his imperfections.

And I love him.

I choose love. I choose joy. I choose adventure and laughter and *him*.

"Thank you for being so patient with me," I whisper.

"It's what you do for the people you love. And Addie Bloom, I love you more than I ever have or ever will love anyone or anything else."

If you'd told me six months ago that I'd be madly in love with Duncan Lavoie and happy about it, I would've laughed until I cried.

But there's nowhere else I'd rather be than here, with him, peppering his face with kisses and whispering *I love you* until he straightens, carrying me into his bedroom and making me feel like a dainty, delicate flower.

We still have things to deal with and issues to overcome, but for the first time in my life, I believe in love.

I believe we're supposed to be together.

And I finally believe in happy endings.

28

Duncan

ONLY THING better than winning a game is leaving the locker room afterward to find my girlfriend wearing my jersey and waiting for me in the family room at the arena.

"I'm sorry, who was that complaining that he was old this morning?" she asks with a grin as she lifts herself the few inches necessary to press a kiss to my lips. "Because that guy out there on the ice tonight looked about twenty-three."

I grab her around the waist and spin her in a hug. "One of the rookies was telling you he felt old this morning? When? Which one? I'll have a talk with him."

"You two are gross," Paisley says.

"But it's a cute gross," my sister replies.

She gets the next hug. My family's visiting for American Thanksgiving.

So is Addie's.

I'm getting the brother glare times four.

All of them are in Minnesota jerseys.

It's funny as hell.

"How'd you like the front-row seats?" I ask them as Addie introduces me to all of them, their wives, and their kids.

They don't answer.

Her brothers don't, anyway.

They just keep staring.

I try to suck in a smile and fail. "You know you have nothing on your sister when it comes to intimidation factor, right?"

It's safe to say Addie's sisters-in-law like me far more than her brothers do.

I'm good with that.

We all head out to Chester Green's, the sports bar dedicated to all things Thrusters, for a postgame drink, where Nick and Kami, Ares and Felicity, Zeus and Joey, and some other old teammates are waiting.

I stop at the bar and order drinks. When I get to the table, Felicity and Kami have already cornered Addie. Paisley's grilling Zeus about Joey's airplane. My sister is chatting with Addie's sisters-in-law, and Ares and Nick are staring down Addie's brothers.

I shove between Addie and Kami, who lights up.

"Duncan! I saw the cutest dog today. Shelter guy. Total mutt. He needs a new home."

"Look, he's so cute," Addie says, showing me her phone.

Kami's already been working on her, it seems, likely with the help of Muffy, who's also nearby. Tyler's at the bar, getting drinks and talking to a few fans.

For all of my friends' worries about me falling for Addie again a few months ago, all is well now. Once baseball season ended—massive tough loss in the first round of the playoffs—and Addie had five minutes to catch her breath and catch up on sleep, we made our official debut as a couple on a double date with Nick and Kami.

You win Kami over, you win over the whole group.

And Addie won them over by telling Nick the details of the prank she played in college to get her asshat of an ex kicked off campus.

After hearing a few more of the things the douchemuffin did, not just to her, I'm even prouder.

"Why's he at the shelter?" I ask Kami, nodding at the picture.

"He was wandering a neighborhood. No collar, no chip. Just a lonely guy looking for love. You should go meet him. Bet Paisley would pet-sit for you anytime you need her to when Addie leaves for spring training."

"We should go meet him," Addie says. "Look at that face. And those eyes! How can you resist those eyes?"

I can't resist *her* eyes.

Her smile. Her snark. Her laughter.

She makes my life brighter every single day.

She keeps me on my toes. She challenges me. She loves me.

Ares asked me the other day if I'm sure.

If I'm sure I'm ready to retire.

That's an easy yes.

I'll still play hockey. Still get my time on the ice. There's a league with former pros and high-level amateurs that were matched up by the Thrusters' and Fireballs' adult sports community outreach program.

Have more time to fool around with my guitar.

Get a little less famous around town so I can return to some of my favorite bars from over the years.

Start a podcast about *Croaking Creatures*.

Walk my dog, apparently.

"Shelter open tomorrow?" I ask Kami.

"It's Thanksgiving tomorrow."

"Next day?"

"I'll make a phone call and get you in."

"*We make so many exceptions for these big-headed hockey players,*" Felicity says without moving her mouth.

"That's still incredibly freaky," Addie tells her.

"Wait until she makes your brother's balls talk," Nick says, still having a stare-down with Addie's brothers.

Ares grunts in agreement.

It's impressive to watch two grown men outstare four grown men, but that's exactly what's happening.

"Yo, Duncan, can I get an autograph?" a guy says behind us.

I get distracted with fans—happens when we're out at Chester Green's—and only have to tell people I'm not *Daddie* four times.

"You really couldn't have better names," Paisley's saying to Addie when I finally get to sit back down. "Your couple name is epic. But please don't call him *Daddy* when I'm around, okay?"

Those two are besties.

Even better besties than Addie and half the staff at CVU's athletics department.

They weren't thrilled the first time they met her, but that might've been my fault.

She did all of the talking.

I did all of the growling.

Neither of us told Paisley about our visit. She probably suspects—Addie's been on campus multiple times for various events since the Fireballs were knocked out of the playoffs—but she hasn't asked.

Instead, she takes lunch dates with Addie every time.

Sometimes I think my niece knows more about my girlfriend than I do.

"You going on the next road trip?" Felicity asks Addie.

"I was planning on it, but—"

"I'll dog-sit if you get a dog," Paisley says. "Uncle Duncan's house is way more comfortable than my dorm."

This is my life.

Hockey for one last season.

Family. Friends.

Addie.

Home.

Other than a dog, what more could a guy ask for?

EPILOGUE

Duncan

IN THE THREE years since Addie let me back into her life, I've discovered there are things I love doing with her.

And then there are things I hate doing with her.

Dress shopping falls into the *hate* category.

Mostly because it involves a lot of unsatisfied boners coupled with fears that I'll hurt her again.

"No," I say to her as she holds up a slinky silver dress in the same dress shop where we re-met. "If you want that one, just put it on my card right now because I'll be cutting it off of you in the dressing room."

She snickers.

Paisley does too.

"I'm *kidding*," she tells me. "I don't want to try on that dress."

"Why are you so cranky?" Paisley asks. "You always say you love it when Addie wears dresses."

"He's a total caveman when he sees naked women, and he won't let me go into the changing room alone," Addie tells her.

Paisley sticks out her tongue and crosses her eyes. "Filed under *things I will never ask again because ew*."

"Have you found anything?"

"No, I—actually, hand over that silver dress. What size is it?"

We leave the shop two hours later with the silver dress for Paisley for her sorority's fall formal and with Addie texting Waverly to ask how much it'll cost us to get another custom gown.

It's baseball's All-Star break again, but we're not shopping for a gown for an auction.

We're shopping for a gown for an awards dinner hosted by the city, where my beautiful fiancée will be receiving the highest service award you can get in Copper Valley. And then we're shopping for wedding dresses.

And no, I don't let her shop for wedding dresses alone either.

Which is why she's having it custom-made by her own favorite seamstress back in Minnesota.

Addie's still texting with Waverly when her phone rings.

Paisley and I stop when Addie stops, a frown wrinkling her forehead. "Two seconds, it's my boss," she says.

"Tell him no if he wants you to auction something off," I tell her.

She shushes me and swipes to answer. "Hey, Lila. How's your break?"

"She should've been coaching at the All-Star game," Paisley whispers to me.

Loudly.

Addie freezes, her mouth forming an O before a smile starts to take over. "He—but—oh. Well, yes. Of course. Absolutely, I'm ready… Tomorrow? You're sure? I can be free today… Okay. Okay. Yes. Tomorrow. I'll see you then. And Lila? Thank you."

She hangs up the phone and stares at it.

After a moment, she lifts her face, and her eyes lock with mine.

And then she bursts into tears.

"H-happy," she sobs as Paisley and I both attack her with hugs. "H-happy t-tears."

"Why are we crying happy tears?" Paisley asks with a sniffle. "*Dammit*, Addie, you know I'm a sympathetic crier."

I'm getting wet in the eyes too.

There are approximately three things in life that make Addie weepy.

Baseball movies.

Sometimes sex.

361

And hard-fought victories of her own or of someone she loves.

We're not watching a movie.

We're not having sex.

The Fireballs aren't playing.

Which means—

"Dusty's on leave," she says.

"On leave?"

"His dad's sick. Has to go home."

Dusty was chosen for the Fireballs' manager position when Addie withdrew her name three years ago. He's done a pretty good job too.

Playoffs every year.

Went to the World Series last year but didn't quite get the job done.

Team still misses Cooper. Diego's good, but *no one* can be Cooper Rock.

"They want me," she whispers. *"Next week. I start next week to finish the season."*

"Oh my god, you did it!" Paisley shrieks.

"Temporary," Addie says. "It's temporary."

She swipes at her eyes while she's crunched in between Paisley and me.

"But if you do a good job…" Paisley whispers.

"Yeah," she whispers back.

"And if he doesn't come back…"

"He'll come back."

But he won't stay long.

We already know that.

Dusty's been making noises about settling down with a woman he met in Seattle last year.

"What can I do to help?" I ask.

She shifts the Addie sandwich to squeeze me in a tight hug. "Keep being you."

Easy enough.

"I need tickets for next week's game," Paisley says while she lets Addie go so I can hug her back just as tightly. "There's zero chance I'm missing seeing my aunt be the team's manager for the first time."

"This is temporary," Addie says into my neck.

It's not.

I can feel it in my gut.

But if that's what she needs me to agree with right now, then that's what I'll do.

"I'm so fucking proud of you," I tell her.

"I'm so fucking grateful for you," she replies.

"And I'm hungry," Paisley announces. "Good news makes me want good food. Where can a girl get some poutine around here?"

"Loaded fries," Addie and I say together.

And that's how we end up celebrating her temporary-maybe-not-temporary promotion at the same little bar I used to play at every now and again.

Chuck's still there.

I don't like how he looks at my niece.

But that's okay.

I'm retired.

I have time to make sure he doesn't try anything he'll regret.

When I'm not playing at little bars like this. Or walking our dog. Or helping the *Croaking Creatures* creators come up with even more new and inventive ways to make the creatures croak.

And podcasting about it.

And sometimes playing hockey in the old retired guys' league.

This wasn't where I thought life would take me.

It's better.

BONUS EPILOGUE

Addie

THE GOOD NEWS?

I am highly unlikely to die of mortification.

The bad news?

My baseball team is crashing my honeymoon.

"What's going on?" I whisper to Duncan as we lounge by the pool in paradise.

"I think the privacy settings on your calendar need work," he whispers back.

I narrow in on Brooks Elliott.

His sister-in-law is a hacker. And he and Luca Rossi both retired at the end of the season.

Right after we won another championship.

Making history again.

"Whoa, Skipper, who knew you'd be here?" Brooks says as he and Mackenzie stroll past with their little ones—who are getting bigger by the day—in tow.

Mackenzie grins at me. "Hi, Addie. Can we be friends now that you don't hold my husband's fate in the palm of your hand?"

I like Mackenzie. If she had an athletic bone in her body and hadn't been terrified to talk to baseball players before she conquered her fear for the sake of being the team's most superstitious fan, she would've been an even better player than Cooper Rock.

But I don't know that I like her *here*. "That depends on how much more you plan on interrupting my honeymoon."

"Oh my gosh, is this your honeymoon?"

"She's as bad as Kami," Duncan murmurs to me.

"We had no idea," Luca says as he and Henri and their kids traipse past too.

Everyone's in swimsuits and coverups and hauling pool toys.

"Hey, Coach Addie, we didn't know you'd be here," another familiar voice says.

I sit up and spin to look at this one.

Cooper.

Cooper freaking Rock.

And Waverly.

She blows me a kiss, then grabs Cooper's arm and pulls him in the other direction. "Don't worry," she calls to us. "I rented the whole place out so no one can bother you."

And there's Max and Tillie Jean and their children.

"I should've thought of that," Duncan says.

"Whoa, my dude, who saw this coming?"

Duncan and I stare at each other for a split second, then turn and look behind us.

Zeus Berger's here.

And Ares.

Their wives.

Their kids.

"What the fuck is going on?" I whisper.

Duncan looks at me.

Back at the Berger twins.

They're blocking our view, but I'm pretty sure I just saw Nick and Kami Murphy too.

Duncan pulls off his sunglasses and stares.

We saw every last one of these people two days ago at our wedding.

"It's a Thrusters paradise." That was definitely Nick Murphy. "Nice weather. I like it."

No question.

"We picked the wrong resort," Duncan says.

"Cannonball!" Zeus yells.

Before he can leap in, all four of his kids get a running start and they go first.

The splash coming off the pool gets all of us.

"Don't worry, we won't crash your meals," Felicity

says as she takes the open lounger next to me. "Unless you want us to. But when we heard the Fireballs were coming, we cleared our schedules so we could be here as a protective layer between you and your players."

I glance around the pool again.

The only players here are retired.

They're not *mine* anymore.

"We can be friends," I say quietly.

"I hope so," Duncan says. "You *did* marry me. That implies a certain level of friendship."

"No, you goof. My former players. I can be friends with them."

He grins at me. "Yes, you can."

"And their wives. And their kids."

"Yep. *Next* week. This week, we're finding a new resort."

"You don't want friends on your honeymoon?" Felicity says in one of her puppet voices, which is less freaky now than it used to be.

"Did you have friends on your honeymoon?" I ask her.

She grins. "We got married here with everyone hanging out. It was the *best*. Except for the morning sickness. That part wasn't the best. But getting married and hanging out with everyone we loved most in the world for a whole week...until I found out my best friend was shagging my brother the whole time, but I ultimately didn't have to murder my brother, so that was fine too. Eventually."

I look at Duncan. "Were you here for it?"

"Great time," he confirms. "But I was not among those who were shagging other people's sisters. In case you were wondering."

Zeus cannonballs into the pool now that his kids have made room, and we all get even more soaked.

But that's not what has my eyes watering.

"Addie?" Duncan says softly.

"These people love us," I whisper.

He smiles and nods. "They do."

"Why?"

"Because you're awesome and they tolerate me."

Felicity and Ares grunt an objection in unison.

"You're both awesome," Felicity says.

"Not to be creepy, but I make a good friend too," Luca's partner, Henri, says behind us, making us all jump.

"Sorry," she adds. "I saw something on the back of your chair, and I needed to get a better look. It's all book research. *Not* more farm animal research."

"I'm not allowed to do farm animal research either," Nick says.

I get to be friends with Henri.

Not just friendly acquaintances, but *friends*.

Dammit.

My eyes are starting to leak.

Duncan slides off his lounger and joins me on mine. "Happy?" he murmurs.

"More than I ever thought possible."

He strokes my arm and kisses my head. "Our friends don't have very good boundaries, do they?"

"That's probably for the best." I succeed in wrangling the tears and smile up at him. "Once we're back home, I'll be too busy to remember to make new friends."

"Hey, Coach Addie, you wanna check out my form with pool noodle baseball?" Cooper yells. "I might need some tips so I can take down these puckheads."

"I think I'm going to enjoy being friends with these people," I tell Duncan.

"Hope so. I'm inviting them all over for dinner to compensate for how busy you'll be."

"But I think right now, I'd prefer to have some alone time with my husband."

He's on his feet in seconds, pulling me to mine, and then tossing me over his shoulder as Ares cannonballs into the pool, drenching us all once again.

"Leave some water in there for the kids to play in, eh?" Duncan calls to him. "See you suckers later. We have things to do."

Things to do.

Like being happier than I ever thought possible.

"I'm so glad you came back into my life," I tell Duncan as he carries me out of the pool area. "And not just because you can carry me like this so I can ogle your ass upside down."

He pats my ass. "I'm glad you gave me another chance."

"I can't imagine what my life would've been like if I hadn't."

"Boring," he replies without hesitation, which makes me laugh.

"Then thank goodness you saved me from that."

"Always, Addie. Always."

PIPPA GRANT BOOK LIST

The Girl Band Series (Complete)

Mister McHottie

Stud in the Stacks

Rockaway Bride

The Hero and the Hacktivist

The Thrusters Hockey Series

The Pilot and the Puck-Up

Royally Pucked

Beauty and the Beefcake

Charming as Puck

I Pucking Love You

The Bro Code Series

Flirting with the Frenemy

America's Geekheart

Liar, Liar, Hearts on Fire

The Hot Mess and the Heartthrob

Copper Valley Fireballs Series (Complete)

Jock Blocked

Real Fake Love

The Grumpy Player Next Door

Irresistible Trouble

Three BFFs and a Wedding Series (Complete)

The Worst Wedding Date

The Gossip and the Grump

The Bride's Runaway Billionaire

The Tickled Pink Series

The One Who Loves You

Rich In Your Love

A Thrusters x Fireballs Mash-Up

The Secret Hook-Up

Standalones

Until It Was Love

The Last Eligible Billionaire

Not My Kind of Hero

Dirty Talking Rival (*Bro Code Spin-Off*)

A Royally Inconvenient Marriage (*Royally Pucked Spin-Off*)

Exes and Ho Ho Hos

The Happy Cat Series (Complete)

Hosed

Hammered

Hitched

Humbugged

Happily Ever Aftered

The Bluewater Billionaires Series (Complete)

The Price of Scandal by Lucy Score

The Mogul and the Muscle by Claire Kingsley

Wild Open Hearts by Kathryn Nolan

Crazy for Loving You by Pippa Grant

Pippa Grant writing as Jamie Farrell:

The Misfit Brides Series (Complete)

Blissed

Matched

Smittened

Sugared

Merried

Spiced

Unhitched

The Officers' Ex-Wives Club Series (Complete)

Her Rebel Heart

Southern Fried Blues

ABOUT THE AUTHOR

Pippa Grant wanted to write books, so she did.

Before she became a *USA Today* and #1 Amazon best-selling romantic comedy author, she was a young military spouse who got into writing as self-therapy. That happened around the time she discovered reading romance novels, and the two eventually merged into a career. Today, she has more than 30 knee-slapping Pippa Grant titles and nine published under the name Jamie Farrell.

When she's not writing romantic comedies, she's fumbling through being a mom, wife, and mountain woman, and sometimes tries to find hobbies. Her crowning achievement? Having impeccable timing for telling stories that will make people snort beverages out of their noses. Consider yourself warned.

Find Pippa at...
www.pippagrant.com
pippa@pippagrant.com

Made in the USA
Monee, IL
24 September 2024

66497473R00222